IN A SECRET ROOM IN WASHINGTON, D.C., a man named John Tanner is asked to stake his life and those of his wife and children in a gamble whose goal and risks no one will fully reveal to him.

IN A SMALL SUBURBAN TOWN, where only the nicest people live, friends, neighbors, everyone and anyone may be part of a monstrous conspiracy of international evil.

ROBERT LUDLUM
THE OSTERMAN WEEKEND

"*Shattering* . . . it will cost you the night and the cold hours of the morning!"

—*Cincinnati Enquirer.*

Bantam Books by Robert Ludlum
Ask your bookseller for the books you have missed

THE BOURNE IDENTITY

THE CHANCELLOR MANUSCRIPT

THE HOLCROFT COVENANT

THE MATARESE CIRCLE

THE OSTERMAN WEEKEND

THE SCARLATTI INHERITANCE

The Osterman Weekend

Robert Ludlum

BANTAM BOOKS
TORONTO · NEW YORK · LONDON · SYDNEY

FOR MICHAEL, JONATHAN, GLYNIS—
three extraordinary people who
possess, among so many talents,
the gifts of laughter and perception...

THE OSTERMAN WEEKEND
*A Bantam Book | published by arrangement with
the Author*
Bantam edition | February 1982

ISBN 0–553–20276–6

Published simultaneously in the United States and Canada

PRINTED IN THE UNITED STATES OF AMERICA

09876543

PART ONE

SUNDAY AFTERNOON

1

Saddle Valley, New Jersey, is a Village.

At least real estate developers, hearing alarm signals from a decaying upper middle-class Manhattan, found a Village when they invaded its wooded acres in the late 1930's.

The white, shield-shaped sign on Valley Road reads

SADDLE VALLEY
VILLAGE INCORPORATED 1862
Welcome

The "Welcome" is in smaller lettering than any of the words preceding it, for Saddle Valley does not really welcome outsiders, those Sunday afternoon drivers who like to watch the Villagers at play. Two Saddle Valley police cars patrol the roads on Sunday afternoon.

It might also be noted that the sign on Valley Road does not read

SADDLE VALLEY, NEW JERSEY

or even

SADDLE VALLEY, N.J.

merely

SADDLE VALLEY

The Village does not acknowledge a higher authority; it is its own master. Isolated, secure, inviolate.

On a recent July Sunday afternoon, one of the two Saddle Valley patrol cars seemed to be extraordinarily thorough. The white car with blue lines roamed the roads just a bit faster than usual. It went from one end of the Village to the other—cruising into the residential areas—in front of, behind and to the sides of the spacious, tastefully landscaped one-acre lots.

This particular patrol car on this particular Sunday afternoon was noticed by several residents of Saddle Valley.

It was meant to be.

It was part of the plan.

John Tanner, in old tennis shorts and yesterday's shirt, sneakers and no socks, was clearing out his two-car garage with half an ear cocked to the sounds coming from his pool. His twelve-year-old son, Raymond, had friends over, and periodically Tanner walked far enough out on the driveway so he could see past the backyard patio to the pool and make sure the children were all right. Actually, he only walked out when the level of shouting was reduced to conversation—or periods of silence.

Tanner's wife, Alice, with irritating regularity, came into the garage through the laundry-room entrance to tell her husband what to throw out next. John hated getting rid of things, and the resulting accumulation of junk exasperated her. This time she motioned toward a broken lawn spreader which had lain for weeks at the back of the garage.

John noticed her gesture. "I could mount it on a piece of wrought iron and sell it to the Museum of Modern Art," he said. "Remnants of past inequities. Pre-gardener period."

Alice Tanner laughed. Her husband noted once again, as he had for so many years, that it was a nice laugh.

"I'll haul it to the curb. They pick up Mondays." Alice reached for the relic.

"That's okay. I'll do it."

"No, you won't. You'll change your mind halfway down."

Her husband lifted the spreader over a Briggs and Stratton rotary lawn mower while Alice sidled past the small Triumph she proudly referred to as her "status symbol." As she started pushing the spreader down the driveway, the right wheel fell off. Both of them laughed.

"That'd clinch the deal with the museum. It's irresistible."

Alice looked up and stopped laughing. Forty

yards away, in front of their house on Orchard Drive, the white patrol car was slowly cruising.

"The gestapo's screening the peasants this afternoon," she said.

"What?" Tanner picked up the wheel and threw it into the well of the spreader.

"Saddle Valley's finest is on the job. That's the second or third time they've gone down Orchard."

Tanner glanced at the passing patrol car. The driver, Officer Jenkins, returned his stare. There was no wave, no gesture of greeting. No acknowledgment. Yet they were acquaintances, if not friends.

"Maybe the dog barked too much last night."

"The baby-sitter didn't say anything."

"A dollar fifty an hour is hush money."

"You'd better get this down, darling." Alice's thoughts turned from the police car. "Without a wheel it becomes father's job. I'll check the kids."

Tanner, pulling the spreader behind him, went down the driveway to the curb, his eyes drawn to a bright light about sixty yards away. Orchard Drive, going west, bore to the left around a cluster of trees. Several hundred feet beyond the midpoint of the bend were Tanner's nearest neighbors, the Scanlans.

The light was the reflection of sun off the patrol car. It was parked by the side of the road.

The two policemen were turned around in their seats, staring out the rear window, staring, he was sure, at *him*. For a second or two, he remained motionless. Then he started to walk toward the car. The two officers turned, started the engine and sped off.

Tanner looked after it, puzzled, then walked slowly back toward his house.

The Saddle Valley police car raced out toward Peachtree Lane; there it slowed and resumed cruising speed.

Richard Tremayne sat in his air-conditioned living room watching the Mets blow a six-run lead. The curtains of the large bay windows were open.

Suddenly Tremayne rose from his chair and went to the window. The patrol car was there again. Only now it was hardly moving.

"Hey, Ginny!" he called to his wife. "Come here a minute."

Virginia Tremayne walked gracefully down the three steps into the living room. "What is it? Now you didn't call me to tell me your Mets or Jets hit something?"

"When John and Alice were over last night . . . were he and I . . . all right? I mean, we weren't too loud or anything, were we?"

"You were both plastered. But pleasant. Why?"

"I know we were drunk. It was a lousy week. But we didn't do anything outlandish?"

"Of course not. Attorneys and newsmen are models of decorum. Why do you ask?"

"Goddamn police car's gone by the house for the fifth time."

"Oh." Virginia felt a knot in the pit of her stomach. "Are you sure?"

"You can't miss *that* car in the sunlight."

"No, I guess you can't. . . . You said it was a rotten week. Would that awful man be trying to . . ."

"Oh, Jesus, no! I told you to forget that. He's a loudmouth. He took the case too personally." Tremayne continued looking out the window. The police car was leaving.

"He did threaten you, though. You said he did. He said he had connections. . . ."

Tremayne turned slowly and faced his wife. "We all have connections, don't we? Some as far away as Switzerland?"

"Dick, please. That's absurd."

"Of course it is. Car's gone now . . . probably nothing. They're due for another raise in October. Probably checking out houses to buy. The bastards! They make more than I did five years out of law school."

"I think you're a little edgy with a bad head. That's what I think."

"I think you're probably right."

Virginia watched her husband. He kept staring out the window. "The maid wants Wednesday off. We'll eat out, all right?"

"Sure." He did not turn around.

His wife started up into the hall. She looked back at her husband; he was now looking at her. Beads of perspiration had formed on his forehead. And the room was cool.

The Saddle Valley patrol car headed east toward Route Five, the main link with Manhattan twenty-six miles away. It stopped on a road overlooking Exit 10A. The patrolman to the right of the driver took a pair of binoculars from the glove compartment and began scanning the cars coming off the exit ramp. The binoculars had Zeiss-Ikon lenses.

After several minutes he tapped the sleeve of the driver, Jenkins, who looked over through the open window. He motioned the other man to give him the binoculars, and put them to his eyes, tracking the automobile specified by his fellow officer. He spoke one word: "Confirmed."

Jenkins started the car and headed south. He picked up the radio phone. "Two car calling in. Heading south on Register Road. Tailing green Ford sedan. New York plates. Filled with niggers or P.R.'s."

The crackling reply came over the speaker. "Read you, two car. Chase 'em the hell out."

"Will do. No sweat. Out."

The patrol car then turned left and sped down the long incline into Route Five. Once on the highway, Jenkins pressed the accelerator to the floor and the car plunged forward on the smooth surface. In sixty seconds the speedometer read ninety-two.

Four minutes later the patrol car slowed down rounding a long curve. A few hundred yards beyond the curve stood two aluminum-framed telephone booths, glass and metal reflecting the harsh glare of the July sun.

The police car came to a stop and Jenkins' companion climbed out.

"Got a dime?"

"Oh, Christ, McDermott!" Jenkins laughed. "Fifteen years in the field and you don't carry the change to make contact."

"Don't be a smartass. I've got nickels, but one of them's an Indian head."

"Here." Jenkins took a coin from his pocket and handed it to McDermott. "An ABM could be stuck and you wouldn't use a Roosevelt dime to alert operations."

"Don't know that I would." McDermott walked to the phone booth, pushed in the squeaky, shiny door, and dialed "0". The booth was stifling, the still air so close that he kept the door open with his foot.

"I'll head down to the U-turn," yelled Jenkins from the car window. "Pick you up on the other side."

"Okay. . . . Operator. A collect call to New Hampshire. Area Code three-one-two. Six-five-four-oh-one. The name is Mr. Leather."

There was no mistaking the words. McDermott had placed a call to the state of New Hampshire and the telephone operator put it through. However, what the operator could not know was that this particular number did not cause a telephone to ring in the state of New Hampshire. For somewhere, in some underground complex housing thousands of trunk lines, a tiny relay was activated and a small magnetized bar fell across a quarter-inch space and made another connection. This connection caused—not a bell—but a low humming sound to emanate from a telephone two hundred and sixty-three miles *south* of Saddle Valley, New Jersey.

The telephone was in a second-floor office in a red brick building fifty yards inside a twelve-foot-high electrified fence. The building was one of perhaps ten, all connected with one another to form a single complex. Outside the fence the woods were thick with summer foliage. The location was McLean, Virginia. The complex was the Central Intelligence Agency. Isolated, secure, inviolate.

The man sitting behind the desk in the second-floor office crushed out his cigarette in relief. He'd been waiting anxiously for the call. He noted with satisfaction that the small wheels of the recording device automatically started revolving. He picked up the telephone.

"Andrews speaking. Yes, operator, I accept the charges."

"Leather reporting," came the words rerouted from the state of New Hampshire.

"You're cleared. Tape going, Leather."

"Confirming the presence of all suspects. The Cardones just arrived from Kennedy Airport."

"We knew he landed . . ."

"Then why the hell did we have to race down here?"

"That's a rotten highway, Route Five. He could have an accident."

"On Sunday afternoon?"

"Or any other time. You want the statistics on accidents for that route?"

"Go back to your Goddamn computers . . ."

Andrews shrugged. Men in the field were always irritated over one thing or another. "As I read you, all three suspects are present. Correct?"

"Correct. Tanners, Tremaynes and the Cardones. All accounted for. All waiting. The first two are primed. We'll get to Cardone in a few minutes."

"Anything else?"

"Not for now."

"How's the wife?"

"Jenkins is lucky. He's a bachelor. Lillian keeps looking at those houses and wants one."

"Not on our salary, McDermott."

"That's what I tell her. She wants me to defect."

For the briefest of seconds Andrews reacted painfully to McDermott's joke. "The pay's worse, I'm told."

"Couldn't be. . . . There's Jenkins. Be in touch."

Joseph Cardone drove his Cadillac into the circular drive and parked in front of the stone steps leading to the huge oak door. He turned off the engine and stretched, bending his elbows beneath the roof. He sighed and woke his boys of six and seven. A third child, a girl of ten, was reading a comic book.

Sitting beside Cardone was his wife, Betty. She looked out the window at the house. "It's good to get away, but it's better to get home."

Cardone laughed and put his large hand on his wife's shoulder. "You must mean that."

16

"I do."

"You must. You say it every time we come home. The exact words."

"It's a nice home."

Cardone opened the door. "Hey, Princess . . . get your brothers out and help your mother with the smaller bags." Cardone reached in and withdrew the keys from the ignition. He started toward the trunk. "Where's Louise?"

"She probably won't be here till Tuesday. We're three days early, remember? I gave her off till then."

Cardone winced. The thought of his wife's cooking was not pleasant. "We eat out."

"We'll have to today. It takes too long to defrost things." Betty Cardone walked up the stone steps, taking the front-door key out of her purse.

Joe dismissed his wife's remark. He liked food and he did not like his wife's preparation of it. Rich debutantes from Chestnut Hill couldn't begin to cook like good South Side Italian mamas from Philadelphia.

One hour later he had the central air-conditioning going full blast throughout the large house, and the stuffy air, unchanged for nearly two weeks, was becoming bearable again. He was aware of such things. He'd been an exceptionally successful athlete—his route to success, both social and financial. He stepped out on the front porch and looked at the lawn with the huge willow tree centered in the grass within the circular drive. The gardeners had kept it all up nicely. They should.

Their prices were ridiculous. Not that price ever concerned him any more.

Suddenly there it was again. The patrol car. This was the third time he'd seen it since leaving the highway.

"Hey, you! Hold it!"

The two officers in the car looked briefly at one another, about to race away. But Cardone had run to the curb.

"Hey!"

The patrol car stopped.

"Yes, Mr. Cardone?"

"What's with the police routine? Any trouble around here?"

"No, Mr. Cardone. It's vacation time. We're just checking against our schedules when residents return. You were due this afternoon, so we just wanted to make sure it was you. Take your house off the check list."

Joe watched the policemen carefully. He knew the officer was lying, and the policeman knew he knew.

"You earn your money."

"Do our best, Mr. Cardone."

"I'll bet you do."

"Good day, sir." The patrol car sped off.

Joe looked after it. He hadn't intended to go to the office until mid-week, but that had to be changed now. He'd go into New York in the morning.

On Sunday afternoons, between the hours of five

and six, Tanner closeted himself in his study, a walnut-paneled room with three television sets, and watched three different interview shows simultaneously.

Alice knew her husband had to watch. As Director of News for Standard Mutual, it was part of his job to be aware of the competition. But Alice thought there was something sinister about a man sitting alone in a half-lit room watching three television sets at the same time, and she constantly chided him for it.

Today, Tanner reminded his wife that he'd have to miss next Sunday—Bernie and Leila would be there, and nothing ever disturbed an Osterman weekend. So he sat in the darkened room, knowing all too well what he was going to see.

Every Director of News for every network had his favorite program, the one to which he gave extra attention. For Tanner it was the Woodward show. A half hour on Sunday afternoon during which the best news analyst in the business interviewed a single subject, usually a controversial figure currently in the headlines.

Today Charles Woodward was interviewing a substitute, Undersecretary Ralph Ashton from the State Department. The Secretary himself was suddenly unavailable, so Ashton had been recruited.

It was a gargantuan mistake by the Department. Ashton was a witless, prosaic former businessman whose main asset was his ability to raise money. That he was even considered to represent the Administration was a major error on someone's part.

19

Unless there were other motives.

Woodward would crucify him.

As Tanner listened to Ashton's evasive, hollow replies, he realized that a great many people in Washington were soon going to be telephoning each other. Woodward's polite inflections couldn't hide his growing antagonism toward the Undersecretary. The reportorial instinct was being frustrated; soon Woodward's tones would turn to ice and Ashton would be slaughtered. Politely, to be sure, but slaughtered nevertheless.

It was the sort of thing Tanner felt embarrassed watching.

He turned up the volume of the second set. In ponderous, nasal tones a moderator was describing the backgrounds and positions of the panels of experts who were about to question the U.N. delegate from Ghana. The black diplomat looked for all the world as if he were being driven to the guillotine in front of a collection of male Madame Defarges. Very white, well-paid Madame Defarges.

No competition there.

The third network was better, but not good enough. No competition there either.

Tanner decided he had had enough. He was too far ahead to worry, and he'd see Woodward's tape in the morning. It was only five-twenty, and the sun was still on the pool. He heard his daughter's shouts as she returned from the country club, and the reluctant departure of Raymond's friends from the backyard. His family was together. The three of them were probably sitting outside waiting till he finished watching and started the fire for the steaks.

He'd surprise them.

He turned off the sets, put the pad and pencil on his desk. It was time for a drink.

Tanner opened the door of his study and walked into the living room. Through the rear windows, he saw Alice and the children playing follow-the-leader off the pool diving board. They were laughing, at peace.

Alice deserved it. Christ! She deserved it!

He watched his wife. She jumped—toes pointed —into the water, bobbing up quickly to make sure that eight-year-old Janet would be all right when she followed her.

Remarkable! After all the years he was more in love with his wife than ever.

He remembered the patrol car, then dismissed the thought. The policemen were simply finding a secluded spot in which to rest, or listen to the ball game undisturbed. He'd heard that policemen did that sort of thing in New York. Then why not in Saddle Valley? Saddle Valley was a lot safer than New York.

Saddle Valley was probably the safest place in the world. At least it seemed that way to John Tanner on this particular Sunday afternoon.

Richard Tremayne turned off his one television set within ten seconds after John Tanner had shut off his three. The Mets had won it after all.

His headache had left him and with it his irritability. Ginny had been right, he thought. He was simply edgy. No reason to take it out on the family. His stomach felt stronger now. A little food would fix him up again. Maybe he'd call Johnny and Ali and take Ginny over for a swim in the Tanners' pool.

Ginny kept asking why they didn't have one of their own. Heaven knew they had an income several times that of the Tanners. Everybody could see that. But Tremayne knew why.

A pool would be that one symbol too much. Too much at age forty-four. It was enough that they had moved into Saddle Valley when he was only thirty-eight. A seventy-four-thousand-dollar house at thirty-eight years of age. With a fifty-thousand-dollar down payment. A pool could wait until his forty-fifth birthday. It would make sense then.

Of course what people—clients—didn't think about was that he had graduated from Yale Law in the top five percent of his class, had clerked for Learned Hand, had spent three years at the bottom of his present firm's ladder before any real money came his way. When it came, however, it came rapidly.

Tremayne walked out to the patio. Ginny and their thirteen-year-old daughter Peg were cutting roses near a white arbor. His entire backyard, nearly half an acre, was cultivated and manicured. There were flowers everywhere. The garden was Ginny's pastime, hobby, avocation—next to sex, her passion. Nothing really replaced sex, thought her husband with an unconscious chuckle.

"Here! Let me give you a hand," shouted Tremayne as he walked toward his wife and daughter.

"You're feeling better," said Virginia smiling.

"Look at these, daddy! Aren't they beautiful?" His daughter held up a bunch of red and yellow roses.

"They're lovely, sweetheart."

"Dick, did I tell you? Bernie and Leila are flying east next week. They'll be here Friday."

"Johnny told me. . . . An Osterman weekend. I'll have to get in shape."

"I thought you were practicing last night."

Tremayne laughed. He never apologized for getting drunk, it happened too seldom, and he was never really difficult. Besides, last night he had deserved it. It *had* been a rotten week.

The three of them walked back to the patio. Virginia slipped her hand under her husband's arm. Peggy, growing so tall, her father thought, smiled brightly. The patio phone rang.

"I'll get it!" Peg dashed ahead.

"Why not?" shouted her father in mock exasperation. "It's never for us!"

"We've simply got to get her her own telephone." Virginia Tremayne pinched her husband's arm playfully.

"You're both driving me on welfare."

"It's for you, mother. It's Mrs. Cardone." Peggy suddenly covered the receiver with her hand. *"Please* don't talk too long, Mother. Carol Brown said she'd call me when she got home. You know, I told you. The Choate boy."

Virginia Tremayne smiled knowingly, exchanging a conspiratorial look with her daughter. "Carol won't elope without telling you, darling. She may need more than her week's allowance."

"Oh, mother!"

Richard watched them with amusement. It was comfortable and comforting at the same time. His wife was doing a good job with their child. No one could argue with that. He knew there were those who criticized Ginny, said she dressed a little . . . flamboyantly. He'd heard that word and knew it meant something else. But the kids. The kids all flocked around Ginny. That was important these days. Perhaps his wife knew something most other women didn't know.

Things . . . "things" were working out, thought Tremayne. Even the ultimate security, if Bernie Osterman was to be believed.

It was a good life.

He'd get on the phone with Joe if Ginny and Betty ever finished with their conversation. Then he'd call John and Ali. After Johnny's television shows were over. Perhaps the six of them could go over to the Club for the Sunday buffet.

Suddenly the memory of the patrol car flashed across his mind. He dismissed it. He had been nervous, edgy, hung over. Let's face it, he thought. It *was* Sunday afternoon and the town council *had* insisted that the police thoroughly check out the residential areas on Sunday afternoons.

Funny, he mused. He didn't think the Cardones were due back so early. Joe must have been called by his office to get in on Monday. The market was crazy these days. Especially commodities, Joe's specialty.

Betty nodded yes to Joe's question from the telephone. It solved the dinner problem. The buffet wasn't bad, even if the Club had never learned the secret of a good antipasto. Joe kept telling the manager that you had to use Genoa salami, not Hebrew National, but the chef had a deal with a Jewish supplier, so what could a mere member do? Even Joe, probably the richest of them all. On the other hand he was Italian—not Catholic, but nevertheless Italian—and it had only been a decade since the Saddle Valley Country Club first let Italians join. One of these days they'd let Jews in—that'd be the time for some kind of celebration.

It was this silent intolerance—never spelled out —that caused the Cardones, the Tanners and the Tremaynes to make it a special point to have Bernie and Leila Osterman very much in evidence at the Club whenever they came east. One thing could be said for the six of them. They weren't bigots.

It was strange, thought Cardone as he hung up the phone and started toward the small gym on the side of his house, strange that the Tanners had brought them all together. It had been John and Ali Tanner who had known the Ostermans in Los Angeles when Tanner was just starting out. Now Joe wondered whether John and Ali really understood the bond between Bernie Osterman and

25

him and Dick Tremayne. It was a bond one didn't discuss with outsiders.

Eventually it would spell out the kind of independence every man sought, every worried citizen might pray for; there were dangers, risks, but it was right for him and Betty. Right for the Tremaynes and the Ostermans. They had discussed it among themselves, analyzed it, thought it through carefully, and collectively reached the decision.

It might have been right for the Tanners. But Joe, Dick and Bernie agreed that the first signal had to come from John himself. That was paramount. Enough hints had been dropped and Tanner had not responded.

Joe closed the heavy, matted door of his personal gymnasium, turned on the steam dials and stripped. He put on a pair of sweatpants and took his sweatshirt off the stainless-steel rack. He smiled as he noticed the embroidered initials on the flannel. Only a girl from Chestnut Hill would have a monogram sewn on a sweatshirt.

J. A. C.

Joseph Ambruzzio Cardone.

Guiseppe Ambruzzio Cardione. Second of eight children from the union of Angela and Umberto Cardione, once of Sicily and later South Philadelphia. Eventually, citizens. American flags alongside countless, cosmeticized pictures of the Virgin Mary holding a cherubic Christ-child with blue eyes and red lips.

Guiseppe Ambruzzio Cardione grew into a large, immensely strong young man who was just about the best athlete South Philadelphia High had ever seen. He was president of his senior class and twice elected to the All-City Student Council.

Of the many college scholarships offered he chose the most prestigious, Princeton, also the nearest to Philadelphia. As a Princeton halfback he accomplished the seemingly impossible for his alma mater. He was chosen All-American, the first Princeton football player in years to be so honored.

Several grateful alumni brought him to Wall Street. He'd shortened his name to Cardone, the last vowel pronounced very slightly. It had a kind of majesty, he thought. Like Cardozo. But no one was fooled; soon he didn't care. The market was expanding, exploding to the point where *everyone* was buying securities. At first he was merely a good customers' man. An Italian boy who had made good, a fellow who could talk to the emerging new-rich with money to spend; talk in ways the new-rich, still nervous about investments, could understand.

And it had to happen.

The Italians are sensitive people. They're more comfortable doing business with their own kind. A number of the construction boys—the Castelanos, the Latronas, the Battellas—who had made fortunes in industrial developments, gravitated to Cardone. Two syllables only. "Joey Cardone," they called him. And Joey found them tax shelters, Joey found them capital gains, Joey found them security.

The money poured in. The gross of the brokerage house nearly doubled, thanks to Joey's friends. Worthington and Bennett, members, N. Y. Stock Exchange, became Worthington, Bennett and Cardone. From that point it was a short leap to Bennett-Cardone, Ltd.

Cardone was grateful to his *compares*. But the reason for his gratitude was also the reason why he shuddered just a bit when a patrol car appeared too frequently around his house. For a few of his *compares,* perhaps more than a few, were on the fringes—perhaps more than the fringes—of the underworld.

He finished with the weights and climbed on his rowing machine. The perspiration was pouring out and he felt better now. The menace of the patrol car began to diminish. After all, ninety-nine percent of the Saddle Valley families returned from vacations on Sunday. Who ever heard of people coming back from a vacation on a Wednesday? Even if the day were listed as such at the police station, a conscientious desk sergeant might well consider it an error and change it to Sunday. No one returned on Wednesday. Wednesday was a business day.

And who would ever take seriously the idea that Joseph Cardone had anything to do with the Cosa Nostra? He was the living proof of the work ethic. The American Success Story. A Princeton All-American.

Joe removed his sweatsuit and walked into the steam room, now dense with vapor. He sat on the bench and breathed deeply. The steam was purifying. After nearly two weeks of French-Canadian cooking, his body needed purifying.

He laughed aloud in his steam room. It was good to be home, his wife was right about that. And Tremayne told him the Ostermans would be flying in Friday morning. It'd be good to see Bernie and Leila again. It had been nearly four months. But they'd kept in touch.

Two hundred and fifty miles south of Saddle Valley, New Jersey, is that section of the nation's capital known as Georgetown. In Georgetown the pace of life changes every day at 5:30 P.M. Before, the pace is gradual, aristocratic, even delicate. After, there is a quickening—not sudden, but with a growing momentum. The residents, for the most part men and women of power and wealth and commitments to both, are dedicated to the propagation of their influence.

After five-thirty, the games begin.

After five-thirty in Georgetown, it is time for stratagems.

Who is where? . . . Why are they there?

Except on Sunday afternoon, when the power-brokers survey their creations of the previous week, and take the time to restore their strength for the next six days of strategy.

Let there be light and there *was* light. Let there be rest and there *is* rest.

Except, again, not for all.

For instance, not for Alexander Danforth, aide

29

to the President of the United States. An aide without portfolio and without specified activities.

Danforth was the liaison between the all-securities communications room in the underground levels of the White House and the Central Intelligence Agency in McLean, Virginia. He was the compleat power-broker because he was never in evidence, yet his decisions were among the most important in Washington. Regardless of administrations, his quiet voice was heeded by all. It had been for years.

On this particular Sunday afternoon, Danforth sat with the Central Intelligence Agency's Deputy Administrator, George Grover, beneath the bougainvillea tree on Danforth's small backyard patio, watching television. The two men had reached the same conclusion John Tanner had reached two hundred and fifty miles north: Charles Woodward was going to make news tomorrow morning.

"State's going to use up a month's supply of toilet tissue," Danforth said.

"They should. Whoever let Ashton go on? He's not only stupid, he *looks* stupid. Stupid and slippery. John Tanner's responsible for this program, isn't he?"

"He is."

"Smart son of a bitch. It'd be nice to be certain he's on our side," Grover said.

"Fassett's assured us." The two men exchanged looks. "Well, you've seen the file. Don't you agree?"

"Yes. Yes, I do. Fassett's right."

"He generally is."

There were two telephones on the ceramic table in front of Danforth. One was black with an outdoor plug-in jack on the ground. The other was red and a red cable extended from inside the house. The red phone hummed—it did not ring. Danforth picked it up.

"Yes. . . . Yes, Andrews. Good. . . . Fine. Ring Fassett on Redder and tell him to come over. Has Los Angeles confirmed the Ostermans? No change? . . . Excellent. We're on schedule."

Bernard Osterman, C.C.N.Y., Class of '46, pulled the page out of his typewriter and glanced at it. Adding it to the bottom of a thin sheaf of papers, he stood up. He walked around his kidney-shaped pool and handed the manuscript to his wife, Leila, who sat naked in her lounge chair.

Osterman was naked too.

"You know, an undressed woman's not particularly attractive in sunlight."

"You think you're a portrait in beige? . . . Give." She took the pages and reached for her large, tinted glasses. "Is this the finish?"

Bernie nodded. "When are the kids getting home?"

"They'll call from the beach before they start back. I told Marie to make sure they phone. I wouldn't want Merwyn to find out about naked girls in sunlight at his age. There's enough aversion to that in this town."

"You've got a point. Read." Bernie dove into the

31

pool. He swam back and forth rapidly for three minutes . . . until he was out of breath. He was a good swimmer. In the Army they made him a swimming instructor at Fort Dix. "Speed-Jew" they had called him at the Army pool. But never to his face. He was a thin man, but tough. If C.C.N.Y. had had a football team instead of a joke, he would have been its captain. An end. Joe Cardone told Bernie he could have used him at Princeton.

Bernie had laughed when Joe told him that. In spite of the surface democratization of the Army experience—and it was surface—it had never occurred to Bernard Osterman, of the Tremont Avenue Ostermans, Bronx, New York, to vault time-honored barriers and enter the Ivy League. He might have been able to, he was bright and there was the G.I. Bill, but it simply never entered his thinking.

It wouldn't have been comfortable then—in 1946. It would be now; things had changed.

Osterman climbed up the ladder. It was good that he and Leila were going to the east coast, back to Saddle Valley for a few days. It was somehow akin to taking a brief, concentrated course in pleasant living whenever they returned. Everyone always said the east was hectic, pressurized—far more so than Los Angeles; but that wasn't so. It only seemed that way because the area of action was more confined.

Los Angeles, *his* Los Angeles, which meant Burbank, Hollywood, Beverly Hills, was where the real insanity was practiced. Men and women racing crazily up and down the aisles of a palm-lined drug store. Everything on sale, everything labeled, everyone competing in their psychedelic shirts and orange slacks.

There were times when Bernie just wanted to see someone dressed in a Brooks Brothers suit and a buttondown broadcloth. It didn't really mean anything, not actually; he didn't give much of a damn what costumes the tribes of Los Angeles wore. Perhaps it was just the continual, overbearing assault on the eyes.

Or perhaps he was entering one of his downswings again. He was wearying of it all.

Which was unfair. The palm-lined drug store had treated him very well.

"How is it?" he asked his wife.

"Pretty good. You may even have a problem."

"What?" Bernie grabbed a towel from a stack on the table. "What problem?"

"You could be stripping too many layers away. Too much pain, maybe." Leila flipped over a page as her husband smiled. "Be quiet a minute and let me finish. Perhaps you'll snap out of it."

Bernie Osterman sat down in a webbed chair and let the warm California sun wash over his body. There was still a smile on his lips; he knew what his wife meant and it was comforting to him. The years of formula writing hadn't destroyed his ability to strip away the layers—when he wanted to.

And there were times when there was nothing more important to him than to want to. To prove to himself that he could still do it. The way he used to back in the days when they lived in New York.

They were good days. Provocative, exciting, filled with commitment and purpose. Only there was never anything else really—just commitment, just purpose. A few flattering reviews written by other intense young writers. He'd been called *penetrating* then; *perceptive, incisive.* Once, even, *extraordinary.*

It hadn't been enough. And so he and Leila came to the palm-lined drug store and willingly, happily trained their talents for the exploding world of the television residual.

Someday, though. Someday, thought Bernard Osterman, it would happen again. The luxury of sitting down with all the time in the world to really do it. Make a big mistake if he had to. It was important to be able to think like that.

"Bernie?"

"Yes?"

Leila draped a towel over her front and pushed the latch on the lounge chair so the back raised itself. "It's beautiful, sweetie. I mean really very beautiful, and I think you know it's not going to work."

"It does work!"

"They won't sit still for it."

"Fuck 'em!"

"We're being paid thirty thousand for a one-hour drama, Bernie. Not a two-hour exorcism ending in a funeral home."

"It's not an exorcism. It happens to be a sad

story based on very real conditions, and the conditions don't change. You want to drive down to the barrio and take a look?"

"They won't buy it. They'll want rewrites."

"I won't make them!"

"And they'll hold the balance. There's fifteen thousand coming to us."

"Son of a bitch!"

"You know I'm right."

"Talk! All Goddamned talk! This season we'll have *meaning! Controversy!* . . . Talk!"

"They look at the figures. A rave in *The Times* doesn't sell deodorant in Kansas."

"Fuck 'em."

"Relax. Take another swim. It's a big pool." Leila Osterman looked at her husband. He knew what that look meant and couldn't help smiling. A little sadly.

"O.K., fix it then."

Leila reached for the pencil and yellow pad on the table next to her chair. Bernie stood up and approached the edge of the pool.

"You think Tanner might want to join us? You think maybe I can approach him?"

His wife put down her pencil and looked up at her husband. "I don't know. Johnny's different from us . . ."

"Different from Joe and Betty? Dick and Ginny? I don't see he's so different."

"I wouldn't jump at him. He's still a newshawk. Vulture they used to call him, remember? The vulture of San Diego. He's got a spine. I wouldn't want to bend it. It might snap back."

35

"He thinks like we do. He thinks like Joe and Dick. Like us."

"I repeat. Don't jump. Call it the well-advertised woman's intuition, but don't jump. . . . We could get hurt."

Osterman dove into the pool and swam thirty-six feet under water to the far end. Leila was only half right, he thought. Tanner was an uncompromising newsman but he was also a sensible and sensitive human being. Tanner wasn't a fool, he saw what was happening—everywhere. It was inevitable.

It all came down to individual survival.

It reduced itself to being able to do what one wanted to do. To write an "exorcism" if he was capable of it. Without worrying about deodorants in the state of Kansas.

Bernie surfaced and held onto the side of the pool, breathing deeply. He pushed himself off and slowly breast-stroked back toward his wife.

"Did I box you into a corner?"

"You never could." Leila spoke while writing on the yellow pad. "There was a time in my life when I thought thirty thousand dollars was all the money in the world. Brooklyn's house of Weintraub was not Chase Manhattan's biggest client." She tore off a page and secured it under a Pepsi-Cola bottle.

"I never had that problem," said Bernie treading water. "The Ostermans are really a silent branch of the Rothschilds."

"I know. Your racing colors are puce and pumpkin orange."

36

"Hey!" Bernie suddenly grasped the ledge and looked excitedly at his wife. "Did I tell you? The trainer called this morning from Palm Springs. That two-year-old we bought did three furlongs in forty-one seconds!"

Leila Osterman dropped the pad on her lap and laughed. "You know, we're really too much! And you want to play Dostoyevski!"

"I see what you mean. . . . Well, someday."

"Sure. In the meantime keep one eye on Kansas and the other on those cockamamie horses of yours."

Osterman chuckled and plunged toward the opposite side of the pool. He thought once more about the Tanners. John and Ali Tanner. He'd cleared their names with Switzerland. Zurich was enthusiastic.

Bernard Osterman had made up his mind. Somehow he'd convince his wife.

He was going to talk seriously to John Tanner next weekend.

Danforth walked through the narrow front hallway of his Georgetown house and opened the door. Laurence Fassett, of the Central Intelligence Agency, smiled and extended his hand.

"Good afternoon, Mr. Danforth. Andrews called me from McLean. We've only met once before—I'm sure you don't remember. It's an honor, sir."

Danforth looked at this extraordinary man and returned the smile. The C.I.A. dossier said Fassett was forty-seven, but to Danforth he seemed much younger. The broad shoulders, the muscular neck, the unwrinkled face beneath the short-cropped blond hair: this all reminded Danforth of his own approaching seventieth birthday.

"Of course I remember. Come in, please."

As Fassett stepped into the hallway, his gaze fell on several Degas watercolors on the wall. He took a step closer. "These are beautiful."

"Yes, they are. Are you an expert, Mr. Fassett?"

"Oh, no. Just an enthusiastic amateur. . . . My wife was an artist. We used to spend a lot of time in the Louvre."

Danforth knew he shouldn't dwell on Fassett's wife. She had been German—with ties in East Berlin. She had been killed in East Berlin.

"Yes, yes, of course. Come this way, please. Grover's out back. We were watching the Woodward program on the patio."

The two men walked out onto the flagstone and brick back yard. George Grover rose from his chair.

"Hello, Larry. Things are beginning to move."

"Looks that way. It can't be too quick for me."

"Nor for any of us, I shouldn't think," said Danforth. "Drink?"

"No, thank you, sir. If you don't mind, I'd rather make this as quick as possible."

The three men sat down around the ceramic table. "Then let's pick up from where we are right now," Danforth said. "What is the immediate plan?"

Fassett looked bewildered. "I thought it had all been cleared through you."

"Oh, I've read the reports. I just want the information firsthand from the man in charge."

"All right, sir. Phase one is complete. The Tanners, the Tremaynes and the Cardones are all in Saddle Valley. No immediate vacations planned, they'll be there throughout the coming week. This information is confirmed from all our sources. There are thirteen agents in the town and the three families will be under constant surveillance. . . . Intercepts have been placed on all telephones. Untaceable.

"Los Angeles has established the Ostermans' flight on Friday to be Number 509, arriving Kennedy at 4:50 Eastern Daylight Time. Their usual procedure is to take a taxi directly out to the suburbs. The cab will be followed, of course . . ."

"If, by then, they're adhering to normal patterns," interrupted Grover.

"If they're not, they won't be on that plane. . . . Tomorrow we bring Tanner down to Washington."

"He has no inkling at the moment, does he?" asked Danforth.

"None at all—other than the patrol car, which we'll use if he balks tomorrow morning."

"How do you think he'll take it?" Grover leaned forward on his seat.

"I think it'll blow his mind."

"He may refuse to cooperate," Danforth said.

"That's not likely. If I do my job, he won't have a choice."

Danforth looked at the intense, muscular man who spoke so confidently. "You're anxious that we succeed, aren't you? You're very committed."

"I have reason to be." Fassett returned the old man's stare. When he continued it was in a matter-of-fact tone. "They killed my wife. They ran her down on the Kurfürstendamm at two o'clock in the morning—while I was being 'detained.' She was trying to find me. Did you know that?"

"I've read the file. You have my deepest sympathy. . . ."

"I don't want your sympathy. Those orders came from Moscow. I want them. I want Omega."

PART TWO

MONDAY
TUESDAY
WEDNESDAY
THURSDAY

2

Tanner left the elevator and walked down the thickly carpeted corridor toward his office. He'd spent twenty-five minutes in the screening room watching the Woodward tape. It confirmed what the newspapers had reported: Charles Woodward had exposed Undersecretary Ashton as a political hack.

There had to be a lot of embarrassed men in Washington, he thought.

"Quite a show, wasn't it?" his secretary said.

"Out-of-sight, as my son would put it. I don't think we can expect many dinner invitations to the White House. Any calls?"

"From all over town. Mainly congratulations; I left the names on your desk."

"That's comforting. I may need them. Anything else?"

"Yes, sir. The F.C.C. called twice. A man called Fassett."

"Who?"

43

"Mr. Laurence Fassett."

"We've always dealt with Cranston down there."

"That's what I thought, but he said it was urgent."

"Maybe the State Department's trying to get us arrested before sundown."

"I doubt it. They'd at least wait a day or two; it'd look less political."

"You'd better get him back. To the F.C.C. everything's urgent." Tanner crossed into his office, sat down at his desk, and read through the messages. He smiled; even his competition had been impressed.

The telephone intercom buzzed. "Mr. Fassett's on one, sir."

"Thanks." Tanner pushed the appropriate button. "Mr. Fassett? Sorry I was out of the office when you called."

"It's my place to apologize," said the polite voice at the other end of the line. "It's just that I have a difficult schedule today, and you're a priority."

"What's the problem?"

"Routine but urgent is the best way I can describe it. The papers you filed with us in May for Standard's news division were incomplete."

"What?" John remembered something F.C.C.'s Cranston had said to him a few weeks ago. He also recalled that Cranston had said it was unimportant. "What's missing?"

"Two signatures of yours for one thing. On pages seventeen and eighteen. And the breakdown of projected public service features for the six-month period commencing in January."

John Tanner did remember now. It had been Cranston's fault. Pages seventeen and eighteen had been missing from the folder sent from Washington for Tanner's signature—a point which the network's legal department had made to Tanner's office—and the service feature blanks were to be left open for another month, pending network decisions. Cranston, again, had agreed.

"If you'll check, you'll find your Mr. Cranston omitted the pages you refer to and the specific service features were postponed. He agreed to that."

There was a momentary pause from Washington. When Fassett spoke his voice held a touch less politeness than it had previously.

"In all deference to Cranston, he had no authority to make such a decision. Surely you have the information now." It was a statement.

"Yes, as a matter of fact, we do. I'll send it out Special Delivery."

"I'm afraid that's not good enough. We'll have to ask you to get down here this afternoon."

"Now, wait a minute. That's kind of short notice, isn't it?"

"I don't make the rules. I just carry them out. As of two months ago Standard Mutual Network is operating in violation of the F.C.C. code. We can't allow ourselves to be put in that position. Regardless of who's responsible, that is a fact. You're in violation. Let's get it cleared up today."

"All right. But I warn you, if this action is in any

45

way a harassment emanating from the State Department, I'll bring down the network attorneys and label it for what it is."

"I not only don't like your insinuation, but I don't know what you're talking about."

"I think you do. The Woodward Show yesterday afternoon."

Fassett laughed. "Oh, I heard about that. The *Post* did quite a story on it. . . . And I think you can put your mind at ease. I tried to reach you twice last Friday."

"You did?"

"Yes."

"Wait a minute." Tanner pushed the *hold* button and then the *local*. "Norma? Did this Fassett try to get me Friday?"

There was a short silence while Tanner's secretary checked Friday's call sheet. "Could be. There were two calls from Washington, an Operator thirty-six in D. C. for you to reach if you returned by four. You were in the studio till five-thirty."

"Didn't you ask who was calling?"

"Of course I did. The only answer I got was that it could wait until Monday."

"Thanks." Tanner got back on the line with Fassett. "Did you leave an operator's number?"

"Operator three-six, Washington. Till 4:00 P.M."

"You didn't give your name or identify the agency. . . ."

"It was Friday. I wanted to get out early. Would you have felt better if I'd left an urgent call you couldn't return?"

46

"Okay, okay. And this can't wait for the mails?"

"I'm sorry, Mr. Tanner. I mean I'm really very sorry, but I have my instructions. Standard Mutual's not a small local station. This filing should have been completed weeks ago. . . . Also," here Fassett laughed again, "the way you keep stepping on exposed toes, I wouldn't want to be you if some wheels in the State Department found out your whole damn news department was in violation. . . . And that's no threat. It couldn't be. We're both at fault."

John Tanner smiled at the telephone. Fassett was right. The filing *was* overdue. And there was no sense risking bureaucratic reprisals. He sighed. "I'll catch the one o'clock shuttle and be at the F.C.C. by three or a little after. Where's your office?"

"I'll be with Cranston. We'll have the papers, and don't forget the schedules. They're only projections, we won't hold you to them."

"Right. See you then." Tanner pushed another button and dialed his home number.

"Hi, darling."

"I've got to hop down to Washington this afternoon."

"Any problems?"

"No. 'Routine but urgent' was the description. Some F.C.C. business. I'll catch a shuttle back to Newark by seven. I just wanted you to know that I'd be late."

"Okay, darling. Do you want me to pick you up?"

"No, I'll get a cab."

"Sure?"

"Very. It'll make me feel good to think Standard's paying the twenty bucks."

"You're worth it. By the way, I read the reviews on the Woodward Show. You're a regular triumph."

"That's what I wrote across my jacket. Tanner the Triumph."

"I wish you would," said Alice quietly.

Even in jest she could never let it go. They had no real money problems, but Alice Tanner forever thought her husband was underpaid. It was the only serious argument between them. He could never explain that to seek more from a corporation like Standard Mutual meant just that much more obligation to the faceless giant.

"See you tonight, Ali."

"Bye. I love you."

As if in silent deference to his wife's complaint, Tanner commandeered one of the news cars to take him to LaGuardia Airport in an hour. No one argued. Tanner was, indeed, a triumph this morning.

During the next forty-five minutes, Tanner tied together a number of administrative loose ends. The last order of business was a call to Standard Mutual's legal department.

"Mr. Harrison, please. . . . Hello, Andy? John Tanner. I'm in a hurry, Andy; I've got to catch a plane. I just want to find out something. Do we have anything pending with the F.C.C. I don't know about? Any problems? I know about the public service features but Cranston said we could hold on those. . . . Sure, I'll wait." Tanner fingered the telephone cord, his thoughts still on Fassett. "Yes, Andy, I'm here. . . . Pages seventeen and eighteen. The signatures. . . . I see. Okay. Thanks. No, no problems here. Thanks again."

Tanner replaced the phone and got out of his chair slowly. Harrison had added fuel to his vague suspicions. It all seemed just a bit too contrived. The F.C.C. filing had been complete except for the final two pages on the fourth and fifth copies of the document. They were merely duplicates, important to no one, easily Xeroxed. Yet those pages had been missing from the file. Harrison had just commented:

"I remember, John. I sent you a memo about it. It looked to me as though they had been deliberately left out. Can't imagine why. . . ."

Neither could Tanner.

3

Monday—3:25 P.M.

To Tanner's amazement, the F.C.C. sent a limousine to meet his plane.

Cranston's offices were on the sixth floor of the F.C.C. Building; at one time or another every major network news director had been summoned there. Cranston was a career man—respected by the networks as well as the changing administrations—and because of this Tanner found himself resenting the unknown Laurence Fassett, who could say with indignation, ". . . Cranston had no authority to make such a decision."

He'd never heard of Laurence Fassett.

Tanner pushed open the door to Cranston's waiting room. It was empty. The secretary's desk was bare—no pads, no pencils, no papers of any kind. What light there was came from Cranston's office door. It was open and he could hear the quiet whirr of an air conditioner. The window shades in the office were down, probably to keep out the summer sunlight. And then, against the office wall, he saw the shadow of a figure walking towards the door.

"Good afternoon," said the man as he came into view. He was shorter than Tanner by several inches, probably five ten or eleven, but very broad in the shoulders. His blond hair was cut short, his eyes set far apart beneath bushy light-brown eyebrows. He was, perhaps, Tanner's age, but without question a more physical man. Even his stance had a potential spring to it, thought Tanner.

"Mr. Fassett?"

"That's right. Won't you come in?" Fassett, instead of retreating into Cranston's office, crossed in front of Tanner to the door and locked it. "We'd rather not have any interruptions."

"Why not?" asked Tanner, startled.

Laurence Fassett looked about the room. "Yes. Yes. I see what you mean. Good point. Come in, please." Fassett walked in front of Tanner into Cranston's office. The shades of the two windows overlooking the street were pulled all the way down; Cranston's desk was as bare as his secretary's, except for two ashtrays and one other item. In the center of the cleared surface was a small Wollensak tape recorder with two cords—one in front of Cranston's chair, the other by the chair in front of Cranston's desk.

"Is that a tape recorder?" asked the news director, following Fassett into the office.

"Yes, it is. Won't you sit down, please?"

John Tanner remained standing. When he spoke it was with quiet anger. "No, I will *not* sit down. I don't like any of this. Your methods are very unclear, or maybe *too* clear. If you intend putting anything I say down on tape, you know perfectly well I won't allow it without the presence of a network attorney."

Fassett stood behind Cranston's desk. "This is not F.C.C. business. When I explain, you'll understand my . . . methods."

"You'd better explain quickly, because I'm about to leave. I was called by the F.C.C. to deliver the public service hours projected by Standard Mutual—which I have in my briefcase—and to sign two copies of our filing which *your* office omitted sending. You made it clear that you would be with Cranston when I arrived. Instead, I find an office which obviously is not in use. . . . I'd say you'd better have a good explanation or you'll be hearing from our attorneys within an hour. And if this is any kind of reprisal against Standard Mutual's news division, I'll blast you from coast to coast."

"I'm sorry. . . . These things are never easy."

"They shouldn't be!"

"Now hold it. Cranston's on vacation. We used his name because you've dealt with him before."

"You're telling me you intentionally lied?"

"Yes. The key, Mr. Tanner, is in the phrase you employed just now . . . 'I was called by the F.C.C.,' I believe you said. May I present my credentials?" Laurence Fassett reached into his breast pocket and withdrew a small black plastic case. He held it across the desk.

Tanner opened it.

The top card identified Laurence C. Fassett as an employee of the Central Intelligence Agency.

The other car was Fassett's priority permit to enter the McLean complex at any hour of day or night.

"What's this all about? Why am I here?" Tanner handed back Fassett's identification.

"That's the reason for the tape recorder. Let me show you. Before I explain our business I have to ask you a number of questions. There are two switches which can shut off the machine. One here by me, the other there by you. If at any time I ask you a question you do not care to answer, all you have to do is push the OFF switch and the machine stops. On the other hand—and, again, for your protection—if I feel you are including private information which is no concern of ours, *I* shall stop the machine." Fassett started up the recorder with his switch and then reached across the desk for the cord in front of Tanner's chair and stopped it. "See? Quite simple. I've been through hundreds of these interviews. You've got nothing to worry about."

"This sounds like a pretrial examination without benefit of counsel or mandate of subpoena! What's the point? If you think you're going to intimidate me, you're crazy!"

"The *point* is one of completely positive identification. . . . And you're absolutely right. If it was our intention to intimidate anyone, we picked about as vulnerable a subject as J. Edgar Hoover. And even *he* doesn't have control of a network news program."

Tanner looked at the C.I.A. man standing politely behind Cranston's desk. Fassett had a point. The C.I.A. wouldn't allow itself to use so blatant a tactic on someone in his position.

"What do you mean, 'completely positive identification'? You know who I am."

"It should give you some idea of the magnitude of the information I'm empowered to deliver. Just extraordinary precaution in line with the importance of the data. . . . Did you know that in the Second World War an actor—a corporal in the British army, to be exact—impersonated Field Marshall Montgomery at high-level conferences in Africa and even some of Montgomery's Sandhurst classmates didn't catch on?"

The news director picked up the cord and pushed the ON and OFF switches. The machine started and stopped. John Tanner's curiosity—mingled with fear—was growing. He sat down. "Go ahead. Just remember, I'll shut off the tape and leave any time I want to."

"I understand. That's your privilege—up to a point."

"What do you mean by that? No qualifications, please."

"Trust me. You'll understand." Fassett's reassuring look served its purpose.

"Go ahead," said Tanner. The C.I.A. man picked up a manila folder and opened it. He then started the machine.

54

"Your full name is John Raymond Tanner?"

"Incorrect. My legal name is John Tanner. The Raymond was a baptismal name and is not registered on my birth certificate."

Fassett smiled from across the desk. "Very good."

"Thank you."

"You currently reside at 22 Orchard Drive, Saddle Valley, New Jersey?"

"I do."

"You were born on May 21, 1924, in Springfield, Illinois, to Lucas and Margaret Tanner?"

"Yes."

"Your family moved to San Mateo, California, when you were seven years old?"

"Yes."

"For what purpose?"

"My father's firm transferred him to Northern California. He was a personnel executive for a department-store chain. The Bryant Stores."

"Comfortable circumstances?"

"Reasonably so."

"You were educated in the San Mateo public school system?"

"No. I went through the second year of San Mateo High and transferred to a private school for the final two years of secondary school. Winston Preparatory."

"Upon graduation you enrolled at Stanford University?"

"Yes."

"Were you a member of any fraternities or clubs?"

"Yes. Alpha Kappa fraternity. The Trylon News Society, several others I can't recall. . . . Photography club, I think, but I didn't stay. I worked on the campus magazine, but quit."

"Any reason?"

Tanner looked at the C.I.A. man. "Yes. I strenuously objected to the Nisei situation. The prison camps. The magazine supported them. My objection still stands."

Fassett smiled again. "Your education was interrupted?"

"Most educations were. I enlisted in the Army at the end of my sophomore year."

"Where were you trained?"

"Fort Benning, Georgia. Infantry."

"Third Army? Fourteenth Division?"

"Yes."

"You saw service in the European theatre of operations?"

"Yes."

"Your highest rank was First Lieutenant?"

"Yes."

"O.C.S. training at Fort Benning?"

"No. I received a Field Commission in France."

"I see you also received several decorations."

"They were unit citations, battalion commendations. Not individual."

"You were hospitalized for a period of three weeks in St. Lô. Was this a result of wounds?"

Tanner looked momentarily embarrassed. "You know perfectly well it wasn't. There's no Purple Heart on my Army record," he said quietly.

"Would you explain?"

"I fell out of a jeep on the road to St. Lô. Dislocated hip."

Both men smiled.

"You were discharged in July of 1945 and returned to Stanford the following September?"

"I did. . . . To anticipate you, Mr. Fassett, I switched from an English major to the journalism school. I graduated in 1947 with a Bachelor of Arts degree."

Laurence Fassett's eyes remained on the folder in front of him. "You were married in your junior year to one Alice McCall?"

Tanner reached for his switch and shut off the machine. "This may be where I walk out."

"Relax, Mr. Tanner. Just identification. . . . We don't subscribe to the theory that the sins of the parents are visited upon their daughters. A simple yes or no will suffice."

Tanner started the machine again. "That is correct."

At this point, Laurence Fassett picked the cord off the desk and pushed the OFF switch. Tanner watched the reels stop, and then looked at the C.I.A. man.

"My next two questions concern the circumstances leading up to your marriage. I presume you do not care to answer them."

"You presume correctly."

"Believe me, they aren't important."

"If you told me they were, I'd leave right now."
Ali had been through enough. Tanner would not

allow his wife's personal tragedy to be brought up again, by anyone.

Fassett started the machine again. "Two children were born to you and Alice Mc . . . Tanner. A boy, Raymond, now age thirteen, and a girl, Janet, now eight."

"My son is twelve."

"His birthday is day after tomorrow. To go back a bit, your first employment after graduation was with *The Sacramento Daily News.*"

"Reporter. Rewrite man, office boy, movie critic and space salesman when time permitted."

"You stayed with the Sacramento paper for three and a half years and then obtained a position with *The Los Angeles Times?*"

"No. I was in Sacramento for . . . two and a half years—I had an interim job with the *San Francisco Chronicle* for about a year before I got the job at *The Times.*"

"On *The Los Angeles Times* you were quite successful as an investigative reporter. . . ."

"I was fortunate. I assume you're referring to my work on the San Diego waterfront operations."

"I am. You were nominated for a Pulitzer, I believe."

"I didn't get it."

"And then elevated to an editorial position with *The Times?*"

"An assistant editor. Nothing spectacular."

"You remained with *The Times* for a period of five years. . . ."

"Nearer six, I think."

"Until January of 1958 when you joined Standard Mutual in Los Angeles?"

"Correct."

"You remained on the Los Angeles staff until March of 1963 when you were transferred to New York City. Since that time you have received several promotions?"

"I came east as a network editor for the seven o'clock news program. I expanded into documentaries and specials until I reached my present position."

"Which is?"

"Director of News for Standard Mutual."

Laurence Fassett closed the folder and shut off the tape recorder. He leaned back and smiled at John Tanner. "That wasn't so painful, was it?"

"You mean that's it?"

"No, not . . . *it,* but the completion of the identity section. You passed. You gave me just enough slightly wrong answers to pass the test."

"What?"

"These things," Fassett slapped the folder, "are designed by the Interrogations Division. Fellows with high foreheads bring in other fellows with beards and they put the stuff through computers. You couldn't possibly answer everything correctly. If you did it would mean you had studied too hard. . . . For instance, you were with *The Sacramento Daily News* for three years almost to the day. Not two and a half or three and a half. Your family moved to San Mateo when you were eight years, two months, not seven years old."

59

"I'll be Goddamned. . . ."

"Frankly, even if you had answered everything correctly, we might have passed you. But it's nice to know you're normal. In your case, we had to have it all on tape. . . . Now, I'm afraid, comes the tough part."

"Tough compared to what?" asked the news editor.

"Just rough. . . . I have to start the machine now." He did so and picked up a single sheet of paper. "John Tanner, I must inform you that what I am about to discuss with you comes under the heading of classified information of the highest priority. In no way is this information a reflection on you or your family and to that I do so swear. The revealing of this information to anyone would be against the interests of the United States Government in the severest sense. So much so that those in the government service aware of this information can be prosecuted under the National Security Act, Title eighteen, Section seven-nine-three, should they violate the demands of secrecy. . . . Is everything I've said so far completely clear?"

"It is. . . . However, I am neither bound nor am I indictable."

"I realize that. It is my intention to take you in three stages toward the essential, classified information. At the end of stages one and two you may ask to be excused from this interview and we can only rely on your intelligence and loyalty to your government to keep silent about what has been said. However, if you agree to the third stage,

60

in which identities are revealed to you, you accept the same responsibility as those in government service and can be prosecuted under the National Security Act should you violate the aforementioned demands of secrecy. Is this clear, Mr. Tanner?"

Tanner shifted in his seat before speaking. He looked at the revolving wheels of the tape recorder and then up at Fassett. "It's clear, but I'll be damned if I agree to it. You don't have any right calling me down here under false pretenses and then setting up conditions that make me indictable."

"I didn't ask if you agreed. Only if you understood clearly what I said."

"And if that's a threat, you can go to hell."

"All I'm doing is spelling out conditions. Is that a threat? Is it any more than you do every day with contracts? You can walk out any time you like until you give me your consent to reveal names. Is that so illogical?"

Tanner reasoned that it wasn't, really. And his curiosity now had to be satisfied.

"You said earlier that whatever this thing is, it has nothing to do with my family? Nothing to do with my wife? . . . Or me?"

"I swore to it on this tape." Fassett realized that Tanner had added the "or me" as an afterthought. He was protecting his wife.

"Go ahead."

Fassett rose from the chair and walked toward the window shades. "By the way, you don't have to stay sitting down. They're high-impedance microphones. Miniaturized, of course."

"I'll sit."

"Suit yourself. A number of years ago we heard rumors of a Soviet NKVD operation which could have widespread, damaging effects on the American economy should it ever amount to anything. We tried to trace it down, tried to learn something about it. We couldn't. It remained rumor. It was a better-kept secret than the Russian space program.

"Then in 1966 an East German intelligence officer defected. He gave us our first concrete knowledge of the operation. He informed us that East German Intelligence maintained contact with agents in the West—or a cell—known only as *Omega*. I'll give you the geographical code name in a minute . . . or maybe I won't. It's in step two. That's up to you. Omega would regularly forward sealed files to East German Intelligence. Two armed couriers would fly them to Moscow under the strictest secrecy.

"The function of Omega is as old as espionage itself, and extremely effective in these days of large corporations and huge conglomerates. . . . Omega is a doomsday book."

"A what?"

"Doomsday book. Lists containing hundreds, perhaps by now thousands, of individuals marked for the plague. In this case not bubonic, but blackmail. The men and women on these lists are people in decision-making positions in scores of giant companies in key fields. Many have enormous economic power. Purchasing as well as refusal-to-purchase power. Forty or fifty, acting in concert, could create economic chaos."

"I don't understand. Why would they? Why should they?"

"I told you. Blackmail. Each of these people is vulnerable, exploitable for any of a thousand reasons. Sex, extracurricular or deviate; legal misrepresentation; business malpractice; price-fixing; stock manipulations; tax evasion. The book touches a great many people. Men and women whose reputations, businesses, professions, even their families could be destroyed. Unless they comply."

"It's also a pretty low view of the business world, and I'm not at all sure it's an accurate one. Not to the extent you describe it. Not to the point of economic chaos."

"Oh? The Crawford Foundation made an in-depth study of industry leadership in the United States from 1925 to 1945. The results are still classified a quarter of a century later. The study determined that during this period thirty-two percent of the corporate financial power in this country was obtained by questionable, if not illegal, means. *Thirty-two percent!*"

"I don't believe that. If it's true it should be made public."

"Impossible. There'd be legal massacre. Courts and money are not an immaculate combination. . . . Today it's the conglomerates. Pick up the newspaper any day. Turn to the financial pages and read about the manipulators. Look at the charges and countercharges. It's a mother lode for Omega.

A directory of candidates. None of those boys lives in a deep freeze. Not one of them. An unsecured loan is granted, a stock margin is expanded—temporarily—girls are provided to a good customer. Omega digs just a little with the right people and a lot of slime gets in the bucket. It's not very hard to do. You just have to be accurate. Enough so to frighten."

Tanner looked away from the blond man who spoke with such precision. With such relaxed confidence. "I don't like to think you're right."

Suddenly, Fassett crossed back to the table and turned off the tape recorder. The wheels stopped. "Why not? It's not just the information uncovered —that could be relatively harmless—but the way it's applied. Take *you*, for instance. Suppose, just suppose, a story based on occurrences around twenty some-odd years ago outside Los Angeles were printed in the Saddle Valley paper. Your children are in school there, your wife happy in the community. . . . How long do you think you'd stay there?"

Tanner lurched out of his chair and faced the shorter man across the desk. His rage was such that his hands trembled. He spoke with deep feeling, barely audible.

"That's filthy!"

"That's Omega, Mr. Tanner. Relax, I was only making a point." Fassett turned the recorder back on and continued as Tanner returned warily to his chair. "Omega exists. Which brings me to the last part of . . . stage one."

"What's that?"

Laurence Fassett sat down behind the desk. He crushed out his cigarette, while Tanner reached into his pocket and withdrew a pack. "We know now that there's a timetable for Omega. A date for the chaos to begin. . . . I'm not telling you anything you don't know when I admit that my agency is often involved in exchange of personnel with the Soviets."

"Nothing I don't know."

"One of ours for two or three of theirs is the normal ratio. . . ."

"I know that, too."

"Twelve months ago on the border of Albania such an exchange took place. Forty-five days of haggling. I was there, which is why I'm here now. During the exchange our team was approached by several members of the Soviet Foreign Service. The best way I can describe them to you is to call them moderates. The same as our moderates."

"I understand what our moderates oppose. What do the Soviet moderates oppose?"

"Same thing. Instead of a Pentagon—and an elusive military-industrial complex—it's the hard-liners in the Presidium. The militarists."

"I see."

"We were informed that the Soviet militarists have issued a target date for the final phase of Operation Omega. On that date the plan will be implemented. Untold hundreds of powerful executives in the American business community will be reached and threatened with personal destruction if they do not follow the orders given them. A major financial crisis could be the result. An economic disaster is not impossible. . . . It's the truth.

"That is the end of stage one."

Tanner got out of his chair, drawing on his cigarette. He paced up and down in front of the desk. "And with that information I have the option to get out of here?"

"You do."

"You're too much. Honest to Christ, you're too much! . . . The tape's running. Go on."

"Very well. Stage two. We knew that Omega was made up of the very same type of individual it will attack. It had to be, otherwise the contacts could never have been made, the vulnerabilities never established. In essence, we basically knew what to look for. Men who could infiltrate large companies, men who worked either in or for them, who could associate with their subjects. . . . As I mentioned previously, Omega is a code name for a cell or a group of agents. There is also a geographical code name; a clearing house for the forwarding of information. Having passed through this source, the authenticity is presumably established because of its operational secrecy. The geographical code name for Omega is difficult to give an accurate translation of, but the nearest is 'Chasm of . . . Leather' or 'Goat Skin.' "

" 'Chasm of Leather'?" Tanner put out his cigarette.

"Yes. Remember, we learned this over three years ago. After eighteen months of concentrated research we pinpointed the 'Chasm of Leather' as one of eleven locations throughout the country. . . ."

"One of them being Saddle Valley, New Jersey?"

"Let's not get ahead of ourselves."

"Am I right?"

"We placed agents within these communities," continued the C.I.A. man, disregarding Tanner's question. "We ran checks on thousands of citizens —a very expensive exercise—and the more we researched, the more evidence we turned up that the Village of Saddle Valley was the 'Chasm of Leather.' It was a thorough job. Watermarks on stationery, analysis of dust particles the East German officer brought out in the sealed folders he gave us when he defected, a thousand different items checked and rechecked. . . . But mainly, the information about certain residents unearthed in the research."

"I think you'd better get to the point."

"That will be *your* decision. I've just about concluded stage two." Tanner remained silent, so Fassett continued. "You are in a position to give us incalculable assistance. In one of the most sensitive operations in current U.S.-Soviet relations, you can do what no one else can do. It might even appeal to you, for as you must have gathered from what I've said, the moderates on both sides are at this moment working together."

"Please clarify that."

"Only fanatics subscribe to this type of insurgency. It's far too dangerous for both countries. There's a power struggle in the Soviet Presidium. The moderates must prevail for all our sakes. One way to accomplish this is to expose even part of Omega and kill the target date."

"How can I do anything?"

"You know Omega, Mr. Tanner. You know Omega very well."

Tanner caught his breath. For a moment he believed his heart had stopped. He felt the blood rush to his head. He felt, for an instant, somewhat sick.

"I find that an *incredible* statement."

"I would, too, if I were you. Nevertheless, it's true."

"And I gather this is the end of stage two? . . . You bastard. You son of a bitch!" Tanner spoke hardly above a whisper.

"Call me anything you like. Hit me if you want to. I won't hit back. . . . I told you, I've been through this before."

Tanner got out of the chair and pressed his fingers against his forehead. He turned away from Fassett, then whipped around. "Suppose you're *wrong?*" he whispered. "Suppose you Goddamn idiots have made another *mistake!*"

"We haven't. . . . We don't claim to have flushed Omega out completely. However, we *have* narrowed it down. You're in a unique position."

Tanner walked to the window and started to pull up the shade.

"Don't *touch* that! Hold it *down!*" Fassett leaped

from his chair and grabbed Tanner's wrist with one hand and the string of the shade with his other. Tanner looked into the agent's eyes.

"And if I walk out of here now, I live with what you've told me? Never knowing who's in my house, who I'm talking to in the street? Living with the knowledge that you think someone might fire a rifle into this room if I lift up the shade?"

"Don't over-dramatize. These are merely precautions."

Tanner walked back to his side of the desk but did not sit down. "Goddamn you," he said softly. "You know I can't leave. . . ."

"Do you accept the conditions?"

"I do."

"I must ask you to sign this affidavit." He took out a page from the manila folder and placed it in front of Tanner. It was a concise statement on the nature and penalties of the National Security Act. It referred to Omega in unspecific terms—Exhibit A, defined as the tape recording. Tanner scribbled his name and remained standing, staring at Fassett.

"I shall now ask you the following questions." Fassett picked up the folder and flipped to the back pages. "Are you familiar with the individuals I now specify? Richard Tremayne and his wife, Virginia. . . . Please reply."

Astounded, Tanner spoke softly, "I am."

"Joseph Cardone, born Guiseppe Ambruzzio Cardione, and his wife, Elizabeth?"

"I am."

"Bernard Osterman and his wife, Leila?"

"Yes."

"Louder, please, Mr. Tanner."

"I said, yes."

"I now inform you that one, two, or all three of the couples specified are essential to the Omega operation."

"You're out of your mind! You're insane!"

"We're not. . . . I spoke of our exchange on the Albanian border. It was made known to us then that Omega, Chasm of Leather, operated out of a Manhattan suburb—and that confirmed our analysis. That Omega was comprised of couples—men and women fanatically devoted to the militaristic policies of the Soviet expansionists. These couples were well paid for their services. The couples specified—the Tremaynes, the Cardones, and the Ostermans—currently possess coded bank accounts in Zurich, Switzerland, with amounts far exceeding any incomes ever reported."

"You can't mean what you're saying!"

"Even allowing for coincidence, and we have thoroughly researched each party involved, it is our opinion that you are being used as a very successful cover for Omega. You're a newsman above reproach.

"We don't claim that all three couples are involved. It's conceivable that one or possibly two of the couples are being used as decoys, as you are. But it's doubtful. The evidence—the Swiss accounts, the professions, the unusual circumstances of your association—point to a cell."

"Then how did you disqualify me?" asked Tanner numbly.

"Your life from the day you were born has been microscopically inspected by professionals. If we're wrong about you, we have no business doing what we're doing."

Tanner, exhausted, sat down with difficulty in the chair. "What do you want me to do?"

"If our information is correct, the Ostermans are flying east on Friday and will stay with you and your family over the weekend. Is that right?"

"It *was*."

"Don't change it. Don't alter the situation."

"That's impossible now. . . ."

"It's the only way you can help us. *All* of us."

"Why?"

"We believe we can trap Omega during this coming weekend. *If* we have your cooperation. Without it, we can't."

"How?"

"There are four days remaining before the Ostermans arrive. During this period our subjects—the Ostermans, the Tremaynes, and the Cardones—will be harassed. Each couple will receive untraceable telephone calls, cablegrams routed through Zurich, chance meetings with strangers in restaurants, in cocktail lounges, on the street. The point of all this is to deliver a common message. That John Tanner is *not* what he appears to be. You are something else. Perhaps a double agent, or a Politbureau informer, or even a bona fide member of my own organization. The information they receive will be confusing, designed to throw them off balance."

"And make my family a set of targets. I won't permit it! They'd kill us!"

"That's the one thing they won't do."

"Why not? If anything you say is true—and I'm by no means convinced that it is. I *know* these people. I can't believe it!"

"In that event, there's no risk at all."

"Why not?"

"If they—any one or all couples—are not involved with Omega, they'll do the normal thing. They'll report the incidents to the police or the F.B.I. We'll take over then. If one or two couples make such reports and the other or others do not, we'll know who Omega is."

"And . . . supposing you *are* right. What then? What are your built-in guarantees?"

"Several factors. All fool-proof. I told you the 'information' about you will be false. Whoever Omega is will use his resources and check out what he learns with the Kremlin itself. Our confederates there are prepared. They will intercept. The information Omega gets back from Moscow will be the truth. The truth until this afternoon, that is. You are simply John Tanner, news director, and no part of any conspiracy. What will be added is the trap. Moscow will inform whoever runs a check on you to be suspicious of the *other* couples. *They* may be defectors. We divide. We bring about a confrontation and walk in."

"That's awfully glib. It sounds too easy."

"If any attempt was made on your life or the lives of your family, the entire Omega operation would be in jeopardy. They're not willing to take that risk. They've worked too hard. I told you, they're fanatics. The target date for Omega is less than one month away."

"That's not good enough."

"There's something else. A minimum of two armed agents will be assigned to each member of your family. Twenty-four-hour surveillance. They'll never be more than fifty yards away. At any time."

"Now I know you're insane. You don't know Saddle Valley. Strangers lurking around are spotted quickly and chased out! We'd be sitting ducks."

Fassett smiled. "At this moment we have thirteen men in Saddle Valley. Thirteen. They're daily residents of your community."

"Sweet Jesus!" Tanner spoke softly. "Nineteen-eighty-four is creeping up on us, isn't it?"

"The times we live in often call for it."

"I don't have a choice, do I? I don't have a choice at all." He pointed to the tape recorder and the affidavit lying beside it. "I'm hung now, aren't I?"

"I think you're over-dramatizing again."

"No, I'm not. I'm not dramatizing anything. . . . I have to do exactly what you want me to do, don't I? I *have* to go through with it. . . . The only alternative I have is to disappear . . . and be hunted. Hunted by you and—if you're right—by this Omega."

Fassett returned Tanner's look without a trace of deceit. Tanner had spoken the truth and both men knew it.

"It's only six days. Six days out of a lifetime."

4

Monday—8:05 P.M.

The flight from Dulles Airport to Newark seemed unreal. He wasn't tired. He was terrified. His mind kept darting from one image to another, each visual picture pushing the previous one out into the distance. There were the sharp staring eyes of Laurence Fassett above the tape recorder's turning reels. The drone of Fassett's voice asking those interminable questions; then the voice growing louder and louder.

"Omega!"

And the faces of Bernie and Leila Osterman, Dick and Ginny Tremayne, Joe and Betty Cardone.

None of it made sense! He'd get to Newark and suddenly the nightmare would be over and he'd remember giving Laurence Fassett the public service features and signing the absent pages of the F.C.C. filing.

Only he knew he wouldn't.

The hour's ride from Newark to Saddle Valley

was made in silence, the taxi driver taking his cue from his fare in the back seat who kept lighting cigarettes and who hadn't answered him when he'd asked how the flight had been.

SADDLE VALLEY
VILLAGE INCORPORATED 1862
Welcome

Tanner stared at the sign as it caught the cab's headlights. As it receded he could only think of the words "Chasm of Leather."

Unreal.

Ten minutes later the taxi pulled up to his house. He got out and absently handed the driver the fare agreed upon.

"Thanks, Mr. Tanner," said the driver, leaning over the seat to take the money through the window.

"What? What did you say?" demanded John Tanner.

"I said 'Thanks, Mr. Tanner.' "

Tanner leaned down and gripped the door handle, pulling the door open with all his strength.

"How did you know my name? You tell me how you knew my *name!*"

The taxi driver could see beads of perspiration rolling down his passenger's face, the crazy look in the man's eyes. A weirdo, thought the driver. He carefully moved his left hand toward the floor beneath his feet. He always kept a thin lead pipe there.

76

"Look, Mac," he said, his fingers around the pipe. "You don't want nobody to use your name, take the sign off your lawn."

Tanner stepped back and looked over his shoulder. On the lawn was the wrought-iron lantern, a weatherproof hurricane lamp hanging from a crossbar by a chain. Above the lamp, reflected in the light, were the words:

THE TANNERS
22 ORCHARD DRIVE

He'd looked at that lamp and those words a thousand times. *The Tanners. 22 Orchard Drive.* At that moment they, too, seemed unreal. As if he had never seen them before.

"I'm sorry, fella. I'm a little on edge. I don't like flying." He closed the door as the driver began rolling up the window. The driver spoke curtly.

"Take the train then, Mister. Or walk, for Christ's sake!"

The taxi roared off, and Tanner turned and looked at his house. The door opened. The dog bounded out to meet him. His wife stood in the hall light, and he could see her smile.

5

Tuesday—3:30 A.M. *California Time*

The white French telephone, with its muted Hollywood bell, had rung at least five times. Leila thought sleepily that it was foolish to have it on Bernie's side of the bed. It never woke him, only her.

She nudged her husband's ribs with her elbow. "Darling.... Bernie. Bernie! It's the phone."

"What?" Osterman opened his eyes, confused. "The phone? Oh, the Goddamn phone. Who can hear it?"

He reached over in the darkness and found the thin cradle with his fingers.

"Yes? . . . Yes, this is Bernard Osterman. . . . Long distance?" He covered the phone with his hand and pushed himself up against the headboard. He turned toward his wife. "What time is it?"

Leila snapped on her bedside lamp and looked at the table clock. "Three-thirty. My God!"

"Probably some bastard on that Hawaiian series. It's not even midnight there yet." Bernie was listening at the phone. "Yes, operator, I'm waiting. . . . It's very long distance, honey. If it *is* Hawaii, they can put that producer on the typewriter; we've had it. We never should have touched it. . . . Yes, operator? Please hurry, will you?"

"You said you wanted to see those islands without a uniform on, remember?"

"I apologize. . . . Yes, operator, this *is* Bernard Osterman, damn it! Yes? Yes? Thank you, operator. . . . Hello? I can hardly hear you. Hello? . . . Yes, that's better. Who's this? . . . What? What did you say? . . . Who *is* this? What's your name? I don't understand you. Yes, I *heard* you, but I don't understand. . . . Hello? . . . Hello! Wait a minute! I said *wait* a minute!" Osterman shot up and flung his legs over the side of the bed. The blankets came after him and fell on the floor at his feet. He began punching the center bar on the white French telephone. "Operator! Operator! The Goddamn line's dead!"

"Who was it? Why are you shouting? What did they say?"

"He . . . the son of a bitch grunted like a bull. He said, he said we were to watch out for the . . . *Tan One*. That's what he said. He made sure I heard the words. The *Tan One*. What the hell is that?"

"The *what?*"

"The Tan One! That's all he kept repeating!"

"It doesn't make sense. . . . Was it Hawaii? Did the operator say where the call came from?"

Osterman stared at his wife in the dim light of the bedroom. "Yes. I heard that clearly. It was overseas. . . . It was Lisbon. Lisbon, Portugal."

"We don't know anyone in Portugal!"

"Lisbon, Lisbon, Lisbon . . ." Osterman kept repeating the name quietly to himself. "Lisbon. Neutral. Lisbon was neutral."

"What do you mean?"

"Tan One . . ."

"Tan . . . tan. Tanner. Could it be John Tanner? John Tanner!"

"Neutral!"

"It's John Tanner," said Leila quietly.

"Johnny? . . . What did he mean, 'Watch out'? Why should we watch out? Why place a call at three-thirty in the morning?"

Leila sat up and reached for a cigarette. "Johnny's got enemies. The San Diego waterfront still hurts because of him."

"San Diego, sure! But Lisbon?"

"Daily Variety said last week that we're going to New York," continued Leila, inhaling smoke deeply. "That we'd probably stay with our ex-neighbors, the Tanners."

"So?"

"Perhaps we're too well advertised." She looked at her husband.

"Maybe I'll call Johnny." Osterman reached for the phone.

Leila grabbed his wrist. "Are you out of your *mind?*"

Osterman lay back down.

Joe opened his eyes and glanced at his watch: six-twenty-two. Time to get up, have a short workout in his gym and perhaps walk over to the Club for an hour's practice on the golf range.

He was an early riser, Betty the opposite. She would sleep till noon whenever she had the chance. They had two double beds, one for each of them, because Joe knew the debilitating effects of two separate body temperatures under the same set of covers. The benefits of a person's sleep were diminished by nearly fifty percent when he shared a bed all night with somebody else. And since the purpose of the marriage bed was exclusively sexual, there was no point in losing the benefits of sleep.

A pair of double beds was just fine.

He finished ten minutes on the exercycle and five with seven-and-a-half-pound handbells. He looked through the thick glass window of the steam bath and saw that the room was ready.

A panel light above the gym's wall clock flashed on. It was the front doorbell. Joe had the device installed in case he was home alone and working out.

The clock read six-fifty-one, much too early for anyone in Saddle Valley to be ringing front doorbells. He put the small weights on the floor and walked to his house intercom.

"Yes? Who is it?"

"Telegram, Mr. Cardione."

"Who?"

"Cardione, it says."

"The name is Cardone."

"Isn't this Eleven Apple Place?"

"I'll be right there."

He flicked off the intercom and grabbed a towel from the rack, draping it around him as he walked rapidly out of the gym. He didn't like what he had just heard. He reached the front door and opened it. A small man in uniform stood there chewing gum.

"Why didn't you telephone? It's pretty early, isn't it?"

"Instructions were to deliver. I had to drive out here, Mr. Cardione. Almost fifteen miles. We keep twenty-four-hour service."

Cardone signed for the envelope. "Why fifteen miles? Western Union's got a branch in Ridge Park."

"Not Western Union, Mister. This is a cablegram . . . from Europe."

Cardone grabbed the envelope out of the uniformed man's hand. "Wait a minute." He didn't want to appear excited, so he walked normally into the living room where he remembered seeing Betty's purse on the piano. He took out two one-dollar bills and returned to the door. "Here you are. Sorry about the trip." He closed the door and ripped open the cablegram.

L'UOMO BRUNO PALIDO NON È AMICO DEL ITALIANO. GUARDA BENE VICINI DI QUESTA MANIERA. PROTECIATE PER LA FINA DELLA SETTIMANA.

DA VINCI

Cardone walked into the kitchen, found a pencil

on the telephone shelf and sat down at the table. He wrote out the translation on the back of a magazine.

> The light-brown man is no friend of the Italian. Be cautious of such neighbors. Protect yourself against the end of the week. Da Vinci.

What did it mean? What "light-brown . . . neighbors"? There were no blacks in Saddle Valley. The message didn't make sense.

Suddenly Joe Cardone froze. The light-brown neighbor could only mean John Tanner. The end of the week—Friday—the Ostermans were arriving. Someone in Europe was telling him to protect himself against John Tanner and the upcoming Osterman weekend.

He snatched up the cablegram and looked at the dateline.

Zurich.

Oh, Jesus Christ! Zurich!

Someone in Zurich—someone who called himself Da Vinci, someone who knew his real name, who knew John Tanner, who knew about the Ostermans—was warning him!

Joe Cardone stared out the window at his backyard lawn. Da Vinci, Da Vinci!

Leonardo.

Artist, soldier, architect of war—all things to all men.

Mafia!

Oh, Christ! Which of them?

The Costellanos? The Batellas? The Latronas, maybe.

Which of them had turned on him? And *why?* He was their *friend!*

His hands shook as he spread the cablegram on the kitchen table. He read it once more. Each sentence conjured up progressively more dangerous meanings.

Tanner!

John Tanner had found out something! But *what?*

And why did the message come from Zurich?

What would any of them have to do with Zurich?

Or the Ostermans?

What had Tanner discovered? What was he going to do? ... One of the Battella men called Tanner something once; what was it?

"Volturno!"

Vulture.

". . . no friend of the Italian. . . . Be cautious. . . . Protect yourself. . . ."

How? From *what?* Tanner wouldn't confide in him. Why should he?

He, Joe Cardone, wasn't syndicate; he wasn't *famiglia.* What could *he* know?

But "Da Vinci's" message had come from Switzerland.

And that left one remaining possibility, a frightening one. The Cosa Nostra had learned about Zurich! They'd use it against him unless he was able to control the "light-brown man," the Italian's enemy. Unless he could stop whatever it was John Tanner was about to do, he'd be destroyed.

Zurich! The Ostermans!

He had done what he thought was right! What he had to do to *survive*. Osterman had pointed that out in a way that left no doubts. But it was in other hands now. Not his. He couldn't be touched any more.

Joe Cardone walked out of the kitchen and returned to his miniature gymnasium. Without putting on gloves he started pounding the bag. Faster and faster, harder and harder.

There was a screeching in his brain.

"Zurich! Zurich! Zurich!"

Virginia Tremayne heard her husband get out of bed at six-fifteen, and knew immediately that something was wrong. Her husband rarely stirred that early.

She waited several minutes. When he didn't return, she rose, put on her bathrobe, and went downstairs. He was in the living room standing by the bay window, smoking a cigarette and reading something on a piece of paper.

"What *are* you doing?"

"Look at this," he answered quietly.

"At what?" She took the paper from his hand.

Take extreme caution with your editorial friend. His friendship does not extend beyond his zeal. He is not what he appears to be. We

"What is this? When did you get it?"

"I heard noises outside the window about twenty minutes ago. Just enough to wake me up. Then there was the gunning of a car engine. It kept racing up and down. . . . I thought you heard it, too. You pulled the covers up."

"I think I did. I didn't pay any attention. . . ."

"I came down and opened the door. This envelope was on the doormat."

"What does it mean?"

"I'm not sure yet."

"Who's Blackstone?"

"The commentaries. Basis of the legal system. . . ." Richard Tremayne flung himself down in an armchair and brought his hand up to his forehead. With the other he rolled his cigarette delicately along the rim of an ashtray. "Please. . . . Let me think."

Virginia Tremayne looked again at the paper with the cryptic message. " 'Editorial friend.' Does that mean? . . ."

"Tanner's onto something and whoever delivered this is in panic. Now they're trying to make me panic, too."

"Why?"

"I don't know. Maybe they think I can help them. And if I don't, they're threatening me. All of us."

"The Ostermans."

"Exactly. They're threatening us with Zurich."

"Oh, my God! They know! Someone's found out!"

"It looks that way."

"Do you think Bernie got frightened? Talked about it?"

Tremayne's eye twitched. "He'd be insane if he did. He'd be crucified on both sides of the Atlantic. . . . No, that's not it."

"What is it, then?"

"Whoever wrote this is someone I've either worked with in the past or refused to handle. Maybe it's one of the current cases. Maybe one of the files on my desk right now. And Tanner got wind of it and is making noises. They expect me to stop him. If I don't, I'm finished. Before I can afford it. . . . Before Zurich goes to work for us."

"They couldn't *touch* you!" said Tremayne's wife with fierce, artificial defiance.

"Come on, darling. Let's not kid each *other*. In polite circles I'm a merger analyst. In the boardrooms I'm a corporate raider. To paraphrase Judge Hand, the merger market is currently insane with false purchase. False. That means fake. Buying with paper. Pieces of fiction."

"Are you in trouble?"

"Not really—I could always say I was given wrong information. The courts like me."

"They respect you! You've worked harder than any man I know. You're the best damned lawyer there is!"

"I'd like to think so."

"You *are!*"

Richard Tremayne stood at the large bay window looking out at the lawn of his seventy-four-thousand-dollar ranch house. "Isn't it funny. You're probably right. I'm one of the best there is in a system I despise. . . . A system Tanner would rip apart piece by piece on one of his programs if he knew what really made it go. That's what the little message is all about."

"I think you're wrong. I think it's someone you've beaten who wants to get even. Who's trying to frighten you."

"Then he's succeeded. What this . . . Blackstone is telling me isn't anything I don't know. What I *am* and what I *do* makes me Tanner's natural enemy. At least, he'd think so. . . . If only he knew the truth."

He looked at her and forced a smile. "They know the truth in Zurich."

6

Osterman wandered aimlessly around the studio lot, trying to get his mind off the pre-dawn phone call. He was obsessed by it.

Neither he nor Leila had slept again. They'd kept trying to narrow down the possibilities and when those were exhausted they explored the more important question of why.

Why had *he* been called? What was behind it? Was Tanner onto another one of his exposés?

If he was, it had nothing to do with him. Nothing to do with Bernie Osterman.

Tanner never talked in specifics about his work. Only in generalities. He had a low pressure point when it came to what he considered injustice, and since the two men often disagreed on what constituted fair game in the marketplace, they avoided specifics.

Bernie thought of Tanner as a crusader who had never traveled on foot. He'd never gone through the experience of watching a father come

89

home and announce he had no job the next day. Or a mother staying up half the night sewing wonders into a worn-out garment for a child going to school in the morning. Tanner could afford his indignation, and he had done fine work. But there were some things he would never understand. It was why Bernie had never discussed Zurich with him.

"Hey, Bernie! Wait a minute!" Ed Pomfret, a middle-aged, rotund, insecure producer, caught up with him on the sidewalk.

"Hello, Eddie. How's everything?"

"Great! I tried reaching you at your office. The girl said you were out."

"Nothing to do."

"I got the word, guess you did, too. It'll be good working with you."

"Oh? . . . No, I didn't get the word. What are we working on?"

"What's this? Jokes?" Pomfret was slightly defensive. As if he was aware that Osterman thought he was a second-rater.

"No jokes. I'm wrapping up here this week. What are you talking about? Who gave you the word?"

"That new man from Continuity phoned me this morning. I'm handling half of the segments on *The Interceptor* series. He said you were doing four running shots. I like the idea."

"What idea?"

"The story outline. Three men working on a big, quiet deal in Switzerland. Right away it grabbed me."

Osterman stopped walking and looked down at Pomfret.

"Who put you up to this?"

"Put me up to what?"

"There's no four shots. No outlines. No deal. Now tell me what you're trying to say."

"You've got to be joking. Would I kid powerhouses like you and Leila? I was tickled to death. Continuity told me to phone you, ask for the outlines!"

"Who called you?"

"What's his name. . . . That new exec Continuity brought from New York."

"Who?"

"He told me his name. . . . Tanner. That's it. Tanner. Jim Tanner, John Tanner . . ."

"John Tanner doesn't work here! Now, who told you to tell me this?" He grabbed Pomfret's arm. "Tell me, you son of a bitch!"

"Take your hands off me! You're crazy!"

Osterman recognized his mistake: Pomfret was no more than a messenger boy. He let go of the producer's arm. "I'm sorry, Eddie. I apologize. . . . I've got a lot on my mind. Forgive me, please. I'm a pig."

"Sure, sure. You're uptight, that's all. You're very uptight, man."

"You say this fellow—Tanner—called you this morning?"

"About two hours ago. To tell you the truth, I didn't know him."

"Listen. This is some kind of a practical joke.

You know what I mean? I'm not doing the series, believe me. . . . Just forget it, okay?"

"A joke?"

"Take my word for it, okay? . . . Tell you what; they're talking to Leila and me about a project here. I'll insist on you as the money-man, how about it?"

"Hey, thanks!"

"Don't mention it. Just keep this little joke between the two of us, right?"

Osterman didn't bother to wait for Pomfret's grateful reply. He hurried away down the studio street, toward his car. He had to get home to Leila.

A huge man in a chauffeur's uniform was sitting in the front seat of his car! He got out as Bernie approached and held the back door open for him.

"Mr. Osterman?"

"Who are you? What are you doing in . . ."

"I have a message for you."

"But I don't want to hear it! I want to know why you're sitting in my car!"

"Be very careful of your friend, John Tanner. Be careful what you say to him."

"What in God's name are you talking about?"

The chauffeur shrugged. "I'm just delivering a message, Mr. Osterman. And now would you like me to drive you home?"

"Of course not! I don't know you! I don't understand. . . ."

The back door closed gently. "As you wish, sir. I was simply trying to be friendly." With a smart salute, he turned away.

Bernie stood alone, immobile, staring after him.

7

"Are any of the Mediterranean accounts in trouble?" Joe Cardone asked.

His partner, Sam Bennett, turned in his chair to make sure the office door was shut. "Mediterranean" was their code word for those clients both partners knew were lucrative but dangerous investors. "Not that I know of," he said. "Why? Did you hear something?"

"Nothing direct. . . . Perhaps nothing at all."

"That's why you came back early, though?"

"No, not really." Cardone understood that even for Bennett not all explanations could be given. Sam was no part of Zurich. So Joe hesitated. "Well, partly. I spent some time at the Montreal Exchange."

"What did you hear?"

"That there's a new drive from the Attorney General's office; that the S.E.C. is handing over everything they have. Every possible Mafia connection with a hundred thousand or more is being watched."

93

"That's nothing new. Where've you been?"

"In Montreal. That's where I've been. I don't like it when I hear things like that eight hundred miles from the office. And I'm Goddamned reluctant to pick up a telephone and ask my partner if any of our clients are currently before a grand jury. . . . I mean, telephone conversations aren't guaranteed to be private any more."

"Good Lord!" Bennett laughed. "Your imagination's working overtime, isn't it?"

"I hope so."

"You know damned well I'd have gotten in touch with you if anything like that came up. Or even looked like it *might* come up. You didn't cut a vacation short on those grounds. What's the rest?"

Cardone avoided his partner's eyes as he sat down at his desk. "Okay. I won't lie. Something else did bring me in. . . . I don't think it has anything to do with us. With *you* or the company. If I find out otherwise, I'll come to you, all right?"

Bennett got out of the chair and accepted his partner's non-explanation. Over the years he'd learned not to question Joe too closely. For in spite of his partner's gregariousness, Cardone was a private man. He brought large amounts of capital into the firm and never asked for more than a proper business share. That was good enough for Bennett.

Sam walked to the door, laughing softly. "When are you going to stop running from the phantom of South Philadelphia?"

Cardone returned his partner's smile. "When it stops chasing me into the Bankers' Club with a hot lasagna."

Bennett closed the door behind him, and Joe returned to the ten-day accumulation of mail and messages. There was nothing. Nothing that could be related to a Mediterranean problem. Nothing that even hinted at a Mafia conflict. Yet something had happened during those ten days; something that concerned Tanner.

He picked up his telephone and pushed the button for his secretary. "Is this everything? There weren't any other messages?"

"None you have to return. I told everyone you wouldn't be back until the end of the week. Some said they'd call then, the others will phone you Monday."

"Keep it like that. Any calls, I'll be back Monday."

He replaced the phone and unlocked the second drawer of his desk, in which he kept an index file of three-by-five cards. The Mediterranean clients.

He put the small metal box in front of him and started fingering through the cards. Perhaps a name would trigger a memory, a forgotten fact which might have relevance.

His private telephone rang. Only Betty called him on that line; no one else had the number. Joe loved his wife, but she had a positive genius for irritating him with trivial matters when he wished no interruptions.

"Yes, dear?"

Silence.

"What is it, honey? I'm jammed up."

Still his wife didn't answer.

Cardone was suddenly afraid. No one but Betty had that number!

"Betty? Answer me!"

The voice, when it came, was slow, deep and precise.

"John Tanner flew to Washington yesterday. Mr. Da Vinci is very concerned. Perhaps your friends in California betrayed you. They've been in contact with Tanner."

Joe Cardone heard the click of the disconnected telephone.

Jesus! Oh, Jesus! Oh, Christ! It was the Ostermans! They'd turned!

But *why?* It didn't make sense! What possible connection could there be between Zurich and anything *remotely* Mafia? They were light-years apart!

Or were they? Or was one using the other?

Cardone tried to steady himself but it was impossible. He found himself crushing the small metal box.

What could he do? Who could he talk to?

Tanner himself? Oh, God, of course not!

The Ostermans? Bernie Osterman? Christ, no! Not *now*.

Tremayne. Dick Tremayne.

8

Too shaken to sit in a commuter's seat on the Saddle Valley express, Tremayne decided to drive into New York.

As he sped east on Route Five toward the George Washington Bridge, he noticed a light blue Cadillac in his rearview mirror. When he pulled to the left, racing ahead of the other cars, the Cadillac did the same. When he returned to the right, squeezing into the slower flow, so did the Cadillac —always several automobiles behind him.

At the bridge he neared a tollbooth and saw that the Cadillac, in a faster adjacent lane, came parallel. He tried to see who the driver was.

It was a woman. She turned her face away; he could only see the back of her head. Yet she looked vaguely familiar.

The Cadillac sped off before he could reflect further. Traffic blocked any chance he had to follow. He was certain the Cadillac had followed him, but just as surely, the driver did not want to be recognized.

Why? Who was she?

Was this woman "Blackstone"?

He found it impossible to accomplish anything in his office. He canceled the few appointments he had made, and, instead, reexamined the files of recent corporate mergers he had favorably gotten through the courts. One folder in particular interested him: *The Cameron Woolens.* Three factories in a small Massachusetts town owned for generations by the Cameron family. Raided from the inside by the oldest son. Blackmail had forced him to sell his share of the company to a New York clothing chain who claimed to want the Cameron label.

They got the label, and closed the factories; the town went bankrupt. Tremayne had represented the clothing chain in the Boston courts. The Cameron family had a daughter. An unmarried woman in her early thirties. Headstrong, angry.

The driver of the Cadillac was a woman. About the right age.

Yet to select one was to dismiss so many other possibilities. The merger builders knew whom to call when legal matters got sticky. Tremayne! He was the expert. A forty-four year old magician wielding the new legal machinery, sweeping aside old legal concepts in the exploding economy of the conglomerates.

Was it the Cameron daughter in the light blue Cadillac?

How could he know? There were so many. The Camerons. The Smythes of Atlanta. The Boyntons of Chicago. The Fergusons of Rochester. The corporate raiders preyed upon old families, the moneyed families. The old moneyed families pampered themselves, they were targets. Who among them might be Blackstone?

Tremayne got out of his chair and walked aimlessly around his office. He couldn't stand the confinement any longer; he had to go out.

He wondered what Tanner would say if he called him and suggested a casual lunch. How would Tanner react? Would he accept casually? Would he put him off? Would it be possible—if Tanner accepted—to learn anything related to Blackstone's warning?

Tremayne picked up the phone and dialed. His eyelid twitched, almost painfully.

Tanner was tied up in a meeting. Tremayne was relieved; it had been a foolish thing to do. He left no message and hurried out of his office.

On Fifth Avenue, a Checker cab pulled up directly in front of him, blocking his path at the corner crossing.

"Hey, mister!" The driver put his head out the window.

Tremayne wondered whom he was calling—so did several other pedestrians. They all looked at one another.

"You, mister! Your name Tremayne?"

"Me? Yes. . . ."

"I got a message for you."

"For me? How did you? . . ."

"I gotta hurry, the light's gonna change and I

99

got twenty bucks for this. I'm to tell you to walk east on Fifty-fourth Street. Just keep walking and a Mr. Blackstone will contact you."

Tremayne put his hand on the driver's shoulder. "*Who* told you? Who gave you . . ."

"What do I know? Some wack sits in my cab since nine-thirty this morning with the meter on. He's got a pair of binoculars and smokes thin cigars."

The "Don't Walk" sign began to blink.

"What did he say! . . . Here!" Tremayne reached into his pocket and withdrew some bills. He gave the driver a ten. "Here. Now, *tell* me, please!"

"Just what I said, mister. He got out a few seconds ago, gave me twenty bucks to tell you to walk east on Fifty-fourth. That's all."

"That's *not* all!" Tremayne grabbed the driver's shirt.

"Thanks for the ten." The driver pushed Tremayne's hand away, honked his horn to disperse the jaywalkers in front of him, and drove off.

Tremayne controlled his panic. He stepped back onto the curb and retreated under the awning of the storefront behind him, looking at the men walking north, trying to find a man with a pair of binoculars or a thin cigar.

Finding nobody, he began to edge his way from store entrance to store entrance, towards Fifty-fourth Street. He walked slowly, staring at the passersby. Several collided against him going in the same direction but walking much faster. Several others, heading south, noticed the strange behavior of the blond man in his expensively cut clothes, and smiled.

On the Fifty-fourth Street corner, Tremayne stopped. In spite of the slight breeze and his lightweight suit, he was perspiring. He knew he had to head east. There was no question about it.

One thing was clear. Blackstone was not the driver of the light blue Cadillac. Blackstone was a man with binoculars and thin cigars.

Then who was the woman? He'd seen her before. He knew it!

He started east on Fifty-fourth, walking on the right side of the pavement. He reached Madison and no one stopped him, no one signaled, no one even looked at him. Then across Park Avenue to the center island.

No one.

Lexington Avenue. Past the huge construction sites. No one.

Third Avenue. Second. First.

No one.

Tremayne entered the last block. A dead-end street terminating at the East River, flanked on both sides by the canopies of apartment house entrances. A few men with briefcases and women carrying department store boxes came and went from both buildings. At the end of the street was a light tan Mercedes-Benz sedan parked crossways, as if in the middle of a turn. And near it stood a man in an elegant white suit and Panama hat. He was quite a bit shorter than Tremayne. Even thirty yards away, Tremayne could see he was deeply tanned. He wore thick, wide sunglasses and was looking directly at Tremayne as Tremayne approached him.

"Mr. . . . Blackstone?"

"Mr. Tremayne. I'm sorry you had to walk such a distance. We had to be sure, you see, that you were alone."

"Why wouldn't I be?" Tremayne was trying to place the accent. It was cultivated, but not the sort associated with the northeastern states.

"A man who's in trouble often, mistakenly, looks for company."

"What kind of trouble am I in?"

"You *did* get my note?"

"Of course. What did it mean?"

"Exactly what it said. Your friend Tanner is very dangerous to you. And to us. We simply want to emphasize the point as good businessmen should with one another."

"What business interests are you concerned with, Mr. Blackstone? I assume Blackstone isn't your name so I could hardly connect you with anything familiar."

The man in the white suit and hat and dark glasses took several steps towards the Mercedes.

"We told you. His friends from California . . ."

"The Ostermans?"

"Yes."

"My firm has had no dealings with the Ostermans. None whatever."

"But you have, haven't you?" Blackstone walked in front of the hood and stood on the other side of the Mercedes.

"You can't be serious!"

"Believe me when I say that I am." The man reached for the door handle, but he did not open the door. He was waiting.

"Just a minute! Who *are* you?"

"Blackstone will do."

"No! . . . What you said! You couldn't . . ."

"But we do. That's the point. And since you now know that we do, it should offer some proof of our considerable influence."

"What are you driving at?" Tremayne pressed his hands against the Mercedes' hood and leaned toward Blackstone.

"It's crossed our minds that you may have co-operated with your friend Tanner. That's really why we wanted to see you. It would be most inadvisable. We wouldn't hesitate to make public your contribution to the Osterman interests."

"You're crazy! Why would I cooperate with Tanner? On what? I don't know what you're talking about."

Blackstone removed his dark glasses. His eyes were blue and penetrating, and Tremayne could see freckles about his nose and cheekbones. "If that's true then you have nothing to worry about."

"Of course it's true! There's no earthly reason why I should work with Tanner on anything!"

"That's logical." Blackstone opened the door of the Mercedes. "Just keep it that way."

"For God's sake, you can't just *leave!* I see Tanner every day. At the Club. On the train. What the hell am I supposed to think, what am I supposed to say?"

"You mean what are you supposed to look for? If I were you, I'd act as if nothing had happened. As if we'd never met. . . . He may drop hints—if you're telling the truth—he may probe. Then you'll know."

Tremayne stood up, fighting to remain calm. "For all our sakes, I think you'd better tell me whom you represent. It would be best, it really would."

"Oh, no, counselor." A short laugh accompanied Blackstone's reply. "You see, we've noticed that you've acquired a disturbing habit over the past several years. Nothing serious, not at this time, but to be considered."

"What habit is that?"

"Periodically you drink too much."

"That's ridiculous!"

"I said it wasn't serious. You do brilliant work. Nevertheless, at such times you haven't your normal control. No, it would be a mistake to burden you, especially in your current state of anxiety."

"Don't go. Please! . . ."

"We'll be in touch. Perhaps you'll have learned something that will help us. At any rate, we always watch your . . . merger work with great interest."

Tremayne flinched. "What about the Ostermans? You've got to *tell* me."

"If you've got a brain in your legal head, you won't say a thing to the Ostermans! Or hint at anything! If Osterman is cooperating with Tanner, you'll find out. If he's not, don't give him any ideas about *you*." Blackstone climbed into the driver's seat of the Mercedes and started the motor. He said, just before he drove off, "Keep your head, Mr. Tremayne. We'll be in touch."

Tremayne tried to marshal his thoughts; he could feel his eyelid twitch. Thank Christ he hadn't reached Tanner! Not being prepared, he might have said something—something asinine, dangerous.

Had Osterman been such a gargantuan fool— or coward—to blurt out the truth about Zurich to John Tanner? Without consulting them?

If that were the case, Zurich would have to be alerted. Zurich would take care of Osterman. They'd crucify him!

He had to find Cardone. They had to decide what to do. He ran to a corner telephone.

Betty told him Joe had gone into the office. Cardone's secretary told him Joe was still on vacation.

Joe was playing games. The twitch above Tremayne's left eye nearly blinded him.

9

Tuesday—7:00 A.M.

Unable to sleep, Tanner walked into his study, his eyes drawn to the gray glass of the three television sets. There was something dead about them, empty. He lit a cigarette and sat down on the couch. He thought about Fassett's instructions: remain calm, oblivious, and say nothing to Ali. Fassett had repeated the last command several times.

The only real danger would come if Ali said the wrong thing to the wrong person. There *was* danger in that. Danger to Ali. But Tanner had never withheld anything from his wife. He wasn't sure he could do it. The fact that they were always open with each other was the strongest bond in their strong marriage. Even when they fought, there was never the weapon of unspoken accusations. Alice McCall had had enough of that as a child.

Omega, however, would change their lives, for the next six days, at any rate. He had to accept that because Fassett said it was best for Ali.

The sun was up now. The day was beginning and the Cardones, the Tremaynes and the Ostermans would soon be under fire. Tanner wondered what they'd do, how they'd react. He hoped that all three couples would contact the authorities and prove Fassett wrong. Sanity would return.

But it was possible that the madness had just begun. Whichever the case, he would stay home. If Fassett was right, he'd be there with Ali and the children. Fassett had no control over that decision.

He would let Ali think it was the flu. He'd be in touch with his office by phone, but he would stay with his family.

His telephone rang regularly; questions from the office. Ali and the children complained that the constant ringing of the telephone was enough to drive them crazy, so the three of them retreated to the pool. Except for a few clouds around noon, the day was hot—perfect for swimming. The white patrol car passed the house a number of times. On Sunday Tanner had been concerned over it. Now he was grateful. Fassett was keeping his word.

The telephone rang again. "Yes, Charlie." He didn't bother to say hello.

"Mr. Tanner?"

"Oh, sorry. Yes, this is John Tanner."

"Fassett calling. . . ."

"Wait a minute! Tanner looked out his study window to make sure Ali and the children were still at the pool. They were.

"What is it, Fassett? Have you people started?"

"Can you talk?"

"Yes. . . . Have you found out anything? Has any of them called the police?"

"Negative. If that happens we'll contact you immediately. That's not why I'm calling you. . . . You've done something extremely foolish. I can't emphasize how careless."

"What are you talking about?"

"You didn't go in to your office this morning. . . ."

"I certainly did *not!*"

". . . But there must be no break from your normal routine. No altering of your usual schedule. That's terribly important. For your own protection, you *must* follow our instructions."

"That's asking too much!"

"Listen to me. Your wife and children are at this moment in the swimming pool behind your house. Your son, Raymond, did not go to his tennis lesson. . . ."

"I told him not to. I told him to do some work on the lawn."

"Your wife had groceries delivered, which is not customary."

"I explained that I might need her to take notes for me. She's done that before. . . ."

"The main point is you're not doing what you usually do. It's vital that you keep to your day-to-day routine. I can't stress it enough. You cannot, you *must* not call attention to yourself."

"I'm watching out for my family. I think that's understandable."

"So are we. Far more effectively than you can. None of them have been out of our sight for a single minute. I'll amend that. Neither have you. You walked out into your driveway twice: at nine-thirty-two and eleven-twenty. Your daughter had a friend over for lunch, one Joan Loomis, aged eight. We're extremely thorough and extremely careful."

The news director reached for a cigarette and lit it with the desk lighter. "Guess you are."

"There's nothing for you to worry about. There's no danger to you or your family."

"Probably not. I think you're all crazy. None of them have anything to do with this Omega."

"That's possible. But if we're right, they won't take any action without checking further. They won't panic, too much is at stake. And when they do check further they'll immediately suspect each other. For heaven's sake, don't give them any reason not to. Go about your business as if nothing happened. It's vital. No one could harm your family. They couldn't get near enough."

"All right. You're convincing. But I went out to the driveway three times this morning, not twice."

"No, you didn't. The third time you remained in the garage doorway. You didn't physically walk out onto the driveway. And it wasn't morning, it was twelve-fourteen." Fassett laughed. "Feeling better now?"

"I'd be an awful liar if I didn't admit it."

"You're not a liar. Not generally at any rate. Your file makes that very clear." Fassett laughed again. Even Tanner smiled.

"You're really too much, you know that. I'll go into the office tomorrow."

"When it's all over, you and your wife will have to get together with me and mine for an evening. I think they'd like each other. Drinks will be on me. Dewars White Label with a tall soda for you and Scotch on the rocks with a pinch of water for your wife."

"Good God! If you start describing our sex life. . . ."

"Let me check the index. . . ."

"Go to hell," Tanner laughed, relieved. "We'll take you up on that evening."

"You should. We'd get along."

"Name the date, we'll be there."

"I'll make a point of it on Monday. Be in touch. You have the emergency number for after hours. Don't hesitate to call."

"I won't. I'll be in the office tomorrow."

"Fine. And do me a favor. Don't plan any more programs on us. My employers didn't like the last one."

Tanner remembered. The program Fassett referred to had been a Woodward Show. The writers had come up with the phrase *Caught in the Act* for the letters C.I.A. It was a year ago, almost to the week. "It wasn't bad."

"It wasn't good. I saw that one. I wanted to laugh my head off but I couldn't. I was with the Director, in *his* living room. *Caught in the Act!* Jesus!" Fassett laughed again, putting Tanner more at ease than the news director thought possible.

"Thanks, Fassett."

Tanner put down the telephone and crushed out his cigarette. Fassett was a thorough professional, he thought. And Fassett was right. No one could get near Ali and the kids. For all he knew, the C.I.A. had snipers strapped to the trees. What was left for him to do was precisely what Fassett said: nothing. Just go about business as usual. No break from routine, no deviation from the norm. He felt he could play the role now. The protection was everything Fassett said it would be.

However, one thought bothered him, and the more he considered it, the more it disturbed him.

It was nearly four o'clock in the afternoon. The Tremaynes, the Cardones and the Ostermans had all been contacted by now. The harassment had begun. Yet none had seen fit to call the police. Or even to call *him*.

Was it really possible that six people who had been his friends for years were not what they seemed to be?

10

The Karmann Ghia swung off Wilshire Boulevard onto Beverly Drive. Osterman knew he was exceeding the Los Angeles speed limit; it seemed completely unimportant. He couldn't think about anything except the warning he had just received. He had to get home to Leila. They had to talk seriously now. They had to decide what to do.

Why had they been singled out?

Who was warning them? And about what?

Leila was probably right. Tanner was their friend, as good a friend as they'd ever known. But he was also a man who valued reserve in friendship. There were areas one never touched. There was always the slight quality of distance, a thin glass wall that came between Tanner and any other human being. Except, of course, Ali.

And Tanner now possessed information that touched them somehow, meant something to him and Leila. And Zurich was part of it. But, Christ! *How?*

Osterman reached the foot of the Mulholland hill and drove rapidly to the top, past the huge, early-pastiche mansions that were peopled by those near, or once near, the top of the Hollywood spectrum. A few of the houses were going to seed, decaying relics of past extravagance. The speed limit in the Mulholland section was thirty. Osterman's speedometer read fifty-one. He pressed down on the accelerator. He had decided what to do. He would pick up Leila and head for Malibu. The two of them would find a phone booth on the highway and call Tremayne and Cardone.

The mournful wail of the siren, growing louder, jarred him. It was a sound effect in this town of devices. It wasn't real, nothing here was real. It couldn't be for him.

But, of course, it was.

"Officer, I'm a resident here. Osterman. Bernard Osterman. 260 Caliente. Surely you know my house." It was a statement made positively. Caliente was impressive acreage.

"Sorry, Mr. Osterman. Your license and registration, please."

"Now, look. I had a call at the studio that my wife wasn't feeling well. I think it's understandable I'm in a hurry."

"Not at the expense of pedestrians. Your license and registration."

Osterman gave them to him and stared straight ahead, controlling his anger. The police officer wrote lethargically on the long rectangular traffic summons and when he finished, he stapled Bernie's license to it.

At the sound of the snap, Osterman looked up. "Do you have to mutilate the license?"

The policeman sighed wearily, holding onto the summons. "You could have lost it for thirty days, mister. I lessened the speed; send in ten bucks like a parking ticket." He handed the summons to Bernie. "I hope your wife feels better."

The officer returned to the police car. He spoke once more through the open window. "Don't forget to put your license back in your wallet."

The police car sped off.

Osterman threw down the summons and turned his ignition key. The Karmann Ghia started down the Mulholland slope. Half in disgust, Bernie looked at the summons on the seat next to him.

Then he looked again.

There was something wrong with it. The shape was right, the unreadable print was crowded in the inadequate space as usual, but the paper rang false. It seemed too shiny, too blurred even for a summons from the Motor Vehicle Department of the City of Los Angeles.

Osterman stopped. He picked up the summons and looked at it closely. The violations had been marked carelessly, inaccurately, by the police officer. They hadn't really been marked at all.

And then Osterman realized that the face of the card was only a thin photostat attached to a thicker sheet of paper.

He turned it over and saw that there was a message written in red pencil, partially covered by his stapled license. He ripped the license off and read:

Word received that Tanner's neighbors may have cooperated with him. This is a potentially dangerous situation made worse because our information is incomplete. Use extreme caution and find out what you can. It is vital we know—you know—extent of their involvement. Repeat. Use extreme caution.

                                        Zurich

Osterman stared at the red letters and his fear produced a sudden ache at his temples.

The Tremaynes and the Cardones too!

11

Dick Tremayne wasn't on the four-fifty local to Saddle Valley. Cardone, sitting inside his Cadillac, swore out loud. He had tried to reach Tremayne at his office but was told that the lawyer had gone out for an early lunch. There was no point in having Tremayne call him back. Joe had decided to return to Saddle Valley and meet all the trains from three-thirty on.

Cardone left the station, turned left at the intersection of Saddle Road, and headed west toward the open country. He had thirty-five minutes until the next train was due. Perhaps the drive would help relax him. He couldn't just wait at the station. If anyone was watching him it would look suspicious.

Tremayne would have some answers. Dick was a damned good lawyer, and he'd know the legal alternatives, if there were any.

On the outskirts of Saddle Valley Joe reached a stretch of road bordered by fields. A Silver Cloud

116

Rolls-Royce passed him on his left, and Cardone noted that the huge automobile was traveling extremely fast, much too fast for the narrow country road. He kept driving for several miles, vaguely aware that he was traveling through open country now. He would probably have to turn around in some farmer's driveway. But ahead of him was a long winding curve which, he remembered, had wide shoulders. He'd turn around there. It was time to head back to the station.

He reached the curve and slowed down, prepared to swing hard to his right onto the wide shoulder.

He couldn't.

The Silver Cloud was parked off the road under the trees, blocking him.

Annoyed, Cardone gunned the engine and proceeded several hundred yards ahead where, since there were no other cars in sight, he made the cramped turn.

Back at the station, Cardone looked at his watch. Five-nineteen, almost five-twenty. He could see the entire length of the platform. He'd spot Tremayne if he got off. He hoped the lawyer would be on the five-twenty-five. The waiting was intolerable.

A car pulled up behind his Cadillac, and Cardone looked up.

It was the Silver Cloud. Cardone began to sweat.

A massive man, well over six feet tall, got out of the car and walked slowly toward Cardone's open window. He was dressed in a chauffeur's uniform.

"Mr. Cardione?"

"The name's Cardone." The man's hands, which gripped the base of Joe's window, were immense. Much larger and thicker than his own.

"Okay. Whatever you like. . . ."

"You passed me a little while ago, didn't you? On Saddle Road."

"Yes, sir, I did. I haven't been far from you all day."

Cardone involuntarily swallowed and shifted his weight. "I find that a remarkable statement. Needless to say, very disturbing."

"I'm sorry. . . ."

"I'm not interested in apologies. I want to know why. Why are you following me? I don't know you. I don't like being followed."

"No one does. I'm only doing what I'm told to do."

"What is it? What do you want?"

The chauffeur moved his hands, just slightly, as if to call attention to their size and great strength. "I've been instructed to bring you a message, and then I'll leave. I've a long drive. My employer lives in Maryland."

"What message? Who from?"

"Mr. Da Vinci, sir."

"Da Vinci?"

"Yes sir. I believe he got in touch with you this morning."

"I don't know your Mr. Da Vinci. . . . What message?"

"That you should not confide in Mr. Tremayne."

118

"What are you talking about?"

"Only what Mr. Da Vinci told me, Mr. Cardione."

Cardone stared into the huge man's eyes. There was intelligence behind the blank façade. "Why did you wait until now? You've been following me all day. You could have stopped me hours ago."

"I wasn't instructed to. There's a radio-phone in the car. I was told to make contact just a few minutes ago."

"*Who* told you?"

"Mr. Da Vinci, sir . . ."

"That's not his name! Now, who is he?" Cardone fought his anger. He took a deep breath before speaking. "You tell me who Da Vinci is."

"There's more to the message," said the chauffeur, disregarding Cardone's question. "Mr. Da Vinci says you should know that Tremayne may have talked to Mr. Tanner. No one's sure yet, but that's what it looks like."

"He *what?* Talked to him about *what?*"

"I don't know, sir. It's not my job to know. I'm hired to drive a car and deliver messages."

"Your message isn't *clear!* I don't understand it! What good is a message if it isn't clear!" Cardone strained to keep in control.

"Perhaps the last part will help you, sir. Mr. Da Vinci feels it would be a good idea if you tried to find out the extent of Mr. Tremayne's involvement with Tanner. But you must be careful. Very, very careful. As you must be careful with your friends from California. That's important."

The chauffeur backed away from the Cadillac

119

and slapped two fingers against his cap's visor.

"Wait a minute!" Cardone reached for the door handle, but the huge man in uniform swiftly clamped his hands on the window ledge and held the door shut.

"No, Mr. Cardione. You stay inside there. You shouldn't call attention to yourself. The train's coming in."

"No, please! *Please* . . . I want to talk to Da Vinci! We've got to talk! Where can I reach him?"

"No way, sir." The chauffeur held the door effortlessly.

"You prick!" Cardone pulled the handle and shoved his whole weight against the door. It gave just a bit and then slammed shut again under the chauffeur's hands. "I'll break you in half!"

The train pulled to a stop in front of the platform. Several men got off and the shriek of two whistle blasts pierced the air.

The chauffeur spoke calmly. "He's not on the train, Mr. Cardione. He *drove* into town this morning. We know that, too."

The train slowly started up and rolled down the tracks. Joe stared at the immense human being holding the car door shut. His anger was nearly beyond control but he was realistic enough to know it would do him no good. The chauffeur stepped back, gave Cardone a second informal salute and walked rapidly towards the Rolls-Royce. Cardone pushed the car door open and stepped out onto the hot pavement.

"Hello there, Joe!" The caller was Amos Needham, of the second contingent of Saddle Valley commuters. A vice-president of Manufacturers Hanover Trust and the chairman of the special events committee for the Saddle Valley Country Club. "You market boys have it easy. When it gets rough you stay home and wait for the calm to set in, eh?"

"Sure, sure, Amos." Cardone kept his eye on the chauffeur of the Rolls, who had climbed into the driver's seat and started the engine.

"I tell you," continued Amos, "I don't know where you young fellas are taking us! . . . Did you see the quotes for DuPont? Everybody else takes a bath and it zooms up! Told my trust committee to consult the Ouija board. To hell with you upstart brokers." Needham chuckled and then suddenly waved his small arm, flagging down a Lincoln Continental approaching the depot. "There's Ralph. Can I give you a lift, Joe? . . . But, of course not. You just stepped out of your car."

The Lincoln pulled up to the platform, and Amos Needham's chauffeur started to get out.

"No need, Ralph. I can still manipulate a door handle. By the way, Joe . . . that Rolls you're looking at reminds me of a friend of mine. Couldn't be, though. He lived in Maryland."

Cardone snapped his head around and looked at the innocuous banker. "Maryland? *Who* in Maryland?"

Amos Needham held the car door open and returned Cardone's stare with unconcerned good humor. "Oh, I don't think you'd know him. He's

121

been dead for years. . . . Funny name. Used to kid him a lot. . . . His name was Caesar."

Amos Needham stepped into his Lincoln and closed the door. At the top of Station Parkway the Rolls-Royce turned right and roared off towards the main arteries leading to Manhattan. Cardone stood on the tarred surface of the Saddle Valley railroad station and he was afraid.

Tremayne!

Tremayne was with Tanner!

Osterman was with Tanner!

Da Vinci . . . Caesar!

The architects of war!

And he, Guiseppe Ambruzzio Cardione, was alone!

Oh, Christ! Christ! Son of God! Blessed Mary! Blessed Mary, Mother of Christ! Wash my hands with his blood! The blood of the lamb! Jesus! Jesus! Forgive me my sins! . . . Mary and Jesus! Christ Incarnate! God all holy!

What have I done?

12

Tuesday—5:00 P.M.

Tremayne walked aimlessly for hours; up and down the familiar streets of the East Side. Yet if anyone had stopped him and asked him where he was, he could not have answered.

He was consumed. Frightened. Blackstone had said everything and clarified nothing.

And Cardone had lied. To somebody. His wife or his office, it didn't matter. What mattered was that Cardone couldn't be reached. Tremayne knew that the panic wouldn't stop until he and Cardone figured out between them what Osterman had done.

Had Osterman betrayed them?

Was that really it? Was it *possible?*

He crossed Vanderbilt Avenue, realizing he had walked to the Biltmore Hotel without thinking about a destination.

It was understandable, he thought. The Biltmore brought back memories of the carefree times.

He walked through the lobby almost expecting to

see some forgotten friend from his teens—and suddenly he was staring at a man he hadn't seen in over twenty-five years. He knew the face, changed terribly with the years—bloated, it seemed to Tremayne, lined—but he couldn't remember the name. The man went back to prep-school days.

Awkwardly the two men approached each other.

"Dick . . . Dick Tremayne! It *is* Dick Tremayne, isn't it?"

"Yes. And you're . . . Jim?"

"Jack! Jack Townsend! How are you, Dick?" The men shook hands, Townsend far more enthusiastic. "It must be twenty-five, thirty years! You look great! How the hell do you keep the weight down? Gave up myself."

"You look fine. Really, you look swell. I didn't know you were in New York."

"I'm not. Based in Toledo. Just in for a couple of days. . . . I swear to God, I had a crazy thought coming in on the plane. I canceled the Hilton and thought I'd grab a room here just to see if any of the old crowd ever came in. Insane, huh? . . . And look what I run into!"

"That's funny. Really funny. I was thinking the same sort of thing a few seconds ago."

"Let's get a drink."

Townsend kept spouting opinions that were formed in the traditions of corporate thought. He was being very boring.

Tremayne kept thinking about Cardone. As he

drank his third drink he looked around for the bar telephone booth he remembered from his youth. It was hidden near the kitchen entrance, and only Biltmore habitués-in-good-standing knew of its existence.

It wasn't there any more. And Jack Townsend kept talking, talking, remembering the unmemorable out loud.

There were two Negroes in leather jackets, beads around their necks, standing several feet away from them.

They wouldn't have been there in other days.

The pleasant days.

Tremayne drank his fourth drink in one assault; Townsend *wouldn't* stop talking.

He *had* to call Joe! The panic was starting again. Maybe Joe would, in a single sentence, unravel the puzzle of Osterman.

"What's the matter with you, Dick? You look all upset."

"S'help me God, this is the first time I've been in here in years." Tremayne slurred his words and he knew it. "Have to make a phone call. Excuse me."

Townsend put his hand on Tremayne's arm. He spoke quietly.

"Are you going to call Cardone?"

"What?"

"I asked if you were going to call Cardone."

"Who are you? . . . Who the hell are you?"

"A friend of Blackstone. Don't call Cardone. Don't do that under any circumstances. You put a nail in your own casket if you do. Can you understand that?"

"I don't understand *anything!* Who *are* you? Who's Blackstone?" Tremayne tried to whisper, but his voice carried throughout the room.

"Let's put it this way. Cardone may be dangerous. We don't trust him. We're not sure of him. Any more than we are of the Ostermans."

"What are you saying?"

"They may have gotten together. You may be flying solo now. Play it cool and see what you can find out. We'll be in touch . . . but Mr. Blackstone told you that already, didn't he?"

Then Townsend did a strange thing. He removed a bill from his wallet and placed it in front of Richard Tremayne. He said only two words as he turned and walked through the glass doors.

"Take it."

It was a one-hundred-dollar bill.

What had it bought?

It didn't buy anything, thought Tremayne. It was merely a symbol.

A price. Any price.

When Fassett walked into the hotel room, two men were already bent over a card table, studying various papers and maps. One was Grover. The other man was named Cole. Fassett removed his Panama hat and sunglasses, putting them on the bureau top.

"Everything okay?" asked Grover.

"On schedule. If Tremayne doesn't get too drunk at the Biltmore."

"If he does," said Cole, his attention on a New Jersey road map, "a friendly, bribable cop will correct the situation. He'll get home."

"Have you got men on both sides of the bridge?"

"And the tunnels. He sometimes takes the Lincoln Tunnel and drives up the Parkway. All in radio contact." Cole was making marks on a piece of tracing paper placed over the map.

The telephone rang. Grover crossed to the bedside table to pick it up.

"Grover here. . . . Oh? Yes, we'll double check but I'm sure we would've heard if he had. . . . Don't worry about it. All right. Keep in touch." Grover replaced the receiver and stood by the telephone.

"What's the matter?" Fassett removed his white Palm Beach jacket and began rolling up his sleeves.

"That was Los Angeles logistics. Between the time Osterman left the studio and was picked up on Mulholland, they lost him for about twenty minutes. They're concerned that he may have reached Cardone or Tremayne."

Cole looked up from the table. "Around one o'clock our time—ten in California?"

"Yes."

"Negative. Cardone was in his car and Tremayne on the streets. Neither could be reached. . . ."

"I see what they mean, though," interrupted Fassett. "Tremayne didn't waste any time this noon trying to get to Cardone."

"We calculated that, Larry," said Cole. "We would have intercepted both of them if a meeting had been scheduled."

"Yes, I know. Risky, though."

Cole laughed as he picked up the tracing papers. "You plan—we'll control. Here's every back road link to 'Leather.' "

"We've got them."

"George forgot to bring up a copy, and the others are with the men. A command post should always have a map of the field."

"*Mea culpa.* I was in briefing until two this morning and had to get the shuttle at six-thirty. I also forgot my razor and toothbrush and God knows what else."

The telephone rang once again and Grover reached down for it.

". . . I see . . . wait a minute." He held the phone away from his ear and looked over at Laurence Fassett. "Our second chauffeur had a run-in with Cardone . . ."

"Oh, Christ! Nothing rough, I hope."

"No, no. The hot-tempered All-American tried to get out of the car and start a fight. Nothing happened."

"Tell him to head back to Washington. Get out of the area."

"Go back to D.C., Jim. . . . Sure, you might as well. Okay. See you at camp." Grover replaced the receiver and walked back to the card table.

"What's Jim going to do 'just as well'?" asked Fassett.

"Drop off the Rolls in Maryland. He thinks Cardone got the license number."

"Good. And the Caesar family?"

"Primed beautifully," interrupted Cole. "They can't wait to hear from Guiseppe Ambruzzio Cardione. Like father, unlike son."

"What's that mean?" Grover held his lighter under his cigarette.

"Old man Caesar made a dozen fortunes out of the rackets. His oldest son is with the Attorney General's office and an absolute fanatic about the Mafia."

"Washing away family sins?"

"Something like that."

Fassett walked over to the window and looked down at the long expanse of Central Park South. When he spoke he did so quietly, but the satisfaction in his voice made his companions smile.

"It's all there now. Each one is jolted. They're all confused and frightened. None of them know what to do or whom to talk to. Now we sit and watch. We'll give them a rest for twenty-four hours. A blackout. . . . And Omega has no choice. Omega has to make its move."

13

It was ten-fifteen before Tanner reached his office. He had found it nearly impossible to leave home, but he knew Fassett was right. He sat down and glanced perfunctorily at his mail and messages. Everyone wanted a conference. No one wanted to make a single decision without his say-so.

Corporate musical chairs. The network sub-brass band.

He picked up the phone and dialed New Jersey.

"Hello, Ali?"

"Hi, hon. Did you forget something?"

"No. . . . No. Just felt lonely. What are you doing?"

Inside 22 Orchard Place, Saddle Valley, New Jersey, Alice Tanner smiled and felt warm. "What am I doing? . . . Well, as per the great Khan's orders, I'm overseeing your son's cleaning out the basement. And as the great Khan also instructed, his daughter is spending a hot July morning on her remedial reading. How else could she get into Berkeley by the time she's twelve?"

Tanner caught the complaint. When she was a young girl, his wife's summers were lonely and

130

terrifying. Ali wanted them to be perfect for Janet.

"Well, don't overdo it. Have some kids over."

"I might at that. But Nancy Loomis phoned and asked if Janet could go there for lunch . . ."

"Ali . . ." Tanner switched the phone to his left hand. "I'd rather cool it with the Loomises for a few days . . ."

"What do you mean?"

John remembered Jim Loomis from the daily eight-twenty express. "Jim's trying to boilerplate some market stuff. He's got a lot of fellows on the train to go along with him. If I can avoid him till next week I'm off the hook."

"What does Joe say?"

"He doesn't know about it. Loomis doesn't want Joe to know. Rival houses, I guess."

"I don't see that Janet's going to lunch has anything. . . ."

"Just saves embarrassment. We don't have the kind of money he's looking for."

"Amen to that!"

"And . . . do me a favor. Stay near the phone today."

Alice Tanner's eyes shifted to the telephone in her hand. "Why?"

"I can't go into it, but I may have an important call. . . . What we're always talking about. . . ."

Alice Tanner immediately, unconsciously lowered her voice as she smiled. "Someone's offered you something!"

"Could be. They're going to call at home to set up a lunch."

"Oh, John. That's exciting!"

"It . . . could be interesting." He suddenly found it painful to talk to her. "Speak to you later."

"Sounds marvelous, darling. I'll turn up the bell. It'll be heard in New York."

"I'll call you later."

"Tell me the details then."

Tanner placed the receiver slowly in its cradle. The lies had begun . . . but his family would stay home.

He knew he had to turn his mind to Standard Mutual problems. Fassett had warned him. There could be no break in his normal pattern, and normalcy for any network news director was a condition close to hypertension. Tanner's mark at Standard was his control of potential difficulties. If there was ever a time in his professional life to avoid chaos, it was now.

He picked up his telephone. "Norma. I'll read out the list of those I'll see this morning, and you call them. Tell everyone I want the meetings quick and don't let anyone run over fifteen minutes unless I say otherwise. It would help if all problems and proposals were reduced to written half-pages. Pass the word. I've got a lot to catch up on."

He wasn't free again until 12:30. Then he closed his office door and called his wife.

There was no answer.

He let the phone ring for nearly two minutes, until the spaces between the rings seemed to grow longer and longer.

No answer. No answer at the telephone—the

telephone whose bell was turned up so loud it would be heard in New York.

It was twelve-thirty-five. Ali would figure no one would call between noon and one-thirty. And she probably needed something from the supermarket. Or she might have decided to take the children over to the Club for hamburgers. Or she couldn't refuse Nancy Loomis and had taken Janet over for lunch. Or she had gone to the library—Ali was an inveterate poolside reader during the summer.

Tanner tried to picture Ali doing all these things. That she was doing one, or some, or all, had to be the case.

He dialed again, and again there was no answer. He called the Club.

"I'm sorry, Mr. Tanner. We've paged outside. Mrs. Tanner isn't here."

The Loomises. Of course, she went to the Loomises.

"Golly, John, Alice said Janet had a bad tummy. Maybe she took her to the doctor."

By eight minutes after one, John Tanner had dialed his home twice more. The last time he had let the phone ring for nearly five minutes. Picturing Ali coming through the door breathlessly, always allowing that one last ring, expecting her to answer.

But it did not happen.

He told himself over and over again that he was acting foolishly. He himself had seen the patrol car following them when Ali drove him to the station. Fassett had convinced him yesterday that his watchdogs were thorough.

Fassett.

He picked up the phone and dialed the emergency number Fassett had given him. It was a Manhattan exchange.

"Grover . . ."

Who? thought Tanner.

"Hello? Hello? . . . George Grover speaking."

"My name is John Tanner. I'm trying to find Laurence Fassett."

"Oh, hello, Mr. Tanner. Is something the matter? Fassett's out. Can I help you?"

"Are you an associate of Fassett's?"

"I am, sir."

"I can't reach my wife. I've tried calling a number of times. She doesn't answer."

"She may have stepped out. I wouldn't worry. She's under surveillance."

"Are you positive?"

"Of course."

"I asked her to stay by the phone. She thought I was expecting an important call. . . ."

"I'll contact our men and call you right back. It'll set your mind at ease."

Tanner hung up feeling slightly embarrassed. Yet five minutes went by and the expected ring did not come. He dialed Fassett's number but it was busy. He quickly replaced the phone wondering if his impetuous dialing caused Grover to find his line busy. Was Grover trying to reach him? He had to be. He'd try again right away.

Yet the phone did not ring.

Tanner picked it up and slowly, carefully dialed, making sure every digit was correct.

"Grover."

"This is Tanner. I thought you were going to call right back!"

"I'm sorry, Mr. Tanner. We've been having a little difficulty. Nothing to be concerned about."

"What do you mean, difficulty?"

"Making contact with our men in the field. It's not unusual. We can't expect them to be next to a radio-phone every second. We'll reach them shortly and call you back."

"That's not good enough!" John Tanner slammed the telephone down and got out of his chair. Yesterday afternoon Fassett had detailed every move made by all of them—even to the precise actions at the moment of his phone call. And now this Grover couldn't reach any of the men supposedly watching his family. What had Fassett said?

"We have thirteen agents in Saddle Valley. . . ."

And Grover couldn't reach any of them.

Thirteen men and none could be contacted!

He crossed to the office door. "Something's come up, Norma. Listen for my phone, please. If it's a man named Grover, tell him I've left for home."

SADDLE VALLEY
VILLAGE INCORPORATED 1862
Welcome

"Where to now, Mister?"

"Go straight. I'll show you."

The cab reached Orchard Drive, two blocks from his home; Tanner's pulse was hammering. He kept picturing the station wagon in the driveway. As soon as they made one more turn he'd be able to see it—if it was there. And if it was, everything would be all right. Oh, Christ! Let everything be all right!

The station wagon was not in the driveway.

Tanner looked at his watch.

Two-forty-five. A quarter to three! And Ali wasn't there!

"On the left. The wood-shingled house."

"Nice place, mister. A real nice place."

"Hurry!"

The cab pulled up to the flagstone path. Tanner paid and pulled open the door. He didn't wait for the driver's thanks.

"Ali! Ali!" Tanner raced through the laundry room to check the garage.

Nothing. The small Triumph stood there.

Quiet.

Yet there was something. An odor. A faint, sickening odor that Tanner couldn't place.

"Ali! Ali!" He ran back to the kitchen and saw his pool through the window. Oh, God! He stared at the surface of the water and hurried to the patio door. The lock was stuck and so he slammed against it, breaking the latch, and ran out.

Thank God! There was nothing in the water!

His small Welsh terrier dog stirred from its sleep. The animal was attached to a wire run and immediately started barking in its sharp, hysterical yap.

He sped back into the house, to the cellar door.

"Ray! Janet! Ali!"

Quiet. Except for the incessant barking of the dog outside.

He left the cellar door open and ran to the staircase.

Upstairs!

He leapt up the stairs; the doors to the children's rooms and the guest room were open. The door to his and Ali's room was shut.

And then he heard it. The soft playing of a radio. Ali's clock radio with the automatic timer which shut the radio off at any given time up to an hour. He and Ali always used that timer when they played the radio. Never the ON button. It was a habit. And Ali had been gone over two and a half hours. Someone else had turned on the radio.

He opened the door.

No one.

He was about to turn and search the rest of the house when he saw it. A note written in red pencil next to the clock radio.

He crossed to the bedside table.

> *"Your wife and children went for an unexpected drive. You'll find them by an old railroad depot on Lassiter Road."*

In his panic, Tanner remembered the abandoned

depot. It sat deep in the woods on a rarely used back road.

What had he done? What in Christ's name had he done? He'd killed them! If that was so, he'd kill Fassett! Kill Grover! Kill all those who should have been watching!

He raced out of the bedroom, down the staircase, into the garage. The door was open and he jumped into the seat of the Triumph and started the engine.

Tanner swung the small sports car to the right out of the driveway and sped around the long Orchard Drive curve, trying to remember the quickest way to Lassiter Road. He reached a pond he recognized as Lassiter Lake, used by the Saddle Valley residents for ice skating in winter. Lassiter Road was on the other side and seemed to disappear into a stretch of undisciplined woods.

He kept the accelerator flat against the Triumph's floor. He started talking to himself, then screaming at himself.

Ali! Ali! Janet! Ray!

The road was winding. Blind spots, curves, sun rays coming through the crowded trees. There were no other automobiles, no other signs of life.

The old abandoned depot suddenly appeared. And there was his station wagon—half off the overgrown parking area, into the tall grass. Tanner slammed on his brakes beside the wagon. There was no one in sight.

He jumped out of the Triumph and raced to the car.

In an instant his mind went out of control. The

horror was real. The unbelievable had happened.

On the floor of the front seat was his wife. Slumped, motionless. In the back were little Janet and his son. Heads down. Bodies sprawled off the red seats.

Oh, Christ! Christ! It had happened! His eyes filled with tears. His body shook.

He pulled the door open, screaming in terror. and suddenly a wave of odor washed over him. The sickish odor he had smelled in his garage. He grabbed Ali's head and pulled her up, frightened beyond feeling.

"Ali! Ali! My God! *Please! Ali!*"

His wife opened her eyes slowly. Blinking. Conscious but not conscious. She moved her arms.

"Where . . . where? The *children!*" She drew out the word hysterically. The sound of her scream brought Tanner back to his senses. He leapt up and reached over the seat for his son and daughter.

They moved. They were alive! They *all* were *alive!*

Ali climbed out of the station wagon and stumbled to the ground. Her husband lifted his daughter out of the back seat and held her as she started to cry.

"What *happened?* What *happened?*" Alice Tanner pulled herself up.

"Don't talk, Ali. Breathe. As deeply as you can. Here!" He walked to her and handed her the sobbing Janet. "I'll get Ray."

"What *happened?* Don't tell me *not* to . . ."

"Be quiet! Just breathe. Breathe hard!"

He helped his son out of the back seat. The boy was sick and started to vomit. Tanner cupped his son's forehead with his hand, holding him around the waist with his left arm.

"John, you simply can't . . ."

"Walk around. Try to get Janet to walk! Do as I *say!*"

Obediently, dazedly, Alice Tanner did what her husband commanded. The boy began to shake his head in Tanner's hand.

"Feeling better, son?"

"Wow! . . . Wow! Where are we?" The boy was suddenly frightened.

"It's all right. It's all right. . . . You're all . . . all right."

Tanner looked over at his wife. She had put Janet's feet on the ground, holding her in her arms. The child was crying loudly now, and Tanner watched, filled with hatred and fear. He walked to the station wagon to see if the keys were in the ignition.

They weren't. It didn't make sense.

He looked under the seats, in the glove compartment, in the back. Then he saw them. Wrapped in a piece of white paper, an elastic band holding the paper around the case. The packet was wedged between the collapsible seats, pushed far down, nearly out of sight.

His daughter was screaming now, and Alice Tanner picked the child up, trying to comfort her, repeating over and over again that everything was all right.

Making sure his wife could not see him, Tanner held the small package below the back seat, snapped the elastic band and opened the paper.

It was blank.

He crumpled the paper and stuffed it into his pocket. He would tell Ali what had happened now. They'd go away. Far away. But he would *not* tell her in front of the children.

"Get in the wagon." Tanner spoke to his son softly and went to his wife, taking the hysterical child from her. "Get the keys out of the Triumph, Ali. We're going home."

His wife stood in front of him, her eyes wide with fright, the tears streaming down her face. She tried to control herself, tried with all her strength not to scream. "What happened? What *happened* to us?"

The roar of an engine prevented Tanner from answering. In his anger, he was grateful. The Saddle Valley patrol car sped into the depot and came to a stop less than ten yards from them.

Jenkins and McDermott leapt out of the automobile. Jenkins had his revolver drawn.

"Is everything all right?" He ran up to Tanner. McDermott went rapidly to the station wagon and spoke quietly to the boy in the back seat.

"We found the note in your bedroom. Incidentally, we think we've recovered most of your property."

"Our what?" Alice Tanner stared at the police officer.

"What property?"

"Two television sets, Mrs. Tanner's jewelry, a box of silver, place settings, some cash. There's a list down at the station. We don't know if we got everything. The car was abandoned several blocks from your house. They may have taken other things. You'll have to check."

Tanner handed his daughter to Ali.

"What the hell are you talking about?"

"You were robbed. Your wife must have come back while they were in the process. She and the children were gassed in the garage. . . . They were professionals, no doubt about it. Real professional methods. . . ."

"You're a liar," said Tanner softly. "There was nothing . . ."

"Please!" interrupted Jenkins. "The main thing now is your wife and children."

As if on signal, McDermott called from inside the station wagon. "I want to get this kid to the hospital! *Now!*"

"Oh, my God!" Alice Tanner ran to the automobile, carrying her daughter in her arms.

"Let McDermott take them," said Jenkins.

"How can I trust you? You lied to me. There was nothing missing in my house. No television sets were gone, no signs of any robbery! Why did you lie?"

"There isn't time. I'm sending your wife and children with McDermott." Jenkins spoke rapidly.

"They're going with *me!*"

"No they're not." Jenkins raised his pistol slightly.

142

"I'll kill you, Jenkins."

"Then what stands between you and Omega?" said Jenkins calmly. "Be reasonable. Fassett's on his way out. He wants to see you."

"I'm sorry. Truly, abjectly sorry. It won't, it *can't* happen again."

"What *did* happen? Where was your infallible protection?"

"A logistical error on a surveillance schedule that hadn't been cross-checked. That's the truth. There's no point in lying to you. I'm the one responsible."

"You weren't out here."

"I'm still responsible. The Leather team's my responsibility. Omega saw that a post wasn't covered—for less than fifteen minutes, incidentally—and they moved in."

"I can't tolerate that. You risked the lives of my wife and children!"

"I told you, there's no possibility of recurrence. Also—and in an inverted way, this should be comforting—this afternoon confirms the fact that Omega won't kill. Terror, yes. Murder, no."

"Why? Because you say so? I don't buy it. The C.I.A. track record reads like a disaster file. You're not making any more decisions for *me*, let's get that clear."

"Oh? You are then?"

"Yes."

"Don't be a fool. If not for yourself, for your family."

Tanner got out of the chair. He saw through the

143

venetian blinds that two men were standing guard outside the motel window.

"I'm taking them away."

"Where will you go?"

"I don't know. I just know I'm not staying here."

"You think Omega won't follow you?"

"Why should it . . . they? I'm no part of *you*."

"They won't believe that."

"Then I'll make it clear!"

"Are you going to take out an ad in *The Times?*"

"No!" Tanner swung around and pointed a finger at the C.I.A. man. "You will! However you want to do it. Because if you don't, I'll tell the story of this operation and your inept, malicious handling of it on every network newscast in the country. You won't survive that."

"Neither will you because you'll be dead. Your wife dead. Your son, your daughter . . . dead."

"You can't threaten me . . ."

"For God's sake, look at history! Look at what's *really happened!*" Fassett exploded. Then suddenly he lowered his voice and rised his hand to his chest, speaking slowly. "Take me. . . . My wife was killed in East Berlin. They murdered her for no earthly reason except that she was married to me. I was being . . . taught a lesson. And to teach me that lesson they took my wife. Don't make pronouncements to me. I've been there. You've been safe. Well, you're not safe now."

Tanner was stunned. "What are you trying to say?"

"I'm telling you that you'll do exactly what we've planned. We're too close now. I want Omega."

144

"You can't force me and you know it!"

"Yes, I can. . . . Because if you turn, if you run, I withdraw every agent in Saddle Valley. You'll be alone . . . and I don't think you can cope with the situation by yourself."

"I'm taking my family away . . ."

"Don't be crazy! Omega raced in on a simple logistical error. That means they, whoever they are, are alert. Extremely alert, fast and thorough. What chance do you think you'll have? What chance do you give your family? We've admitted a mistake. We won't make any others."

Tanner knew Fassett was right. If he was abandoned now, he didn't have the resources for control.

"You don't fool around, do you?"

"Did you ever—in a mine field?"

"I guess not. . . . This afternoon. What was it?"

"Terror tactics. Without identification. That's in case you're clean. We realized what had happened and put out a counterexplanation. We'll withhold some of your property—small stuff, like jewelry, until it's over. More authentic."

"Which means you expect me to go along with the 'robbery.' "

"Of course. It's safest."

"Yes. . . . Of course." Tanner reached into his pocket for cigarettes. The telephone rang and Fassett picked it up.

He spoke quietly, then turned to the news director. "Your family's back home. They're okay. Still scared, but okay. Some of our men are straightening up the place. It's a mess. They're trying to lift fingerprints. Naturally, it'll be found the thieves wore gloves. We've told your wife that you're still at headquarters making a statement."

"I see."

"You want us to drive you back?"

"No. . . . No, I don't. I presume I'll be followed anyway."

"Safety surveillance is the proper term."

Tanner entered the Village Pub, Saddle Valley's one fashionable bar, and called the Tremaynes.

"Ginny, this is John. I'd like to talk to Dick. Is he there?"

"John *Tanner?*" Why did she say that? His name. She knew his voice.

"Yes. Is Dick there?"

"No. . . . Of course not. He's at the office. What is it?"

"Nothing important."

"Can't you tell me?"

"I just need a little legal advice. I'll try him at the office. Good-bye." Tanner knew he had done it badly. He had been awkward.

But then, so had Virginia Tremayne.

Tanner dialed New York.

"I'm sorry, Mr. Tanner. Mr. Tremayne's out on Long Island. In conference."

"It's urgent. What's the number?"

Tremayne's secretary gave it to him reluctantly. He dialed it.

"I'm sorry, Mr. Tremayne isn't here."

"His office said he was in conference out there."

"He called this morning and canceled. I'm sorry, sir."

Tanner hung up the phone, then dialed the Cardones.

"Daddy and Mommy are out for the day, Uncle John. They said they'd be back after dinner. Do you want them to call you?"

"No . . . no, that's not necessary. . . ."

There was an empty feeling in his stomach. He dialed the operator, gave her the information, including his credit card number, and three thousand four hundred miles away a telephone rang in Beverly Hills.

"Osterman residence."

"Is Mr. Osterman there?"

"No, he's not. May I ask who's calling, please?"

"Is Mrs. Osterman there?"

"No."

"When do you expect them back?"

"Next week. Who's calling, please?"

"The name's Cardone. Joseph Cardone."

"C-A-R-D-O-N-E. . . ."

"That's right. When did they go?"

"They left for New York last night. The ten o'clock flight, I believe."

John Tanner hung up the receiver. The Ostermans were in New York! They'd gotten in by six o'clock that morning!

The Tremaynes, the Cardones, the Ostermans.

All there. None accounted for.

Any or all.

Omega!

14

Thursday—3:00 A.M.

Fassett had set a convincing scene. By the time Tanner returned home the rooms had been straightened up, but there was still disarray. Chairs were not in their proper places, rugs off center, lamps in different positions; the woman of the house hadn't yet put things to rights.

Ali told him how the police had helped her; if she suspected collusion she didn't let on.

But then Alice McCall had lived with violence as a child. The sight of policemen in her home was not unfamiliar to her. She was conditioned to react with a minimum of hysteria.

Her husband, on the other hand, was not conditioned at all for the role he had to play. For the second night, sleep was fitful, ultimately impossible. He looked at the dial on the clock radio. It was nearly three in the morning and his mind still raced, his eyes refused to stay shut.

It was no use. He had to get up, he had to walk around; perhaps eat something, read something, smoke.

Anything that would help him stop thinking.

He and Ali had had a number of brandies before going to bed—too many drinks for Ali; she was deep in sleep, as much from the alcohol as from exhaustion.

Tanner got out of bed and went downstairs. He wandered aimlessly around; he finished the remains of a cantaloupe in the kitchen, read the junk mail in the hallway, flipped through some magazines in the living room. Finally he went out to the garage. There was still the faint—ever so faint now —odor of the gas which had been used on his wife and children. He returned to the living room, forgetting to turn off the lights in the garage.

Extinguishing his last cigarette, he looked around for another pack; more for the security of knowing there was one than from any immediate need. There was a carton in the study. As he opened the top drawer of his desk, a noise made him look up.

There was a tapping on his study window and the beam of a flashlight waving in small circles against the pane.

"It's Jenkins, Mr. Tanner," said the muffled voice. "Come to your back door."

Tanner, relieved, nodded to the dark figure on the other side of the glass.

"This screen-door latch was broken," said Jenkins softly as Tanner opened the kitchen door. "We don't know how it happened."

"I did it. What are you doing out there?"

"Making sure there's no repetition of this afternoon. There are four of us. We wondered what *you* were doing. The lights are on all over downstairs. Even in the garage. Is anything the matter? Has anyone phoned you?"

"Wouldn't you know if they had?"

Jenkins smiled as he stepped through the door. "We're supposed to, I guess you know that. But there's no accounting for mechanical failures."

"I suppose not. Care for a cup of coffee?"

"Only if you'd make enough for three other guys. They can't leave their posts."

"Sure." Tanner filled the hot water kettle. "Instant be all right?"

"Be great. Thanks." Jenkins sat down at the kitchen table, moving his large police holster so it hung free from the seat. He watched Tanner closely and then looked around the room.

"I'm glad you're outside. I appreciate it, really. I know it's a job, but still . . ."

"Not just a job. We're concerned."

"That's nice to hear. You have a wife and kids?"

"No sir, I don't."

"I thought you were married."

"That's my partner. McDermott."

"Oh, I see. . . . You've been on the force here, let's see . . . a couple of years now, isn't it?"

"Just about."

Tanner turned from the stove and looked at Jenkins. "Are you one of them?"

"I beg your pardon?"

"I asked if you were one of them. This afternoon you used the name Omega. That means you're one of Fassett's men."

"I was instructed what to tell you. I've met Mr. Fassett, of course."

"But you're not a small-town policeman, are you?"

Jenkins did not have time to answer. There was a cry from the grounds outside. Both men in the kitchen had heard that sound before, Tanner in France, Jenkins near the Yalu River. It was a scream in the instant of death.

Jenkins bolted to the screen door and raced outside, Tanner following at his heels. Two other men came out of the darkness.

"It's Ferguson! Ferguson!" They spoke harshly, but they did not yell. Jenkins rounded the pool and ran towards the woods beyond Tanner's property. The news director stumbled and tried to keep up with him.

The mutilated body lay in a clump of weeds. The head was severed; its eyes were wide, as if the lids had been pierced and held with nails.

"Get back, Mr. Tanner! Stay back! Don't look! Don't raise your voice!" Jenkins held the petrified news director by the shoulders, pushing him away from the corpse. The two other men ran into the woods, pistols drawn.

Tanner sank to the ground feeling sick, frightened beyond any fear he'd ever known.

"Listen to me," whispered Jenkins, kneeling over the trembling man. "That body in there wasn't meant for you to see. It has nothing to do with *you!* There are certain rules, certain signs we all know about. That man was killed for Fassett. It was meant for *him.*"

The body was wrapped in canvas and two men

lifted it up to carry it away. Their moves were silent, efficient.

"You're wife's still sleeping," said Fassett quietly. "That's good. . . . The boy got up and came downstairs. McDermott told him you were making coffee for the men."

Tanner sat on the grass on the far side of the pool, trying to make sense out of the last hour. Fassett and Jenkins stood above him.

"For God's sake, how did it happen?" He watched the men carrying the body and his words could hardly be heard. Fassett knelt down.

"He was taken from behind."

"From behind?"

"Someone who knew the woods behind your house." Fassett's eyes bore into Tanner's and the news director understood the unspoken accusation.

"It's my fault, isn't it?"

"Possibly. Jenkins left his post. His position was adjacent. . . . Why were you downstairs? Why were all the first-floor lights on?"

"I couldn't sleep. I got up."

"The lights were on in the garage. Why were you in the garage?"

"I . . . I don't remember. I guess I was thinking about this afternoon."

"You left the garage lights on. . . . I can understand a man who's nervous getting up, going downstairs—having a cigarette, a drink. I can understand that. But I don't understand a man going into his garage and leaving the lights on. . . . Were you going somewhere, Mr. Tanner?"

152

"Going somewhere? . . . No. No, of course not. Where would I go?"

Fassett looked up at Jenkins who was watching Tanner's face in the dim reflection of the light coming from the house. Jenkins spoke.

"Are you sure?"

"My God. . . . You thought I was running away. You thought I was running away and you came in to stop me!"

"Keep your voice down, please." Fassett rose to his feet.

"Do you think I'd *do* that? Do you think for one minute I'd leave my family?"

"You could be taking your family with you," answered Jenkins.

"Oh, Christ! That's why you came to the window. That's why you left your . . ." Tanner couldn't finish the sentence. He felt sick and wondered if he threw up where he could do it. He looked up at the two government men. "Oh, Christ!"

"Chances are it would have happened anyway." Fassett spoke calmly. "It wasn't . . . wasn't part of any original plan. But you've *got* to understand. You behaved *abnormally*. It wasn't *normal* for you to do what you did. You've got to watch every move you make, everything you do or say. You can't forget that. *Ever*."

Tanner awkwardly, unsteadily, got up. "You're not going on with this? You've got to call it off."

"Call it off? One of my men was just killed. We call it off now and you're also dead. So's the rest of your family."

Tanner saw the sadness in the agent's eyes. One didn't argue with such men. They told the truth.

"Have you checked on the others?"

"Yes, we have."

"Where are they?"

"The Cardones are at home. Tremayne stayed in New York; his wife's out here."

"What about the Ostermans?"

"I'll go into that later. You'd better get back inside. We've doubled the patrol."

"No you don't. What about the Ostermans. Aren't they in California?"

"You know they're not. You placed a call to them on your credit card at four-forty-six this afternoon."

"Then where are they?"

Fassett looked at the news director and replied simply. "They obviously made reservations under another name. We know they're in the New York area. We'll find them."

"Then it could have been Osterman."

"It could have been. You'd better get back. And don't worry. We've got an army out here."

Tanner looked over at the woods where Fassett's man had been murdered. His whole body involuntarily shook for a moment. The proximity of such a brutal death appalled him. He nodded to the government men and started towards his house feeling only a sickening emptiness.

"Is it true about Tremayne?" asked Jenkins softly. "He's in the city?"

"Yes. He had a fair amount to drink and took a room at the Biltmore."

"Anyone check the room tonight?"

Fassett turned his attention from the figure of Tanner disappearing into the house. He looked at Jenkins. "Earlier, yes. Our man reported that he went—probably staggered—to his room a little after midnight. We told him to pull out and pick Tremayne up again at seven. What's bothering you?"

"I'm not sure yet. It'll be clearer when we confirm Cardone's situation."

"We did confirm it. He's at home."

"We assume he's at home because we haven't had any reason to think otherwise up to now."

"You'd better explain that."

"The Cardones had dinner guests. Three couples. They all came together in a car with New York plates. Surveillance said they left in a hurry at twelve-thirty. . . . I'm wondering now if Cardone was in that car. It was dark. He could have been."

"Let's check it out. With both. The Biltmore'll be no problem. With Cardone we'll have Da Vinci make another phone call."

Eighteen minutes later the two government men sat in the front seat of an automobile several hundred yards down the road from the Tanner house. The radio came in clearly.

"Information in, Mr. Fassett. The Da Vinci call got us nowhere. Mrs. Cardone said her husband wasn't feeling well; he was sleeping in a guest room and she didn't want to disturb him. Incidentally, she hung up on us. The Biltmore confirmed.

There's no one in room ten-twenty-one. Tremayne didn't even sleep in his bed."

"Thank you, New York," said Laurence Fassett as he flipped the channel button to OFF. He looked over at Jenkins. "Can you imagine a man like Cardone refusing a telephone call at four-thirty in the morning? From Da Vinci?"

"He's not there."

"Neither's Tremayne."

15

Thursday—6:40 A.M.

Fassett told him he could stay home on Thursday. Not that he had to be given permission; nothing could have dragged him away. Fassett also said that he'd contact him in the morning. The final plans for the total protection of the Tanner family would be made clear.

The news director put on a pair of khaki trousers and carried his sneakers and a sportshirt downstairs. He looked at the kitchen clock: twenty minutes to seven. The children wouldn't be up for at least an hour and a half. Ali, with luck, would sleep until nine-thirty or ten.

Tanner wondered how many men were outside. Fassett had said there was an army, but what good would an army be if Omega wanted him dead? What good had an army been for the government man in the woods at three-thirty in the morning? There were too many possibilities. Too many opportunities. Fassett had to understand that now. It had gone too far. If the preposterous were real, if the Ostermans, the Cardones or the Tremaynes really were a part of Omega, he couldn't simply greet them at his door as if nothing had happened. It was absurd!

He went to the kitchen door and quietly let himself out. He'd go towards the woods until he saw someone. He'd reach Fassett.

"Good morning." It was Jenkins, dark circles of weariness under his eyes. He was sitting on the ground just beyond the edge of the woods. He couldn't be seen from the house or even the pool.

"Hello. Aren't you going to get any sleep?"

"I'm relieved at eight. I don't mind. What about you? You're exhausted."

"Look, I want to see Fassett. I've got to see him before he makes any more plans."

The patrolman looked at his wristwatch. "He was going to call you after we gave him the word you were up. I don't think he expected it'd be so early. That may be good though. Wait a sec." Jenkins walked a few feet into the woods and returned with a canvas-pack radio. "Let's go. We'll drive over."

"Why can't he come here?"

"Relax. Nobody could get near your house. Come on. You'll see."

Jenkins picked up the radio by its shoulder strap and led Tanner through a newly created path in the woods surrounding his property. Every thirty to forty feet were men, kneeling, sitting, lying on their stomachs facing the house, unseen but seeing. As Jenkins and Tanner approached each man, weapons were drawn. Jenkins gave the radio to the patrol on the east flank.

158

"Call Fassett. Tell him we're on our way over," he said.

"That agent was killed last night because the killer knew he'd been recognized. One part of Omega was identified and that was unacceptable." Fassett sipped coffee, facing Tanner. "It was also another sort of warning, but that doesn't concern you."

"He was murdered fifty yards from my house, from my family! *Everything* concerns me!"

"All right! . . . Try to understand. We can assume the information on you has been returned; remember, you're just Tanner the newsman, nothing else. They're circling like hawks now, wary of each other. None knowing whether the others have accomplices, scouts of their own. . . . The killer— *one* tentacle of Omega—ran a private surveillance. He collided with the agent; he had no choice but to kill. He didn't know him, he'd never seen him before. The only thing he *could* be sure of was that whoever posted the man would become concerned when he didn't report. Whoever was responsible for that man in the woods would come and find him. That was the warning; his death."

"You can't be sure of that."

"We're not dealing with amateurs. The killer knew the body would be removed before daylight. I told you in Washington, Omega's fanatic. A decapitated body fifty yards from your house is the kind of mistake that would call for an NKVD execution. *If* Omega was responsible. If not . . ."

"How do you know they're not working together? If the Ostermans or the Cardones or the Tremaynes are any part of it, they could have planned it together."

"Impossible. They haven't been in contact since the harassment began. We've fed them all—each of them—contradictory stories, illogical suppositions, half truths. We've had cables routed through Zurich, telephone calls from Lisbon, messages delivered by strangers in dead-end streets. Each couple is in the dark. None know what the others are doing."

The agent named Cole looked up at Fassett from the chair by the motel window. He knew that Fassett could not be absolutely sure of his last statement. They'd lost the Ostermans for nearly twelve hours. There was a surveillance lapse of three and three-and-a-half hours, respectively, with Tremayne and Cardone. Still, thought Cole, Fassett was right to say what he did.

"Where are the Ostermans? You said last night —this morning—that you didn't know where they were."

"We found them. In a New York hotel. From what we've learned, it's doubtful Osterman was in the area last night."

"But, again, you're not sure."

"I said doubtful. Not beyond doubt."

"And you're convinced it had to be one of them?"

"We think so. The killer was male almost certainly. It . . . took enormous strength. . . . He knew the grounds around your property better than we

160

did. And you should know we've studied your place for weeks."

"For God's sake then, *stop* them! Confront them! You can't let it go on!"

"Which one?" Fassett asked quietly.

"*All* of them! A man was *killed!*"

Fassett put his coffee cup down. "If we do as you suggest, which, I admit, is tempting—it was my man who was killed, remember—we not only wash out any chance we have to expose Omega, but we also take a risk with you and your family that I can't justify."

"We couldn't be taking any greater risk and you know it."

"You're in no danger. Not as long as you continue to act in a normal manner. If we walk in now we're admitting the weekend is a trap. That trap couldn't have been set without your assistance. . . . We'd be signing your death warrants."

"I don't understand that."

"Then take my word for it," said Fassett sharply. "Omega *must* come to *us*. There's no other way."

Tanner paused, watching Fassett carefully. "That's not entirely true, is it? What you're saying is . . . it's too late."

"You're very perceptive."

Fassett picked up his cup and went to the table where there was a thermos of coffee. "There's only one more day. At the most two. Some part of Omega will break by then. All we need is one. One defection and it's over."

"And one stick of dynamite in my house blows us to hell."

"There'll be nothing like that. No violence. Not directed at you. Put simply, you're not important. Not any longer. They'll only be concerned about each other."

"What about yesterday afternoon?"

"We've put out a police-blotter story. A robbery. Bizarre to be sure, but a robbery nevertheless. Just what your wife thinks happened, the way she thinks it happened. You don't have to deny anything."

"They'll know it's a lie. They'll call it."

Fassett looked calmly up from the thermos. "Then we'll have Omega, won't we? We'll know which one it is."

"What am I supposed to do? Pick up a telephone and call you? They may have other ideas . . ."

"We'll hear every word said in your house starting with your first guest tomorrow afternoon. Later this morning two television repairmen will come to fix the sets damaged in the robbery. While tracing antenna wiring they'll also install miniaturized pick-ups throughout your home. Starting with the first arrival tomorrow, they'll be activated."

"Are you trying to tell me you won't activate them until then?"

Cole interrupted. "No, we won't. We're not interested in your privacy, only your safety."

"You'd better get back," said Fassett. "Jenkins will drop you off at the south end of your property. You couldn't sleep so you went for a walk."

Tanner crossed slowly to the door. He stopped

and looked back at Fassett. "It's just like it was in Washington, isn't it? You don't give me any alternative."

Fassett turned away. "We'll be in touch. If I were you I'd relax, go to the Club. Play tennis, swim. Get your mind off things. You'll feel better."

Tanner looked at Fassett's back in disbelief. He was being dismissed, as a less-than-respected subordinate is dismissed before a high policy conference.

"Come on," said Cole, standing up, "I'll see you to the car." As they walked, he added, "I think you should know that that man's death last night complicates Fassett's job more than you'll ever realize. That killing was directed at him. It was *his* warning."

The news director looked at Cole closely. "What do you mean?"

"There are signs between old-line professionals and this is one of them. You're insignificant now. . . . Fassett's brilliant. He's set the forces in motion and nothing can stop them. The people who conceived Omega realize what's happened. And they're beginning to see that they may be helpless. They want the man responsible to know they'll be back. Sometime. A severed head means a massacre, Mr. Tanner. They took his wife. Now he's got three kids to worry about."

Tanner felt the sickness coming upon him again.

"What kind of a world do you people live in?"

"The same one you do."

16

Thursday—10:15 A.M.

When Alice awoke at ten-fifteen Thursday morning her immediate reaction was to remain in bed forever. She could hear the children arguing downstairs and the indistinguishable but patient words from her husband settling the dispute. She thought about his remarkable sense of small kindnesses that added up to major concern. That wasn't bad after so many years of marriage.

Perhaps her husband wasn't as quick or dramatic as Dick Tremayne, or as sheerly powerful as Joe Cardone, or as witty or bright as Bernie Osterman, but she wouldn't exchange places with Ginny, Betty, or Leila for anything in the world. Even if everything started all over again, she would wait for John Tanner, or *a* John Tanner. He was that rare man. He wanted to share, *had* to share. *Everything*. None of the others did. Not even Bernie, although he was the most like John. Even Bernie had quiet secrets, according to Leila.

In the beginning, Alice had wondered if her husband's need to share was merely the result of his pity for her. Because she was to be pitied, she realized without any sense of self-indulgence. Most of her life before she met John Tanner had been spent in flight or in pursuit of sanctuary. Her father, a self-professed rectifier of the world's ills, was never able to stay too long in one place. A contemporary John Brown.

The newspapers eventually labeled him . . . lunatic.

The Los Angeles police eventually killed him.
She remembered the words.

Los Angeles, February 10, 1945. Jason McCall, whom authorities believe to have been in the pay of the Communists, was shot down today outside his canyon headquarters when he emerged brandishing what appeared to be a weapon. The Los Angeles police and agents of the Federal Bureau of Investigation unearthed McCall's whereabouts after an extensive search. . . .

The Los Angeles police and the agents of the Federal Bureau of Investigation, however, had not bothered to determine that Jason McCall's weapon was a bent piece of metal he called his "plowshare."

Mercifully, Alice had been with an aunt in Pasadena when the killing took place. She'd met the young journalism student, John Tanner, at the public inquest after her father's death. The Los

Angeles authorities wanted the inquest public. There was no room for a martyr. They wanted it clear that under no circumstances was McCall's death a murder.

Which, of course, it was.

The young journalist—returned from the war—knew it and labeled it as such. And although his story did nothing for the McCall family, it did bring him closer to the sad and bewildered girl who became his wife.

Alice stopped thinking and rolled over on her stomach. It was all past. She was where she wanted to be.

Several minutes later she heard strange male voices downstairs in the hallway. She started to sit up when the door opened and her husband came in. He smiled and bent down, kissing her lightly on the forehead, but in spite of his casualness, there was something strained about him.

"Who's downstairs?" she asked.

"The T.V. men. They're rehooking the sets, but the outside antenna system's loused up. They have to locate the trouble."

"Which means I get up."

"It does. I'm not taking chances with you in bed in front of two well-proportioned men in overalls."

"You once wore overalls. Remember? In your senior year you had that job at the gas station."

"And when I got home I also remember they came off with alarming ease. Now, up you go."

He *was* tense, she thought; he was imposing control on the situation, on himself. He announced that in spite of the pressures which descended on him on Thursdays, on this particular Thursday he was staying at home.

His explanation was simple. After yesterday afternoon, regardless of the continuing police investigation, he wasn't about to leave his family. Not until everything was cleared up.

He took them to the Club, where he and Ali played doubles with their neighbors, Dorothy and Tom Scanlan. Tom was reputed to be so rich he hadn't gone to work in a decade.

What struck Ali was her husband's determination to win. She was embarrassed when he accused Tom of miscalling a line shot and mortified when he made an unusually violent overhead, narrowly missing Dorothy's face.

They won the set, and the Scanlans turned down another. So they went to the pool, where John demanded what amounted to extraordinary service from the waiters. Late in the afternoon he spotted McDermott and insisted he join them for a drink. McDermott had come to the Club—so John told his wife—to tell a member that his car was long overdue at a parking meter in town.

And always, always, Tanner kept going to the telephone inside the Club. He could have had one brought to the poolside table but he wouldn't do so. He claimed that the Woodward conferences were getting heated and he'd rather not talk in public.

Alice didn't believe it. Her husband had many talents and perhaps the most finely honed was his ability to remain calm, even cold, under acute pressure. Yet today he was obviously close to panic.

They returned to Orchard Drive at eight o'clock. Tanner ordered the children to bed; Alice revolted.

"I've had it!" she said firmly. She pulled her husband into the living room and held his arm. "You're being unreasonable, darling. I know how you felt. I felt it, too, but you've been barking orders all day long. Do this! Do that! It's not like you."

Tanner remembered Fassett. He had to remain calm, normal. Even with Ali.

"I'm sorry. It's a delayed reaction, I guess. But you're right. Forgive me."

"It's over and done with," she added, not really accepting his quick apology. "It was frightening, but everything's all right now. It's *over.*"

Oh, Christ, thought Tanner. He wished to God it were that simple. "It's over and I've behaved childishly and I want my wife to say she loves me so we can have a couple of drinks and go to bed together." He kissed her lightly on the lips. "And that, madam, is the best idea I've had all day."

"You took a long time arriving at it," she said as she smiled up at him. "It'll take me a few minutes. I promised Janet I'd read her a story."

"What are you going to read her?"

" 'Beauty and the Beast.' Ponder it." She disengaged herself from his arms, touching his face with her fingers. "Give me ten, fifteen minutes."

Tanner watched her go back into the hall to the

staircase. She'd been through so much, and now this. Now, Omega.

He looked at his watch. It was eight-twenty and Ali would be upstairs for at least ten minutes, probably twice as long. He decided to call Fassett at the motel.

It wasn't going to be the usual conversation with Fassett. No more condescending instructions, no more sermons. It was now the end of the third day; three days of harassment against the suspects of Omega.

John Tanner wanted specifics. He was entitled to them.

Fassett was alarmed, annoyed, at the news director's precise questions.

"I can't take time to phone you whenever someone crosses the street."

"I need answers. The weekend starts tomorrow, and if you want me to go on with this, you'll tell me what's happened. Where are they now? What have their reactions been? I've *got* to know."

For a few seconds there was silence. When Fassett spoke, his voice was resigned. "Very well. . . . Tremayne stayed in New York last night. I told you that, remember? While at the Biltmore he met a man named Townsend. Townsend's a known stock manipulator out of Zurich. Cardone and his wife went to Philadelphia this afternoon. She visited her family in Chestnut Hill and he went out to Bala Cynwyd to meet with a man we know is a high capo in the Mafia. They got back to Saddle Valley an hour ago. The Ostermans are at The Plaza.

169

They're having dinner later tonight with a couple named Bronson. The Bronsons are friends from years ago. They're also on the Attorney General's subversive list."

Fassett stopped and waited for Tanner to speak.

"And none of them have met? They haven't even called each other? They've made no plans? I want the truth!"

"If they've talked it hasn't been on any telephone we can control, which would mean they'd have to be at pay phones at simultaneous times, which they haven't. We know they haven't met—simple surveillance. If any of them has plans, they're individual, not coordinated. . . . We're counting on that as I've told you. That's all there is."

"There doesn't seem to be any relationship. With any of them?"

"That's right. That's what we've concluded."

"But not what you expected. You said they'd panic. Omega would be in panic by now."

"I think they are. Every one of them. Separately. Our projections are positive."

"What the hell does that mean?"

"Think. One couple races to a powerful Mafioso. Another meets with a husband and wife who are as fanatic as anyone in the Presidium. And the lawyer has a sudden conference with an international securities thief out of Zurich. That's panic. The NKVD has many tentacles. Every one of them is on the brink. All we do is sit and wait."

"Beginning tomorrow, sitting and waiting's not going to be so easy."

"Be natural. You'll find yourself functioning on two levels really quite comfortably. It's always like that. There's no danger if you even *half* carry it off. They're too concerned with each other now. Remember, you don't have to hide yesterday afternoon. Talk about it. Be expansive. Do and say what comes naturally about it."

"And you think they'll believe me?"

"They haven't got a choice! Don't you understand that? You make your reputation as an investigative reporter. Do I have to remind you that investigation ends when the subjects collide? That's the age-old wrap-up."

"And I'm the innocent catalyst?"

"You better believe it. The more innocent, the better the wrap-up."

Tanner lit a cigarette. He couldn't deny the government man any longer. His logic was too sound. And the safety, the security, the all-holy well-being of Ali and the children was in this cold professional's hands.

"All right. I greet them all at the door as long-lost brothers and sisters."

"That's the way. And if you feel like it, call them all in the morning, make sure they're coming over. Except the Ostermans, of course. Whatever you'd normally do. . . . And remember, we're right there. The most sophisticated equipment the biggest corporation on earth owns is at work for you. Not even the smallest weapon could get through your front door."

"Is that true?"

"We'd know it if a three-inch blade was in someone's pocket. A four-inch revolver would have you all out of there in sixty seconds."

Tanner replaced the receiver and drew heavily on his cigarette. As he took his hand off the telephone he had the feeling—the physical feeling—of *leaving, jumping, going away.*

It was a strange sensation, an awesome sense of loneliness.

And then he realized what it was, and it disturbed him greatly.

His sanity was now dependent on a man named Fassett. He was utterly in his control.

PART THREE

THE WEEKEND

17

The taxi drew up to the front of the Tanner house. John's dog, the stringy Welsh terrier, ran up and down the driveway, yapping with each advance and retreat, waiting for someone to acknowledge that the visitors were welcome. Janet raced across the front lawn. The taxi door opened; the Ostermans stepped out. Each carried gift-wrapped boxes. The driver brought out a single large suitcase.

From inside the house, Tanner looked at them both: Bernie, in an expensively cut Palm Beach jacket and light-blue slacks; Leila, in a white suit with a gold chain around her waist, the skirt well above her knees, and a wide-brimmed soft hat covering the left side of her face. They were the picture of California success. Yet somehow there was a trace of artifice with Bernie and Leila; they had moved into the real money barely nine years ago.

Or was their success itself a façade, wondered Tanner as he watched the couple bending down to embrace his daughter. Had they, instead, for years and years been inhabitants of a world where scripts and shooting schedules were only secondary——good *covers*, as Fassett might say?

Tanner looked at his watch. It was two minutes past five. The Ostermans were early—according to their original schedule. Perhaps it was their first mistake. Or perhaps they didn't expect him to be there. He always left the Woodward studio early when the Ostermans came, but not always in time to be home before five-thirty. Leila's letter had said plainly their flight from Los Angeles was due at Kennedy around five. A plane being late was understandable, normal. A flight that got in ahead of schedule was improbable.

They'd have to have an explanation. Would they bother?

"Johnny! For heaven's sake! I thought I heard the pup barking. It's Bernie and Leila. What are you standing there for?" Ali had come out of the kitchen.

"Oh, sorry. . . . I just wanted to let Janet have her moment with them."

"Go on out, silly. I'll just set the timer." His wife walked back towards the kitchen as Tanner approached the front door. He stared at the brass knob and felt as he thought an actor might feel before making his first entrance in a difficult part. Unsure—totally unsure—of his reception.

He wet his lips and drew the back of his hand across his forehead. Deliberately he twisted the knob and pulled the door back swiftly. With his other hand he unlatched the aluminum screened panel and stepped outside.

The Osterman weekend had begun.

"Welcome, Schreibers!" he shouted with a wide grin. It was his usual greeting; Bernie considered it the most honorific.

"Johnny!"

"Hi, darling!"

Thirty yards away, they shouted back and smiled broad smiles. Yet even thirty yards away John Tanner could see their unsmiling eyes. Their eyes searched his—briefly, but unmistakably. For a split second Bernie even stopped smiling, stopped any motion whatsoever.

It was over in a moment. And there seemed to be a tacit agreement between them not to pursue the unspoken thoughts.

"Johnny, it's so awfully good to see you!" Leila ran across the lawn.

John Tanner accepted Leila's embrace and found himself responding with more overt affection than he thought he could muster. He knew why. He had passed the first test, the opening seconds of the Osterman weekend. He began to realize that Laurence Fassett could be right, after all. Perhaps he *could* carry it off.

Do as you'd normally do; behave as you'd normally behave. Don't think about anything else.

"John, you look great, just great, man!"

"Where's Ali, sweetie?" asked Leila who stepped aside so Bernie could throw his long thin arms around Tanner.

"Inside. Casserole-doing-time. Come on in! Here, I'll grab the bag. . . . No, Janet, honey, you can't lift Uncle Bernie's suitcase."

"I don't know why not," laughed Bernie. "All it's filled with is towels from The Plaza."

"The Plaza?" Tanner couldn't help himself. "I thought your plane just got in."

Osterman glanced at him. "Uh uh. We flew in a couple of days ago. I'll tell you about it. . . ."

In a strange way it was like old times, and Tanner was astonished that he found himself accepting the fact. There was still the sense of relief at physically seeing each other again, knowing that time and distance were meaningless to their friendship. There was still the feeling that they could take up conversations, continue anecdotes, finish stories begun months previously. And there was still Bernie; gentle, reflective Bernie with his quiet, devastating comments about the palm-lined drug store. Devastating but somehow never condescending; Bernie laughed at himself as well as his professional world, for it *was* his world.

Tanner remembered Fassett's words.

". . . *you'll find yourself functioning on two levels quite comfortably. It's always like that.*"

Again, Fassett was right. . . . In and out; in and out.

It struck Tanner as he watched Bernie that Leila kept shifting her eyes away from her husband to him. Once he returned her look; she lowered her eyes as a child might after a reprimand.

The telephone rang in the study. The sound was jarring to everyone but Alice. There was an extension phone on the table behind the sofa, but John ignored it as he crossed in front of the Ostermans towards the study door.

"I'll take it out here. It's probably the studio."

As he entered the study he heard Leila speak to Ali, her voice lowered.

"Sweetie, Johnny seems tense. Is anything the matter? The way Bernie drawls on no one can get a word in."

"Tense is understating it! You should have seen him yesterday!"

The telephone rang again; Tanner knew it wouldn't be normal to let it ring further. Yet he wanted so much to hear the Ostermans' reaction to Ali's story of the Wednesday terror.

He compromised. He picked the phone out of the cradle, held it to his side and listened for several seconds to the conversation.

Something caught his ear. Bernie and Leila reacted to Ali's words too quickly, with too much anticipation. They were asking questions before she finished sentences! They *did* know something.

"Hello? Hello! Hello, hello!" The anxious voice on the other end of the line belonged to Joe Cardone.

"Hello, Joe? Sorry, I dropped the phone. . . ."

"I didn't hear it drop."

"Very soft, very expensive carpets."

"Where? In that study of yours with the parquet floor?"

"Hey, come on, Joe."

"Sorry. . . . The city was rotten hot today and the market's going to hell."

"That's better. Now you sound like the cheerful fellow we're waiting for."

"You mean everybody's there?"

"No. Just Bernie and Leila."

"They're early. I thought the plane got in at five."

"They flew in a couple of days ago."

Cardone started to speak and then abruptly stopped. He seemed to catch his breath. "Funny they didn't call. I mean, they didn't get in touch with me. Did they with you?"

"No, I guess they had business."

"Sure, but you'd think. . . ." Again Cardone stopped in the middle of a sentence. Tanner wondered whether this hesitation was meant for him; to convince him of the fact that Bernie and Joe hadn't met, hadn't spoken with each other.

"Bernie'll probably tell us all about it."

"Yeah," said Cardone, not really listening. "Well, I just wanted to let you know we'd be late. I'll grab a quick shower; be there soon."

"See you." Tanner hung up the phone, surprised at his own calm. It occurred to him that he had controlled the conversation. *Controlled* it. He had to. Cardone was a nervous man and he hadn't called to say he'd be late. To begin with, he wasn't late.

Cardone had phoned to see if the others had come. Or if they were coming.

Tanner returned to the living room and sat down.

"Darling! Ali just told us! How dreadful! How simply terrifying!"

180

"My God, John! What an awful experience! The police said it was robbery?"

"So did *The New York Times.* Guess that makes it official."

"I didn't see anything in *The Times*," stated Bernie firmly.

"It was only a few lines near the back. We'll get better coverage in the local paper next week."

"I've never heard of any robbery like that," said Leila. "I wouldn't settle for that, I really wouldn't."

Bernie looked at her. "I don't know. It's actually pretty smart. No identification, no harm to anyone."

"What I don't understand is why they didn't just leave us in the garage." Ali turned to her husband. It was a question he hadn't answered satisfactorily.

"Did the police say why?" asked Bernie.

"They said the gas was a low-yield variety. The thieves didn't want Ali or the kids to come to and see them. Very professional."

"Very scary," Leila said. "How did the kids take it?"

"Ray's a neighborhood hero, of course," said Ali. "Janet's still not sure what happened."

"Where *is* Ray?" Bernie pointed to a package in the hall. "I hope he hasn't outgrown model airplanes. That's one of those remote-control things."

"He'll love it," said Ali. "He's in the basement, I think. John's turning it over to him. . . ."

"No, he's outside. In the pool." Tanner realized that his interruption, his sharp correction of Ali, caused Bernie to look at him. Even Ali was startled by the abruptness of his statement.

So be it, thought Tanner. Let them all know the father was aware, every second, of the whereabouts of his own.

The dog began barking in front of the house; the sound of a car could be heard in the driveway. Alice walked to the window.

"It's Dick and Ginny. And Ray's *not* in the pool," she added, smiling at John. "He's in front saying hello."

"He must have heard the car," said Leila for no apparent reason.

Tanner wondered why she made the remark; it was as if she were defending him. He went to the front door and opened it. "Come on in, son. Some other friends of yours are here."

When he saw the Ostermans, the boy's eyes lit up. The Ostermans never arrived empty-handed. "Hello, Aunt Leila, Uncle Bernie!" Raymond Tanner, age twelve, walked into the arms of Leila and then shook hands manfully, shyly, with Bernie.

"We brought you a little something. Actually your buddy Merv suggested it." Bernie crossed to the hall and picked up the package. "Hope you like it."

"Thank you very much." The boy took the gift and went into the dining room to unwrap it.

Virginia Tremayne came in, the picture of cool sensuality. She was dressed in a man-styled shirt with multicolored stripes and a tight knit skirt which accentuated the movements of her body. There were women in Saddle Valley who resented Ginny's appearance, but they weren't in these rooms. Ginny was a good friend.

"I told Dick you called Wednesday," she said to Tanner, "but he says you never reached him. The poor lamb's been holed up in a conference suite with some awful merger people from Cincinnati or Cleveland or somewhere. . . . Leila, darling! Bernie, love!" Ginny pecked Tanner's cheek and choreographed herself past him.

Richard Tremayne came in. He was watching Tanner and what he saw obviously pleased him.

Tanner, on the other hand, felt the look and whipped his head around too quickly. Tremayne didn't have time to shift his eyes away. The news director recognized in the lawyer's stare the look of a doctor studying a medical chart.

For a split second both men silently, unwillingly, acknowledged the tension. And then it passed, as it had passed with the Ostermans. Neither man dared sustain it.

"Hey, John! Sorry I didn't get your message. Ginny mentioned something legal."

"I thought you might have read about it."

"What, for God's sake?"

"We didn't get much coverage in the New York papers, but wait'll you read next Monday's weekly. We'll be celebrities."

"What the hell are you talking about?"

"We were robbed Wednesday. Robbed and kidnapped and chloroformed and God knows what else!"

"You're joking!"

"The hell he is!" Osterman walked into the hallway. "How are you, Dick?"

"Bernie! How are you, buddy?" The men grasped hands, but Tremayne could not seem to take his attention from John Tanner.

"Did you hear what he said? Did you hear that? What happened, for Christ's sake? I've been in town since Tuesday. Didn't even have time to get home."

"We'll tell you all about it. Later. Let me get your drinks." Tanner walked away rapidly. He couldn't fault Tremayne's reaction. The lawyer was not only shocked by what he'd heard, he was frightened. So much so that he had to make clear he had been gone since Tuesday.

Tanner made drinks for the Tremaynes and then went into the kitchen and looked out past his pool to the edge of the woods. Although there was no one in sight, he knew the men were there. With binoculars, with radios, probably with tiny speakers which magnified conversations taking place in any section of his house.

"Hey, John, I wasn't kidding!" It was Tremayne walking into the kitchen. "Honest to God, I didn't know anything about it. About Wednesday, I mean. Why the hell didn't you reach me?"

"I tried. I even called a number on Long Island. Oyster Bay, I think."

"Oh, shit! You know what I mean! You or Ali should have told Ginny. I'd have left the conference, you know that!"

"It's over with. Here's your drink." Tremayne lifted the glass to his lips. He could drink any of them under any table.

184

"You can't leave it like that. Why did you call me in the first place?"

Tanner, stupidly, wasn't prepared for the question.

"I . . . I didn't like the way the police handled it."

"The police? Fat-cap MacAuliff?"

"I never talked to Captain MacAuliff."

"Didn't you give a statement?"

"Yes . . . yes, I did. To Jenkins and McDermott."

"Where the hell was old law'n'order himself?"

"I don't know. He wasn't there."

"Okay, Mac wasn't there. You say Jenkins and McDermott handled it. Ali told me they were the ones who found you . . ."

"Yes. Yes, that's what I was pissed-off about."

"What?"

"I just didn't like the way they handled it. At least I didn't at the time. I've cooled it now. I was hot then, that's why I tried to reach you."

"What were you figuring? Police negligence? Abridged rights? What?"

"I don't know, Dick! I just panicked, that's all. When you panic you want a lawyer."

"I don't. I want a drink." Tremayne held Tanner's eyes. Tanner blinked—as a small boy defeated in a game of stare.

"It's over with. Let's go back inside."

"Maybe we ought to talk later. Maybe you have some kind of case and I don't see it."

Tanner shrugged, knowing that Dick didn't

really want to talk later at all. The lawyer was frightened, and his fear arrested his professional instinct to probe. As he walked away, Tanner had the feeling that Tremayne was telling the truth about one aspect of Wednesday afternoon. He hadn't been there himself.

But did he know who had been?

By six, the Cardones still hadn't arrived. No one asked why; the hour passed quickly and if anyone was concerned he hid it well. At ten minutes past, Tanner's eyes were drawn to a car driving slowly past his house. It was the Saddle Valley taxi, the sun causing intermittent, sharp flashes off the black enamel. In the rear window of the automobile he saw Joe Cardone's face for a moment. Joe was making sure all the guests had arrived. Or were still there, perhaps.

Forty-five minutes later the Cardones' Cadillac pulled into the driveway. When they entered the house it was obvious that Joe had had several drinks. Obvious because Joe was not a drinker, he didn't really approve of alcohol, and his voice was just a degree louder than it might have been.

"Bernie! Leila! Welcome to the heart of the eastern establishment!"

Betty Cardone, prim, stoutish, Anglican Betty, properly added to her husband's enthusiasm and the four of them exchanged embraces.

"Betty, you look adorable," said Leila. "Joe, my God, Joe! How can a man look so healthy? ... Bernie built a gym and look what *I* got!"

186

"Don't you knock my Bernie!" said Joe, his arm around Osterman's shoulder.

"You tell her, Joe." Bernie moved towards Cardone's wife and asked about the children.

Tanner started towards the kitchen, meeting Ali in the hallway. She carried a plate of hors d'oeuvres.

"Everything's ready. We can eat whenever we want, so I'll sit down for a while. . . . Get me a drink, will you, dear?"

"Sure. Joe and Betty are here."

Ali laughed. "I gathered that. . . . What's the matter, darling? You look funny."

"No, nothing. I was just thinking I'd better call the studio."

Ali looked at her husband. "Please, Everybody's here now. Our best friends. Let's have fun. Forget about Wednesday, *please,* Johnny."

Tanner leaned over the tray of hors d'oeuvres and kissed her. "You're dramatizing," he said, remembering Fassett's admonition. "I really do have to call the studio."

In the kitchen, Tanner walked again to the window. It was a little after seven o'clock and the sun had gone down behind the tall trees in the woods. Shadows lay across the backyard lawn and the pool. And beyond the shadows were Fassett's men.

That was the important thing.

As Ali had said, they were all there now. The best of friends.

The buffet of curry, with a dozen side dishes,

was Ali's usual triumph. The wives asked the usual questions and Ali slighty embossed the culinary answers—as usual. The men fell into the normal arguments about the relative merits of the various baseball teams and, in between, Bernie revealed further the humorous—and extraordinary—working methods of Hollywood television.

While the women cleared out the dining room, Tremayne took the opportunity to press Tanner on the robbery. "What the hell was it last Wednesday? Level with us. I don't buy the burglary story."

"Why not?" asked Tanner.

"It doesn't make sense."

"Nobody uses gas on anybody," added Cardone. "Blackjacks, blindfolds, a shot in the head, maybe. Not gas."

"Advanced thinking, perhaps. I'd rather it was a harmless gas than a blackjack."

"Johnny." Osterman lowered his voice and looked toward the dining room. Betty came out the kitchen door and began removing several dishes and smiled. He smiled back. "Are you working on something that might make you enemies?"

"I imagine I always am in one way or another."

"I mean something like the San Diego thing."

Joe Cardone watched Osterman carefully, wondering if he might elaborate. San Diego had been a Mafia operation.

"Not that I know of. I've got men digging in a lot of areas, but nothing like that. At least I don't think so. Most of my best people have a free rein. . . . Are you trying to tie in Wednesday with something at work?"

"It hadn't struck you?" asked Tremayne.

"Hell, no! I'm a professional newsman. Do you get worried if you're working on a sticky case?"

"Sometimes."

"I read about that show of yours last Sunday." Cardone sat down on the couch next to Tremayne. "Ralph Ashton has friends in high places."

"That's crazy."

"Not necessarily." Cardone had trouble with "necessarily." "I've met him. He's a vindictive man."

"He's not crazy," interjected Osterman. "No, it wouldn't be anything like that."

"Why should it be anything, period? Anything but a robbery?" Tanner lit a cigarette and tried to watch the faces of the three men.

"Because, Goddamn it, it's not a natural way to get robbed," exclaimed Cardone.

"Oh?" Tremayne looked at Cardone, sitting next to him on the sofa. "Are you an expert on robbery?"

"No more than you are, counselor," said Joe.

18

There was something artificial about the start of the weekend; Ali felt it. Perhaps it was that the voices were louder than usual, the laughter more pronounced.

Usually, when Bernie and Leila arrived, they all began calmly, catching up with each family's affairs. Conversations about this or that child, this or that career decision—these always occupied the first few hours. Her husband called it the Osterman syndrome. Bernie and Leila brought out the best in all of them. Made them talk, really *talk* with one another.

Yet no one had volunteered a single important personal experience. No one had brought up a single vital part of their recent lives—except, of course, the horrible thing on Wednesday afternoon.

On the other hand, Ali realized, she was still concerned about her husband—concerned about his staying home from the office, his short temper, his erratic behavior since Wednesday afternoon. Maybe she was imagining things about everybody else.

The other women had rejoined their husbands; Alice had put away the left-overs. The children were in bed now. And she wouldn't listen to any more talk from Betty or Ginny about maids. She *could* afford a maid! *They* could afford a maid! But she wouldn't *have* one!

Her father had had maids. "Disciples" he called them. "Disciples" who cleaned and swept and brought-in and . . .

Her mother had called them "maids."

Ali stopped thinking and wondered if she'd had a drink she couldn't handle. She turned on the faucet and dabbed her face with cold water. Joe Cardone walked through the kitchen door.

"The boss-man told me if I wanted a drink, I pour it myself. Don't tell me where, I've been here before."

"Go right ahead, Joe. Do you see everything you need?"

"Sure do. Lovely gin; beautiful tonic. . . . Hey, what's the matter? You been crying?"

"Why should I be? I just splashed water on my face."

"Your cheeks are all wet."

"Water on the face does that."

Joe put down the bottle of tonic and approached her. "Are you and Johnny in any trouble? . . . This Wednesday afternoon . . . okay, it was a crazy type of robbery, Johnny told me . . . but if it was anything else, you'd let me know, wouldn't you? I mean, if he's playing around with sharks you wouldn't keep it a secret from me, would you?"

"Sharks?"

"Loan-sharks. I've got clients at Standard Mutual. Even a little stock. I know the company. . . . You and Johnny live very well, but sixty thousand dollars after taxes isn't that much any more."

Alice Tanner caught her breath. "John does very well!"

"That's relative. In my opinion, John's in that big middle mess. He can't take over and he won't let go of his little kingdom to try for anything better. That's his business, and yours. But I want you to tell him for me. . . . I'm his friend. His good friend. And I'm clean. Absolutely *clean*. If he needs anything, you tell him to call me, all right?"

"Joe, I'm touched. I really am. But I don't think it's necessary. I don't, really."

"But you'll tell him?"

"Tell him yourself. John and I have an unspoken pact. We don't discuss his salary any more. Frankly because I agree with you."

"Then you've got problems."

"You're not being fair. Problems to you may not be problems for us."

"I hope you're right. Tell him that, too." Cardone walked rapidly back to the bar and picked up his glass. Before Ali could speak he walked through the door back into the living room.

Joe was telling her something and she didn't understand.

"Nobody appointed you or any other member of *any* news media to set yourselves up as infallible

192

guardians of the truth! I'm sick and tired of it! I live with it every day." Tremayne stood in front of the fireplace, his anger obvious to everyone.

"Not infallible, of course not," answered Tanner. "But no one gave the courts the right to stop us from looking for information as objectively as we can."

"When that information is prejudicial to a client *or* his opponent you have no right to make it public. If it's factual, it'll be heard in court. Wait'll the verdict's rendered."

"That's impossible and you know it."

Tremayne paused, smiled thinly, and sighed. "I know I do. Realistically, there's no solution."

"Are you sure you want to find one?" asked Tanner.

"Of course."

"Why? The advantage is yours. You win the verdict, fine. If you lose, you claim the court was corrupted by a biased press. You appeal."

"It's the rare case that's won on appeal," said Bernard Osterman sitting on the floor in front of the sofa. "Even I know that. They get the publicity, but they're rare."

"Appeals cost money," added Tremayne with a shrug. "Most of the time for nothing. Especially corporate appeals."

"Then force the press to restrain itself when there's a lot of heat. It's simple." Joe finished his drink and looked pointedly at Tanner.

"It's not simple," said Leila, sitting in an armchair opposite the sofa. "It becomes judgment.

193

Who defines restraint? That's what Dick means. There's no clear-cut definition."

"At the risk of offending my husband, God forbid," Virginia laughed as she spoke, "I think an informed public is just as important as an unbiased courtroom. Perhaps they're even connected. I'm on your side, John."

"Judgment, again," said her husband. "It's opinion. What's factual information and what's interpreted information?"

"One's truth," said Betty off-handedly. She was watching her husband. He was drinking too much.

"Whose truth? Which truth? . . . Let's create a hypothetical situation. Between John and myself. Say I've been working for six months on a complicated merger. As an ethical attorney I'm dealing with men whose cause I believe in; by putting together a number of companies thousands of jobs are saved, firms which are going bankrupt suddenly have new lives. Then along come several people who are getting hurt—because of their own ineptness—and start shouting for injunctions. Suppose they reach John and start yelling 'Foul!' Because they seem—seem, mind you—like underdogs, John gives their cause one *minute*, just one *minute* of network time across the country. Instantly my case is prejudiced. And don't let anyone tell you the courts aren't subject to media pressure. One *minute* as opposed to *six months*."

"Do you think I'd allow that? Do you think any of us would?"

"You need copy. You always need copy! There

are times when you don't understand!" Tremayne's voice grew louder.

Virginia stood up. "Our John wouldn't do that, darling. . . . I'm for another cup of coffee."

"I'll get it," said Alice, rising from the sofa. She'd been watching Tremayne, startled by his sudden vehemence.

"Don't be silly," answered Ginny going into the hallway.

"I'd like a drink." Cardone held out his glass, expecting someone to take it.

"Sure, Joe." Tanner took his glass. "Gin and tonic?"

"That's what I've been drinking."

"Too much of," added his wife.

Tanner walked into the kitchen and began making Cardone's drink. Ginny was at the stove.

"I'm heating the Chemex; the candle burned out."

"Thanks."

"I always have the same problem. The damn candles go out and the coffee's cold."

Tanner chuckled and poured the tonic. Then he realized that Ginny was making a comment, a rather unattractive comment. "I told Ali to get an electric pot, but she refuses."

"John?"

"Yes?"

"It's a beautiful night. Why don't we all take a swim?"

"Sure. Good idea. I'll backwash the filter. Let me get this to Joe." Tanner returned to the living room in time to hear the opening bars of "Tangerine." Ali had put on an album called "Hits of Yesterday."

There were the proper responses, the laughs of recognition.

"Here you are, Joe. Anyone else for anything?"

There was a chorus of no-thanks. Betty had gotten up and was facing Dick Tremayne by the mantle. Tanner thought they looked as though they'd been arguing. Ali was at the stereo showing Bernie the back of the album cover; Leila Osterman sat opposite Cardone, watching him drink his gin and tonic, seemingly annoyed that he drank so quickly.

"Ginny and I are going to backwash the pool. We'll take a swim, okay? You've all got suits here; if not, there're a dozen extras in the garage."

Dick looked at Tanner. It was a curious look, thought the news editor. "Don't teach Ginny too much about that damned filter. I'm holding firm. No pool."

"Why not?" asked Cardone.

"Too many kids around."

"Build a fence," said Joe with a degree of disdain.

Tanner started out toward the kitchen and the back door. He heard a sudden burst of laughter behind him, but it wasn't the laughter of people enjoying themselves. It was forced, somehow unkind.

Was Fassett right? Was Omega showing the signs? Were the hostilities slowly coming to the surface?

Outside he walked to the edge of the pool, to the filter box. "Ginny?"

"I'm over here, by Ali's tomato plants. This stake fell down and I can't retie the vine."

"Okay." He turned and walked over to her. "Which one? I can't see it."

"Here," said Ginny, pointing.

Tanner knelt down and saw the stake. It hadn't fallen over, it had been snapped. "One of the kids must have run through here." He pulled up the thin broken dowel and placed the tomato vine carefully on the ground. "I'll fix it tomorrow."

He got up. Ginny stood very close to him and put her hand on his arm. He realized they couldn't be seen from the house.

"I broke it," Ginny said.

"Why?"

"I wanted to talk to you. Alone."

She had undone several buttons of her blouse below the neckline. He could see the swell of her breasts. Tanner wondered if Ginny was drunk. But Ginny never got drunk, or if she did, no one ever knew it.

"What do you want to talk about?"

"Dick, for one thing. I apologize for him. He can become gross . . . rude, when he's upset."

"Was he rude? Upset? I didn't notice."

"Of course you did. I was watching you."

"You were wrong."

"I don't think so."

"Let's get the pool done."

"Wait a minute." Ginny laughed softly. "I don't frighten you, do I?"

"My friends don't frighten me," Tanner said, smiling.

"We know a great deal about each other."

Tanner watched Ginny's face closely, her eyes, the slight pinching of her lips. He wondered if this was the moment the unbelievable was about to be revealed to him. If it was, he'd help her say it. "I suppose we always think we know our friends. I sometimes wonder if we ever do."

"I'm very attracted . . . physically attracted to you. Did you know that?"

"No, I didn't," said Tanner, surprised.

"It shouldn't bother you. I wouldn't hurt Ali for the world. I don't think physical attraction necessarily means a commitment, do you?"

"Everyone has fantasies."

"You're sidestepping."

"I certainly am."

"I told you, I wouldn't harm your commitments."

"I'm human. They'd be harmed."

"I'm human, too. May I kiss you? At least I deserve a kiss."

Ginny put her arms around the startled Tanner's neck and pressed her lips against his, opening her mouth. Tanner knew she was doing her best to arouse him. He couldn't understand it. If she meant what she was doing, there was nowhere to complete the act.

Then he did understand. She was promising.

She meant that.

"Oh, Johnny! Oh, God, Johnny!"

198

"All right, Ginny. All right. Don't. . . ." Perhaps she really was drunk, thought Tanner. She'd feel like a fool tomorrow. "We'll talk later."

Ginny pulled slightly back. Her lips to the side of his. "Of course, we'll talk later. . . . Johnny? . . . Who is Blackstone?"

"Blackstone?"

"Please! I've got to know! Nothing will change, I promise you that! *Who is Blackstone?*"

Tanner held her shoulders, forcing her face in front of his own.

She was crying.

"I don't know any Blackstone."

"Don't do this!" she whispered. "Please, for God's sake, don't do this! Tell Blackstone to *stop it!*"

"Did Dick send you out here?"

"He'd kill me," she said softly.

"Let me get it straight. You're offering me . . ."

"Anything you want! Just leave him *alone*. . . . My husband's a good man. A very, very decent man. He's been a good friend to you! Please, don't hurt him!"

"You love him."

"More than my life. So please, don't hurt him. And tell Blackstone to stop!"

She rushed off into the garage.

He wanted to go after her and be kind, but the specter of Omega prevented him. He kept wondering whether Ginny, who was capable of offering herself as a whore, was also capable of things far more dangerous.

But Ginny wasn't a whore. Careless, perhaps, even provocative in a humorous, harmless way, but it had never occurred to Tanner or anybody Tanner knew that she would share her bed with anyone but Dick. She wasn't like that.

Unless she was Omega's whore.

There was the forced laughter again from inside the house. Tanner heard the opening clarinet strains of "Amapola." He knelt down and picked the thermometer out of the water.

Suddenly he was aware that he wasn't alone. Leila Osterman was standing several feet behind him on the grass. She'd come outside silently; or perhaps he was too preoccupied to hear the kitchen door or the sound of her footsteps.

"Oh, hi! You startled me."

"I thought Ginny was helping you."

"She . . . spilled filter powder on her skirt. . . . Look, the temperature's eighty-three. Joe'll say it's too warm."

"If he can tell."

"I see what you mean," said Tanner getting to his feet, smiling. "Joe's no drinker."

"He's trying."

"Leila, how come you and Bernie got in a couple days ago?"

"He hasn't told you?" Leila was hesitant, seemingly annoyed that the explanation was left to her.

"No. Obviously."

"He's looking around. He had conferences, lunches."

"What's he looking for?"

"Oh, projects. You know Bernie; he goes through phases. He never forgets that *The New York Times* once called him exciting . . . or incisive, I never remember which. Unfortunately, he's acquired expensive tastes."

"You've lost me."

"He'd like to find a class series; you know, the old Omnibus type. There's a lot of talk around the agencies about upgrading."

"Is there? I hadn't heard it."

"You're in news, not programming."

Tanner took out a pack of cigarettes and offered one to Leila. As he lit it he could see the concern, the strain, in her eyes. "Bernie has a lot going for him. You and he have made the agencies a great deal of money. He won't have any trouble; he's persuasive as hell."

"It takes more than persuasion, I'm afraid," Leila said. "Unless you want to work for a percentage of nonprofit culture. . . . No, it takes influence. Enormous influence; enough to make the money people change their minds." Leila drew heavily on her cigarette, avoiding Tanner's stare.

"Can he do that?"

"He might be able to. Bernie's word carries more weight than any other writer's on the coast. He has 'clout,' as they say. . . . It extends to New York, take my word for it."

Tanner found himself not wanting to talk. It hurt too much. Leila had all but told him, he thought. All but proclaimed the power of Omega. Of course Bernie was going to do what he wanted to do. Bernie was perfectly capable of making people change their minds, reverse decisions. Or Omega was, and he was part of it—part of them.

"Yes," he said softly. "I'll take your word for it. Bernie's a big man."

They stood quietly for a moment, then Leila spoke sharply. "Are you satisfied?"

"What?"

"I asked if you were satisfied. You've just questioned me like a cop. I can even furnish you with a list of his appointments, if you'd like. And there are hairdressers, department stores, shops—I'm sure they'd confirm my having been there."

"What the hell are you talking about?"

"You know perfectly well! That's not a very nice party in there, in case you haven't noticed. We're all behaving as if we'd never met before, as if we really didn't like our new acquaintances."

"That has nothing to do with me. Maybe you should look to yourselves."

"Why?" Leila stepped back. Tanner thought she looked bewildered, but he didn't trust his appraisal. "Why should we? What *is* it, John?"

"Can't *you* tell *me?*"

"Good Lord, you *are* after him, aren't you? You're after *Bernie.*"

"No, I'm not. I'm not after anyone."

"You listen to me, John! Bernie would give his life for you! Don't you know that?"

Leila Osterman threw the cigarette on the ground and walked away.

As Tanner was about to carry the chlorine bucket to the garage, Ali came outside with Bernie Osterman. For a moment he wondered whether Leila had said anything. Obviously she hadn't. His wife and Bernie simply wanted to know where he kept the club soda and to tell him that everyone was getting into suits.

Tremayne stood in the kitchen doorway, glass in hand, watching the three of them talking. To Tanner he seemed nervous, uneasy.

Tanner walked into the garage and placed the plastic bucket in the corner next to the garage toilet. It was the coolest place. The kitchen door opened and Tremayne walked down the steps.

"I want to see you a minute."

"Sure."

Tremayne turned sideways and slid past the Triumph. "I never see you driving this."

"I hate it. Getting in and out of it's murder."

"You're a big guy."

"It's a small car."

"I . . . I wanted to say I'm sorry about that bullshit I was peddling before. I have no argument with you. I got burned on a case several weeks ago by a reporter on *The Wall Street Journal*. Can you imagine? *The Journal!* My firm decided not to go ahead on the strength of it."

"Free press or fair trial. A damned valid argument. I didn't take it personally."

Tremayne leaned against the Triumph. He spoke cautiously. "A couple of hours ago, Bernie asked you—he was talking about last Wednesday—if you were working on anything like that San Diego story. I never knew much about that except that it's still referred to in the newspapers . . ."

"It's been exaggerated out of proportion. A series of waterfront payoffs. Indigenous to the industry, I think."

"Don't be so modest."

"I'm not. It was a hell of a job and I damned near got the Pulitzer. It's been responsible for my whole career."

"All right. . . . Fine, good. . . . Now, I'm going to stop playing games. Are you digging around something that affects me?"

"Not that I know of. . . . It's what I said to Bernie; I've a staff of seventy-odd directly involved with news gathering. I don't ask for daily reports."

"Are you telling me you don't know what they're doing?"

"I'm better than that," said Tanner with a short laugh. "I approve expenditures; nothing is aired without my clearing it."

Tremayne pushed himself away from the Triumph. "All right, let's level. . . . Ginny came back inside fifteen minutes ago. I've lived with that girl for sixteen years. I know her. . . . She'd been crying. She was outside with you and she came back crying. I want to know why."

"I can't answer you."

"I think you'd better try! . . . You resent the money I make, don't you?"

"That's not true."

"Of course it is! You think I haven't heard Ali

on your back! And now you subtly, off-handedly drop that nothing is *aired* without your *clearing* it! Is that what you told my wife? Am I supposed to hear the details from *her?* A wife can't testify; are you *protecting* us? What do you *want?*"

"Get hold of yourself! Are you into something so rotten you're getting paranoid? Is that it? You want to tell me about it?"

"No. No! Why was she *crying?*"

"Ask her yourself!"

Tremayne turned away and John Tanner could see the lawyer's body begin to shake as he passed his hands on the hood of the small sports car.

"We've known each other a long time; but you've never understood me at all. . . . Don't make judgments unless you understand the men you're judging."

So this was it, thought Tanner. Tremayne was admitting it. He *was* part of Omega.

And then Tremayne spoke again and the conclusion was destroyed. He turned around and the look on his face was pathetic.

"I may not be beyond reproach, I know that, but I'm within the law. That's the system. I may not like it all the time, but I respect that *system!*"

Tanner wondered if Fassett's men had placed one of their electronic pick-ups in the garage. If they had heard the words, spoken in such sorrow, with such a ring of truth. He looked at the broken man in front of him.

"Let's go into the kitchen. You need a drink and so do I."

19

Alice flipped the switch under the living-room windowsill so the music would be heard on the patio speakers. They were all outside now on the pool deck. Even her husband and Dick Tremayne had finally gotten up from the kitchen table; they'd been sitting there for twenty minutes and Ali thought it strange they'd hardly spoken.

"Hello, gracious lady!" The voice was Joe's, and Alice felt herself grow tense. He walked from the hallway into view; he was in swimming trunks. There was something ugly about Joe's body; it dwarfed objects around it. "You're out of ice, so I made a phone call to get some."

"At this hour?"

"It's easier than one of us driving."

"Who'd you call?"

"Rudy at the liquor store."

"It's closed."

Cardone walked towards her, weaving a bit. "I got him at home; he wasn't in bed. . . . He does little favors for me. I told him to leave a couple of bags on the front porch and charge it to me."

"That wasn't necessary. I mean the charging."

"Every little bit helps."

"Please." She walked towards the sofa if for no other reason than to get away from Cardone's gin-laden breath. He followed her.

"Did you think over what I told you?"

"You're very generous, but we don't need any help."

"Is that what John said?"

"It's what he *would* say."

"Then you haven't talked to him?"

"No."

Cardone took her hand gently. She instinctively tried to pull it away, but he held it—firmly, with no trace of hostility, only warmth; but he held it nevertheless. "I may be a little loaded but I want you to take me seriously. . . . I've been a lucky man; it hasn't been hard at all, not really. . . . Frankly, I even feel a little guilty, you know what I mean? I admire Johnny. I think the world of him because he *contributes*. . . . I don't contribute much; I just take. I don't hurt anybody, but I take. . . . You'd make me feel better if you'd let me *give* . . . for a change."

He let her hand go and because she didn't expect it, her forearm snapped back against her waist. She was momentarily embarrassed. And perplexed. "Why are you so determined to give us something. What brought it up?"

Cardone sat down heavily on the arm of the couch. "You hear things. Rumors, gossip, maybe."

"About us? About us and money?"

"Sort of."

"Well, it's not true. It's simply not true."

"Then let's put it another way. Three years ago when Dick and Ginny and Bernie and Leila went skiing with us at Gstaad, you and Johnny didn't want to go. Isn't that right?"

Alice blinked, trying to follow Joe's logic. "Yes, I remember. We thought we'd rather take the children to Nassau."

"But now John's very interested in Switzerland, isn't that right?" Joe's body was swaying slightly.

"Not that I know of. He hasn't told me about it."

"Then if it's not Switzerland, maybe it's Italy. Maybe he's interested in Sicily; it's a very interesting place."

"I simply don't understand you."

Cardone got off the arm of the couch and steadied himself. "You and I aren't so very different, are we? I mean, what credentials we have weren't exactly handed to us, were they? . . . We've earned them, after our own Goddamn fashion. . . ."

"I think that's insulting."

"I'm sorry, I don't mean to be insulting. . . . I just want to be honest, and honesty starts with where you are . . . where you were."

"You're drunk."

"I certainly am. I'm drunk and I'm nervous. Lousy combination. . . . You talk to John. You tell him to see me tomorrow or the next day. You tell him not to worry about Switzerland or Italy, all right? You tell him, no matter what, that I'm clean and I like people who contribute but don't hurt other people. . . . That I'll pay."

Cardone took two steps toward Ali and grabbed her left hand. Gently but insistently, he brought it to his lips, eyes closed, and kissed her palm. Ali had seen that type of kiss before; in her childhood she'd seen her father's fanatical adherents do the same. Then Joe turned and staggered into the hallway.

At the window a shifting of light, a reflection, a change of brightness caught Ali's eye. She turned her head. What she saw caused her to freeze. Outside on the lawn, no more than six feet from the glass, stood Betty Cardone in a white bathing suit, washed in the blue-green light of the swimming pool.

Betty had seen what had happened between Alice and her husband. Her eyes told Ali that.

Joe's wife stared through the window and her look was cruel.

The full tones of the young Sinatra filled the warm summer night as the four couples sat around the pool. Individually—it seemed never by twos to John Tanner—one or another would slip into the water and paddle lazily back and forth.

The women talked of schools and children while the men, on the opposite side of the deck, spoke less quietly of the market, politics, an inscrutable economy.

Tanner sat on the base of the diving board near Joe. He'd never seen him so drunk, and he bore watching. If any or all around the deck were part of Omega, Joe was the weakest link. He'd be the first to break.

Small arguments flared up, quickly subsiding. At one point, Joe's voice was too loud and Betty reacted swiftly but quietly.

"You're drunk, husband-mine. Watch out."

"Joe's all right, Betty," said Bernie, clapping Cardone's knee. "It was rotten-hot in New York to-day, remember?"

"You were in New York, too, Bernie," answered Ginny Tremayne, stretching her legs over the side of the pool. "Was it really that rotten-hot?"

"Rotten-hot, sweetheart." It was Dick who spoke across the water to his wife.

Tanner saw Osterman and Tremayne exchange glances. Their unspoken communication referred to Cardone but it was not meant that he, Tanner, should understand or even notice. Then Dick got up and asked who'd like refills.

Only Joe answered yes.

"I'll get it," said Tanner.

"Hell, no," replied Dick. "You watch the ball-player. I want to call the kid anyway. We told her to be back by one; it's damn near two. These days you have to check."

"You're a mean father," said Leila.

"So long as I'm not a grandfather." Tremayne walked across the grass to the kitchen door.

There was silence for several seconds, then the girls took up their relaxed conversation and Bernie lowered himself over the side into the pool.

Joe Cardone and Tanner did not speak.

Several minutes later, Dick came out of the kitchen door carrying two glasses. "Hey, Ginny! Peg was teed off that I woke her up. What do you think of that?"

"I think she was bored with her date."

Tremayne approached Cardone and handed him his glass. "There you are, fullback."

"I was a Goddamn halfback. I ran circles around your Goddamn Levi Jackson at the Yale Bowl!"

"Sure. But I talked to Levi. He said they could always get you. All they had to do was yell 'tomato sauce' and you went for the sidelines!"

"Pretty Goddamn funny! I murdered that black son of a bitch!"

"He speaks well of you, too," said Bernie, smiling over the side of the pool.

"And I speak well of *you*, Bernie! And big Dick, here!" Cardone clumsily got to his feet. "I speak well of *all* of you!"

"Hey, Joe. . . ." Tanner got off the board.

"Really, Joe, just sit down," ordered Betty. "You'll fall over."

"Da Vinci!"

It was only a name but Cardone shouted it out. And then he shouted it again.

"*Da Vinci*. . . ." He drew out the sound, making the dialect sharply Italian.

"What does *that* mean?" asked Tremayne.

"You tell *me!*" roared Cardone through the tense stillness around the pool.

"He's crazy," said Leila.

"He's positively drunk, if nobody minds my saying so," added Ginny.

211

"Since we can't—at least I can't—tell you what a Da Vinci is, maybe you'll explain." Bernie spoke lightly.

"Cut it out! Just *cut it out!*" Cardone clenched and reclenched his fists.

Osterman climbed out of the water and approached Joe. His hands hung loosely at his sides. "Cool it, Joe. Please. . . . Cool it."

"Zurichchchch!" The scream from Joe Cardone could be heard for miles, thought Tanner. It was happening! He'd said it!

"What do you mean, Joe?" Tremayne took a halting step toward Cardone.

"Zurich! That's what I mean!"

"It's a city in Switzerland! So what the hell else?" Osterman stood facing Cardone; he wasn't about to give quarter. "You say what you mean!"

"No!" Tremayne took Osterman by the shoulder.

"Don't talk to me," yelled Cardone. "You're the one who . . ."

"Stop it! All of you!" Betty stood on the concrete deck at the end of the pool. Tanner would never have believed such strength could come from Cardone's wife.

But there it was. The three men parted from one another, as chastised dogs. The women looked up at Betty, and then Leila and Ginny walked away while Ali stood immobile, uncomprehending.

Betty continued, reverting now to the soft, suburban housewife she seemed to be. "You're all behaving childishly and I know it's time for Joe to go home."

212

"I . . . I think we all can have a nightcap, Betty," said Tanner. "How about it?"

"Make Joe's light," answered Betty with a smile.

"No other way," said Bernie.

"I'll get them." Tanner started back towards the door. "Everyone in?"

"Wait a minute, Johnny!" It was Cardone, a wide grin on his face. "I'm the naughty boy so let me help. Also, I gotta go to the bathroom."

Tanner went into the kitchen ahead of Cardone. He was confused, bewildered. He had expected that when Joe screamed the name "Zurich" it would all be over. Zurich was the key that should have triggered the collapse. Yet it did not happen.

Instead, the opposite occurred.

A control was imposed; imposed by the most unlikely source imaginable, Betty Cardone.

Suddenly, from behind him came a crash. Tremayne was standing in the doorway, looking at the fallen Cardone.

"Well. A mountain of Princeton muscle just passed out! . . . Let's get him into my car. I'm chauffeur tonight."

Passed out? Tanner didn't believe it. Cardone was drunk, yes. But he was nowhere near collapsing.

20

The three men dressed quickly and manhandled the lurching, incoherent Cardone into the front seat of Tremayne's car. Betty and Ginny were in the back. Tanner kept watching Joe's face, especially the eyes, for any signs of pretense. He could see none. And yet there was something false, he thought; there was too much precision in Cardone's exaggerated movements. Was Joe using silence to test the others, he wondered?

Or were his own observations being warped by the progressive tension?

"Damn it!" exclaimed Tremayne. "I left my jacket inside."

"I'll bring it to the Club in the morning," said John. We're scheduled for eleven."

"No, I'd better get it. I left some notes in the pocket; I may need them. . . . Wait here with Bernie. I'll be back in a second."

Dick ran inside and he grabbed his jacket from a hallway chair. He looked at Leila Osterman, who was polishing the top of a table in the living room.

"If I get these rings now maybe the Tanners'll have some furniture left," she said.

"Where's Ali?"

"In the kitchen." Leila continued rubbing the table top.

As Tremayne entered the kitchen, Alice was filling the dishwasher.

"Ali?"

"Oh! . . . Dick. Joe all right?"

"Joe's fine. . . . How's John?"

"Isn't he out there with you?"

"I'm in here."

"It's late; I'm too tired for jokes."

"I couldn't feel less like joking. . . . We've been good friends, Ali. You and Johnny mean a lot to us, to Ginny and me."

"We feel the same; you know that."

"I thought I did. I really believed it. . . . Listen to me. . . ." Tremayne's face was flushed; he swallowed repeatedly, unable to control the pronounced twitch over his left eye. "Don't make judgments. Don't let John make . . . editorial judgments that hurt people unless he understands why they do what they do."

"I don't understand what you're—"

"That's very important," interrupted Tremayne. "He should try to understand. That's one mistake I never commit in court. I always try to understand."

Alice recognized the threat. "I suggest that you say whatever it is you're saying to him."

"I did and he wouldn't answer me. That's why I'm saying it to you. . . . Remember, Ali. No one's ever completely what he seems. Only some of us are more resourceful. Remember that!"

Tremayne turned and left; a second later Ali heard the front door close. As she looked at the empty doorway, she was aware of someone else nearby. There was the unmistakable sound of a quiet footstep. Someone had walked through the dining room and was standing in her pantry, around the corner, out of sight. She walked slowly, silently to the arch. As she turned into the small narrow room she saw Leila standing motionless against the wall, staring straight ahead.

Leila had been listening to the conversation in the kitchen. She gasped when she saw Ali, then laughed with no trace of humor. She knew she'd been caught.

"I came for another cloth." She held up a dust-rag and went back inside the dining room without speaking further.

Alice stood in the center of the pantry wondering what dreadful thing was happening to all of them. Something was affecting the lives of everyone in the house.

They lay in bed; Ali on her back, John on his left side away from her. The Ostermans were across the hall in the guest room. It was the first time they'd been alone together all night.

Alice knew her husband was exhausted but she couldn't postpone the question—or was it a statement—any longer.

"There's some trouble between you and Dick and Joe, isn't there?"

Tanner rolled over; he looked up at the ceiling,

almost relieved. He knew the question was coming and he had rehearsed his answer. It was another lie; he was getting used to the lies. But there was so little time left—Fassett had guaranteed that. He began slowly, trying to speak off-handedly.

"You're too damned smart."

"I am?" She shifted to her side and looked at her husband.

"It's nasty, but it'll pass. You remember my telling you about the stock business Jim Loomis was peddling on the train?"

"Yes. You didn't want Janet to go over for lunch . . . to the Loomis', I mean."

"That's right. . . . Well, Joe and Dick jumped in with Loomis. I told them not to."

"Why?"

"I checked on it."

"What?"

"I checked on it. . . . We've got a few thousand lying around drawing five percent. I figured why not? So I called Andy Harrison—he's head of Legal at Standard, you met him last Easter. He made inquiries."

"What did he find out?"

"The whole thing smells. It's a boilerplate operation. It's rotten."

"Is it illegal?"

"Probably will be by next week. . . . Harrison suggested we do a feature on it. Make a hell of a show. I told that to Joe and Dick."

"Oh, my God! That you'd do a program on it?"

"Don't worry. We're booked for months. There's

no priority here. And even if we did, I'd tell them. They could get out in time."

Ali heard Cardone and Tremayne again: *"Did you speak to him? What did he say?" "Don't let Johnny make judgments. . . ."* They had been panicked and now she understood why. "Joe and Dick are worried sick, you know that, don't you?"

"Yeah. I gathered it."

"You *gathered* it? For heaven's sake, these are your friends! . . . They're frightened! They're scared to death!"

"Okay. Okay. Tomorrow at the Club, I'll tell them to relax. . . . The San Diego vulture isn't vulturing these days."

"Really, that was cruel! No wonder they're all so upset! They think you're doing something terrible." Ali recalled Leila's silent figure pressed against the pantry wall, listening to Tremayne alternately pleading and threatening in the kitchen. "They've told the Ostermans."

"Are you sure? How?"

"Never mind, it's not important. They must think you're a horror. . . . Tomorrow morning, for heaven's sake, tell them not to worry."

"I said I would."

"It explains so much. That silly yelling at the pool, the arguments . . . I'm really very angry with you." But Alice Tanner wasn't angry; the unknown was known to her now. She could cope with it. She lay back, still concerned, still worried, but with a degree of calm she hadn't felt for several hours.

Tanner shut his eyes tight, and let his breath

218

out. The lie had gone well. Better than he had thought it would. It was easier for him now, easier to alter the facts.

Fassett had been right; he could manage them all.

Even Ali.

21

He stood by the bedroom window. There was no moon in the sky, just clouds barely moving. He looked below at the side lawn and the woods beyond, and wondered suddenly if his eyes were playing tricks on him. There was the glow of a cigarette, distinctly seen. Someone was walking and smoking a cigarette in full view! Good Christ! he thought; did whoever it was realize that he was giving away the patrol?

And then he looked more closely. The figure was in a bathrobe. It was Osterman.

Had Bernie seen something? Heard something?

Tanner silently, rapidly went to the bedroom door and let himself out.

"I thought you might be up and around," said Bernie sitting on a deck chair, looking at the water in the pool. "This evening was a disaster."

"I'm not so sure about that."

"Then I assume you've given up your senses of sight and sound. It was a wet night at Malibu. If we all had had knives that pool would be deep red by now."

"Your Hollywood mentality's working over-time." Tanner sat down at the edge of the water.

"I'm a writer. I observe and distill."

"I think you're wrong," Tanner said. "Dick was uptight about business; he told me. Joe got drunk. So what?"

Osterman swung his leg over the deck chair and sat forward. "You're wondering what I'm doing here. . . . It was a hunch, an instinct. I thought you might come down yourself. You didn't look like you could sleep any more than I could."

"You intrigue me."

"No jokes. It's time we talk."

"About what?"

Osterman got up and stood above Tanner. He lit a fresh cigarette with the stub of his first. "What do you want most? I mean for yourself and your family?"

Tanner couldn't believe he'd heard correctly. Osterman had begun with the tritest introduction imaginable. Still, he answered as though he took the question seriously.

"Peace, I guess. Peace, food, shelter, creature comforts. Are those the key words?"

"You've got all that. For your current purposes, anyway."

"Then I *really* don't understand you."

"Has it ever occurred to you that you have no right to select anything anymore? Your whole life is programmed to fulfill a predetermined *function;* do you realize that?"

"It's universal, I imagine. I don't argue with it."

"You can't argue. The system won't permit it. You're trained for something; you gain experience —that's what you do for the rest of your *life*. No arguments."

"I'd be a rotten nuclear physicist; you'd be less than desirable in brain surgery. . . ." Tanner said.

"Of course everything's relative; I'm not talking fantasy. I'm saying that we're controlled by forces we can't control any longer. We've reached the age of specialization, and that's the death knell. We live and work within our given circles; we're not allowed to cross the lines, even to look around. You more than me, I'm afraid. At least I have a degree of choice as to which piece of crap I'll handle. But crap, nevertheless. . . . We're stifled."

"I hold my own; I'm not complaining. Also, my risks are pretty well advertised."

"But you have no back-ups! Nothing! You can't afford to stand up and say *this is me!* Not on the money-line, you can't! Not with *this* to pay for!" Osterman swung his arm to include Tanner's house and grounds.

"Perhaps I can't . . . on the money-line. But who can?"

Osterman drew up the chair and sat down. He held Tanner's eyes with his own and spoke softly. "There's a way. And I'm willing to help." He paused for a moment, as if searching for words, then started to speak again. "Johnny. . . ." Osterman stopped once more. Tanner was afraid he wouldn't continue, wouldn't find the courage.

"Go on."

222

"I've got to have certain . . . assurances; that's very important!" Osterman spoke rapidly, the words tumbling forth on top of each other.

Suddenly both men's attention was drawn to the house. The light in Janet Tanner's bedroom had gone on.

"What's that?" asked Bernie, not bothering to disguise his apprehension.

"Just Janet. That's her room. We finally got it through her head that when she goes to the bathroom she should turn on the lights. Otherwise she bumps into everything and we're all up for twenty minutes."

And then it pierced the air. Terrifyingly, with ear-shattering horror. A child's scream.

Tanner raced around the pool and in the kitchen door. The screams continued and lights went on in the other three bedrooms. Bernie Osterman nearly ran up Tanner's back as the two men raced to the little girl's room. Their speed had been such that Ali and Leila were just then coming out of their rooms.

John rushed against the door, not bothering about the doorknob. The door flew open and the four of them ran inside.

The child stood in the center of the room over the body of the Tanners' Welsh terrier. She could not stop screaming.

The dog lay in a pool of blood.

Its head had been severed from its body.

John Tanner picked up his daughter and ran back into the hallway. His mind stopped functioning. There was only the terrifying picture of the body in the woods alternating with the sight of the small dog. And the horrible words of the man in the parking lot at the Howard Johnson's motel.

"A severed head means a massacre."

He had to get control, he *had* to.

He saw Ali whispering in Janet's ear, rocking her back and forth. He was aware of his son crying several feet away and the outline of Bernie Osterman comforting him.

And then he heard the words from Leila.

"I'll take Janet, Ali. Go to Johnny."

Tanner leapt to his feet in fury. "You touch her, I'll *kill* you! Do you hear me, I'll *kill* you!"

"*John!*" Ali yelled at him in disbelief. "What are you *saying?*"

"*She* was across the hall! Can't you see that? She was *across the hall!*"

Osterman rushed toward Tanner, pushing him back, pinning his shoulders against the wall. Then he slapped him hard across the face.

"That dog's been dead for hours! Now, cut it out!"

For hours. It couldn't be for hours. It had just happened. The lights went on and the head was severed. The little dog's head was cut off. . . . And Leila was across the hall. She and Bernie. Omega! A massacre!

Bernie cradled his head. "I had to hit you. You went a little nuts. . . . Come on, now. Pull yourself together. It's terrible, just terrible, I know. I got a daughter."

224

Tanner tried to focus. First his eyes, then his thoughts. They were all looking at him, even Raymond, still sobbing by the door of his room.

"Isn't anybody here?" Tanner couldn't help himself. Where were Fassett's men? Where in God's name *were* they?

"Who, darling?" Ali put her arm around his waist in case he fell again.

"Nobody here." It was a statement said softly.

"We're here. And we're calling the police. Right now!" Bernie put Tanner's hand on the staircase railing and walked him downstairs.

Tanner looked at the thin, strong man helping him down the steps. *Didn't Bernie understand? He was Omega. His wife was Omega! He couldn't phone the police!*

"The police? You want the police?"

"I certainly do. If that was a joke, it's the sickest I've ever seen. You're damned right I want them. Don't you?"

"Yes. Of course."

They reached the living room; Osterman took command.

"Ali, you call the police! If you don't know the number, dial the operator!" And then he went into the kitchen.

Where were Fassett's men?

Alice crossed to the beige telephone behind the sofa. In an instant it was clear she didn't have to dial.

The beam of a searchlight darted back and forth through the front windows and danced against the wall of the living room. Fassett's men had arrived at last.

At the sound of the front door chimes, Tanner wrenched himself off the couch and into the hallway.

"We heard some yelling and saw the light on. Is everything all right?" It was Jenkins and he barely hid his anxiety.

"You're a little late!" Tanner said quietly. "You'd better come on in! Omega's been here."

"Take it easy." Jenkins walked into the hallway, followed by McDermott.

Osterman came out of the kitchen.

"Jesus! You people are fast!"

"Twelve-to-eight shift, sir," said Jenkins. "Saw the lights on and people running around. That's unusual at this hour."

"You're very alert and we're grateful. . . ."

"Yes, sir." Jenkins interrupted and walked into the living room. "Is anything the matter, Mr. Tanner? Can you tell us or would you rather speak privately?"

"There's nothing private here, officer." Osterman followed the policemen and spoke before Tanner could answer. "There's a dog upstairs in the first bedroom on the right. It's dead."

"Oh?" Jenkins was confused. He turned back to Tanner.

"Its head was cut off. Severed. We don't know who did it."

Jenkins spoke calmly. "I see. . . . We'll take care of it." He looked over at his partner in the hallway. "Get the casualty blanket, Mac."

"Right." McDermott went back outside.

"May I use your phone?"

"Of course."

"Captain MacAuliff should be informed. I'll have to call him at home."

Tanner didn't understand. This wasn't a police matter. It was Omega! What was Jenkins doing? Why was he calling MacAuliff? He should be reaching *Fassett!* MacAuliff was a local police officer; acceptable, perhaps, but fundamentally a political appointment. MacAuliff was responsible to the Saddle Valley town council, not to the United States government. "Do you think that's necessary? At this hour? I mean, is Captain . . ."

Jenkins cut Tanner off abruptly. "Captain Mac-Auliff is the Chief of Police. He'd consider it very abnormal if I didn't report this directly to him."

In an instant Tanner understood. Jenkins had given him the key.

Whatever happened, whenever it happened, however it happened—there could be no deviation from the norm.

This was the Chasm of Leather.

And it struck Tanner further that Jenkins was making his phone call for the benefit of Bernard and Leila Osterman.

Captain Albert MacAuliff entered the Tanner house and immediately made his authority clear. Tanner watched him deliver his instructions to the police officers, in a low, commanding voice. He was a tall, obese man, with a thick neck which made his shirt collar bulge. His hands were thick, too, but strangely immobile, hanging at his sides as he walked—the mark of a man who'd spent years patrolling a beat on foot, shifting his heavy club from one hand to the other.

MacAuliff had been recruited from the New York police and he was a living example of the right man for the right job. Years ago the town council had gone on record that it wanted a no-nonsense man, someone who'd keep Saddle Valley clear of undesirable elements. And the best defense in these days of permissiveness was offense.

Saddle Valley had wanted a mercenary.

It had hired a bigot.

"All right, Mr. Tanner, I'd like a statement. What happened here tonight?"

"We . . . we had a small party for friends."

"How many?"

"Four couples. Eight people."

"Any hired help?"

"No. . . . No, no help."

MacAuliff looked at Tanner, putting his notebook at his side. "No maid?"

"No."

"Did Mrs. Tanner have anyone in during the afternoon? To help out?"

"No."

"You're sure?"

"Ask her yourself." Ali was in the study where they'd made makeshift beds for the children.

"It could be important. While you were at work she might have had some coloreds or P.R.'s here."

Tanner saw Bernie recoil. "I was home all day."

"Okay."

228

"Captain," Osterman stepped forward from Leila's side. "Somebody broke into this house and slit that dog's throat. Isn't it possible that it was a thief? Mr. and Mrs. Tanner were robbed last Wednesday. Shouldn't we check . . ."

It was as far as he got. MacAuliff looked at the writer and scarcely disguised his contempt. "I'll handle this, Mr. . . ." The Police Chief glanced at his notebook. "Mr. Osterman. I'd like Mr. Tanner to explain what happened here tonight. I'd appreciate it if you'd let *him* answer. We'll get to you in good time."

Tanner kept trying to get Jenkins' attention, but the policeman avoided his eyes. The news director didn't know what to say—or what specifically *not* to say.

"Now then, Mr. Tanner," MacAuliff sat down and returned to his notebook, pencil poised. "Let's start at the beginning. And don't forget things like deliveries."

Tanner was about to speak when McDermott's voice could be heard from the second floor.

"Captain! Can I see you a minute? The guest room."

Without saying anything, Bernie started up the stairs in front of MacAuliff, Leila following.

Instantly, Jenkins approached Tanner's chair and bent over. "I've only got time to say this once. Listen and commit! Don't bring up any Omega business. None of it. Nothing! I couldn't say it before, the Ostermans were hovering over you."

"Why not? For Christ's sake, this *is* Omega business! . . . What am I supposed to say? Why shouldn't I?"

"MacAuliff's not one of us. He's not cleared for anything. . . . Just tell the truth about your party. That's *all!*"

"You mean he doesn't *know?*"

"He doesn't. I told you, he's not cleared."

"What about the men outside, the patrols in the woods?"

"They're not his men. . . . If you bring it up he'll think you're crazy. And the Ostermans will know. If you point at me I'll deny everything you say. You'll look like a psycho."

"Do you people think that MacAuliff . . ."

"No. He's a good cop. He's also a small-time Napoleon so we can't use him. Not openly. But he's conscientious, he can help us. Get him to find where the Tremaynes and the Cardones went."

"Cardone was drunk. Tremayne drove them all home."

"Find out if they went *straight* home. MacAuliff loves interrogations; he'll nail them if they're lying."

"How can I . . ."

"You're worried about them. That's good enough. And remember, it's nearly over."

MacAuliff returned. McDermott had "mistaken" the lateral catch in the guest room window as a possible sign of a break-in.

"All right, Mr. Tanner. Let's start with when your guests arrived."

And so John Tanner, functioning on two levels, related the blurred events of the evening. Bernie and Leila Osterman came downstairs and added very little of consequence. Ali came out of the study and contributed nothing.

"Very well, ladies and gentlemen." MacAuliff got out of the chair.

"Aren't you going to question the others?" Tanner also rose and faced the police captain.

"I was going to ask you if we could use your telephone. We have procedures."

"Certainly."

"Jenkins, call the Cardones. We'll see them first."

"Yes, sir."

"What about the Tremaynes?"

"Procedures, Mr. Tanner. After we speak to the Cardones we'll call the Tremaynes and *then* see them."

"That way no one checks with anyone else, right?"

"That's right, Mr. Osterman. You familiar with police work?"

"I write your guidelines every week."

"My husband's a television writer," said Leila.

"Captain." Patrolman Jenkins spoke from the telephone. "The Cardones aren't home. I've got the maid on the line."

"Call the Tremaynes."

The group remained silent while Jenkins dialed. After a brief conversation Jenkins put down the telephone.

"Same story, Captain. The daughter says they're not home either."

231

22

Tanner sat with his wife in the living room. The Ostermans had gone upstairs; the police departed in search of the missing couples. Neither John nor Ali was comfortable. Ali because she had decided in her own mind who had killed the dog, John because he couldn't get out of his mind the implications of the dog's death.

"It was Dick, wasn't it?" Alice asked.

"Dick?"

"He threatened me. He came into the kitchen and threatened me."

"*Threatened* you?" If that was so, thought Tanner, why hadn't Fassett's men come sooner. "When? How?"

"When they were leaving. . . . I don't mean he threatened me personally. Just generally, all of us."

"What did he say?" Tanner hoped Fassett's men were listening now. It would be a point he'd bring up later.

"He said you shouldn't make judgments. Editorial judgments."

"What else?"

"That some . . . some people were more resourceful. That's what he said. That I should remember that people weren't always what they seemed. . . . That some were more resourceful than others."

"He could have meant several things."

"It must be an awful lot of money."

"What's a lot of money?"

"Whatever he and Joe are doing with Jim Loomis. The thing you had looked into."

Oh, God, thought Tanner. The real and the unreal. He'd almost forgotten his lie.

"It's a lot of money," he said softly, realizing he was on dangerous ground. It would occur to Ali that money itself was insufficient. He tried to anticipate her. "More than just money, I think. Their reputations could go down the drain."

Alice stared at the single lighted table lamp. "Upstairs you . . . you thought Leila had done it, didn't you?"

"I was wrong."

"She *was* across the hall . . ."

"That wouldn't make any difference; we went over that with MacAuliff. He agreed. A lot of the blood had dried, congealed. The pup was killed hours ago."

"I guess you're right." Ali kept picturing Leila with her back pressed against the wall, staring straight ahead, listening to the conversation in the kitchen.

The clock on the mantel read five-twenty. They

had agreed they would sleep in the living room, in front of the study, next to their children.

At five-thirty the telephone rang. MacAuliff had not found the Tremaynes or the Cardones. He told Tanner that he had decided to put out a missing persons bulletin.

"They may have decided to go into town, into New York," said Tanner quickly. A missing persons bulletin might drive Omega underground, prolong the nightmare. "Some of those Village spots stay open. Give them more time. They're friends, for heaven's sake!"

"Can't agree. No place stays open after four."

"They may have decided to go to a hotel."

"We'll know soon enough. Hotels and hospitals are the first places M.P.B.'s go to."

Tanner's mind raced. "You've searched the surrounding towns? I know a few private clubs ..."

"So do we. Checked out."

Tanner knew he had to think of something. Anything that would give Fassett enough time to control the situation. Fassett's men were listening on the line, there was no question about that; they'd see the danger instantly.

"Have you searched the area around the old depot? The one on Lassiter Road?"

"Who the hell would go out there? What for?"

"I found my wife and children there on Wednesday. Just a thought."

The hint worked. "Call you back," MacAuliff said. "I'll check that out."

As he hung up the telephone, Ali spoke. "No sign?"

"No. . . . Honey, try to get some rest. I know of a couple of places—clubs—the police may not know about. I'll try them. I'll use the kitchen phone. I don't want to wake the kids."

Fassett answered the phone quickly.

"It's Tanner. Do you know what's happened?"

"Yes. That was damned good thinking. You're hired."

"That's the last thing I want. What are you going to do? You can't have an interstate search."

"We know. Cole and Jenkins are in touch. We'll intercept."

"And then what?"

"There are several alternate moves. I don't have time to explain. Also, I need this line. Thanks, again." Fassett hung up.

"Tried two places," said Tanner coming back into the living room. "No luck. . . . Let's try to get some sleep. They probably found a party and dropped in. Lord knows we've done that."

"Not in years," said Ali.

Both of them pretended to sleep. The tick of the clock was like a metronome, hypnotic, exasperating. Finally, Tanner realized his wife was asleep. He closed his eyes, feeling the heavy weight of his lids, aware of the complete blackness in front of his mind. But his hearing would not rest. At six-forty he heard the sound of a car. It came from in front of his house. Tanner got out of the chair and went quickly to the window. MacAuliff walked up the path, and he was alone. Tanner went out to meet him.

"My wife's asleep. I don't want to wake her."

"Doesn't matter," said MacAuliff ominously. "My business is with you."

"What?"

"The Cardones and the Tremaynes were rendered unconscious by a massive dose of ether. They were left in their car off the road by the Lassiter depot. Now I want to know why you sent us there. How did you know?"

Tanner could only stare at MacAuliff in silence.

"Your answer?"

"So help me, I didn't know! I didn't know *anything*. . . . I'll never forget Wednesday afternoon as long as I live. Neither would you if you were me. The depot just came to mind. I *swear* it!"

"It's one hell of a coincidence, isn't it?"

"Look, if I *had* known I would have told you hours ago! I wouldn't put my wife through this. For Christ's sake, be reasonable!"

MacAuliff looked at him questioningly. Tanner pressed on. "How did it happen? What did they say? Where are they?"

"They're down at the Ridge Park Hospital. They won't be released until tomorrow morning at the earliest."

"You must have talked with them."

According to Tremayne, MacAuliff said, the four of them had driven down Orchard Drive less than a half mile when they saw a red flare in the road and an automobile parked on the shoulder. A man waved them down; a well-dressed man who

236

looked like any resident of Saddle Valley. Only he wasn't. He'd been visiting friends and was on his way back to Westchester. His car had suddenly developed engine trouble and he was stuck. Tremayne offered to drive the man back to his friends' house. The man accepted.

That was the last Tremayne and the two wives remembered. Apparently Cardone had been unconscious throughout the incident.

At the deserted depot the police found an unmarked aerosol can on the floor of Tremayne's car. It would be examined in the morning, but MacAuliff had no doubt it was ether.

"There must be a connection with last Wednesday," said Tanner.

"It's the obvious conclusion. Still, anyone who knows this neck of the woods knows that the old depot area is deserted. Especially anyone who read the papers or heard about Wednesday afternoon."

"I suppose so. Were they robbed . . . too?"

"Not of money, or wallets or jewelry. Tremayne said he was missing some papers from his coat. He was very upset."

"Papers?" Tanner remembered the lawyer saying he had left some notes in his jacket. Notes that he might need. "Did he say which papers?"

"Not directly. He was hysterical—didn't make too much sense. He kept repeating the name 'Zurich.'"

John held his breath and, as he had learned to do, tensed the muscles of his stomach, trying with all his strength to suppress his surprise. It was so

237

like Tremayne to arrive with written-down, pertinent data concerning the Zurich accounts. If there *had* been a confrontation, he was armed with the facts.

MacAuliff caught Tanner's reaction. "Does Zurich mean something to you?"

"No, why should it?"

"You always answer a question with a question?"

"At the risk of offending you again, am I being officially questioned?"

"You certainly are."

"Then, no. The name Zurich means nothing to me. I can't imagine why he'd say it. Of course, his law firm is international."

MacAuliff made no attempt to conceal his anger. "I don't know what's going on, but I'll tell you this much. I'm an experienced police officer and I've had some of the toughest beats a man can have. When I took this job I gave my word I'd keep this town clean. I meant that."

Tanner was tired of him. "I'm sure you did, Captain. I'm sure you always mean what you say." He turned his back and started for the house.

It was MacAuliff's turn to be stunned. The suspect was walking away and there was nothing Saddle Valley's Police Chief could do about it.

Tanner stood on his front porch and watched MacAuliff drive off. The sky was brighter but there'd be no sun. The clouds were low, the rain would come, but not for a while.

No matter. Nothing mattered. It was over for him.

The covenant was broken now. The contract between John Tanner and Laurence Fassett was void.

For Fassett's guarantee had proven false. Omega did not stop with the Tremaynes, the Cardones and the Ostermans. It went beyond the constituency of the weekend.

He was willing to play—*had* to play—under Fassett's rules as long as the other players were the men and women he knew.

Not now.

There was someone else now—someone who could stop a car on a dark road in the early morning hours and create terror.

Someone he didn't know. He couldn't accept that.

Tanner waited until noon before heading towards the woods. The Ostermans had decided to take a nap around eleven-thirty and it was a good time to suggest the same to Ali. They were all exhausted. The children were in the study watching the Saturday morning cartoons.

He walked casually around the pool, holding a six iron, pretending to practice his swing, but actually observing the windows on the rear of the house: the two children's rooms and the upstairs bathroom.

He approached the edge of the woods and lit a cigarette.

No one acknowledged his presence. There was no sign, nothing but silence from the small forest. Tanner spoke softly.

"I'd like to reach Fassett. Please answer. It's an emergency."

He swung his golf club as he said the words.

"I repeat! It's urgent I talk with Fassett! Someone say where you are!"

Still no answer.

Tanner turned, made an improvised gesture toward nothing, and entered the woods. Once in the tall foliage he used his elbows and arms to push deeper into the small forest, toward the tree where Jenkins had gone for the portable radio.

No one!

He walked north; kicking, slashing, searching. Finally he reached the road.

There was no one there! No one was guarding his house! No one was watching the island!

No one!

Fassett's men were gone!

He raced from the road, skirting the edge of the woods, watching the windows fifty yards away on the front of his house.

Fassett's men were gone!

He ran across the back lawn, rounded the pool and let himself into the kitchen. Once inside he stopped at the sink for breath and turned on the cold water. He splashed it in his face and then stood up and arched his back, trying to find a moment of sanity.

No one! No one was guarding his house. No one guarding his wife and his children!

He turned off the water and then decided to let it run slowly, covering whatever footsteps he made.

He walked through the kitchen door, hearing the laughter of his children from the study. Going upstairs, he silently turned the knob of his bedroom door. Ali was lying on top of their bed, her bathrobe fallen away, her nightgown rumpled. She was breathing deeply, steadily, asleep.

He closed the door and listened for any sound from the guest room. There was none.

He went back down into the kitchen, closed the door and walked through the archway into the small pantry to make sure that, too, was shut.

He returned to the telephone on the kitchen wall, lifted the receiver. He did not dial.

"Fassett! If you or any of your men are on this line, cut in and acknowledge! And I mean *now!*"

The dial tone continued; Tanner listened for the slightest break in the circuit.

There was none.

He dialed the motel. "Room twenty-two, please."

"I'm sorry, sir. Room twenty-two is not occupied."

"Not occupied? You're wrong! I spoke to the party at five o'clock this morning!"

"I'm sorry, sir. They checked out."

Tanner replaced the receiver, staring at it in disbelief.

The New York number! The emergency number!

He picked up the telephone, trying to keep his hand from trembling.

The beep of a recording preceded the flat-toned voice.

"The number you have reached is not in service. Please check the directory for the correct number. This is a recording. The number you have reached . . ."

John Tanner closed his eyes. It was inconceivable! Fassett couldn't be reached! Fassett's men had disappeared!

He was alone!

He tried to think. He *had* to think. Fassett had to be found! Some gargantuan error had taken place. The cold, professional government man with his myriad ruses and artifices had made some horrible mistake.

Yet Fassett's men were gone. Perhaps there was no mistake at all.

Tanner suddenly remembered that he, too, had resources. There existed for Standard Mutual Network necessary links to certain government agencies. He dialed Connecticut information and got the Greenwich number of Andrew Harrison, head of Standard's legal department.

"Hello, Andy? . . . John Tanner." He tried to sound as composed as possible. "Sorry as hell to bother you at home but the Asian Bureau just called. There's a story out of Hong Kong I want to clear. . . . I'd rather not go into it now, I'll tell you Monday morning. It may be nothing, but I'd rather check. . . . I guess C.I.A. would be best. It's that kind of thing. They've cooperated with us before. . . . Okay, I'll hold on." The news editor cupped the telephone under his chin and lit a cigarette. Harrison came back with a number and Tanner wrote it down. "That's Virginia, isn't it? . . . Thanks very much, Andy. I'll see you Monday morning."

Once more he dialed.

"Central Intelligence. Mr. Andrews' office." It was a male voice.

"My name is Tanner. John Tanner. Director of News for Standard Mutual in New York."

"Yes, Mr. Tanner? Are you calling Mr. Andrews?"

"Yes. Yes, I guess I am."

"I'm sorry, he's not in today. May I help you?"

"Actually, I'm trying to locate Laurence Fassett."

"Who?"

"Fassett. Laurence Fassett. He's with your agency. It's urgent I speak with him. I believe he's in the New York area."

"Is he connected with this department?"

"I don't know. I only know he's with the Central Intelligence Agency. I told you, it's urgent! An emergency, to be exact!" Tanner was beginning to perspire. This was no time to be talking to a clerk.

"All right, Mr. Tanner. I'll check our directory and locate him. Be right back."

It was a full two minutes before he returned. The voice was hesitant but very precise.

"Are you sure you have the right name?"

"Of course, I am."

"I'm sorry, but there's no Laurence Fassett listed with the switchboard or in any index."

"That's impossible! . . . Look, I've been working

with Fassett! . . . Let me talk with your superior." Tanner remembered how Fassett, even Jenkins, kept referring to those who had been "cleared" for Omega.

"I don't think you understand, Mr. Tanner. This is a priority office. You called for my associate . . . my subordinate, if you like. My name is Dwight. Mr. Andrews refers decisions of this office to me."

"I don't care who you are! I'm telling you this is an emergency! I think you'd better reach someone in much higher authority than yourself, Mr. Dwight. I can't put it plainer. That's *all!* Do it *now!* I'll hold on!"

"Very well. It may take a few minutes . . ."

"I'll hold."

It took seven minutes, an eternity of strain for Tanner, before Dwight returned to the line.

"Mr. Tanner, I took the liberty of checking your own position so I assume you're responsible. However, I can assure you you've been misled. There's no Laurence Fassett with the Central Intelligence Agency. There never has been."

23

Tanner hung up the telephone and supported himself on the edge of the sink. He pushed himself off and walked mindlessly out the kitchen door onto the backyard patio. The sky was dark. A breeze rustled the trees and caused ripples on the surface of the pool. There was going to be a storm, thought Tanner, as he looked up at the clouds. A July thunderstorm was closing in.

Omega was closing in.

With or without Fassett, Omega was real, that much was clear to Tanner. It was real because he had seen and sensed its power, the force it generated, capable of removing a Laurence Fassett, of manipulating the decisions and the personnel of the country's prime intelligence agency.

Tanner knew there was no point trying to reach Jenkins. What had Jenkins said in the living room during the early morning hours? . . . "If you point at me, I'll deny everything. . . ." If Omega could silence Fassett, silencing Jenkins would be like breaking a toy.

There had to be a starting point, a springboard

that could propel him backward through the lies. He didn't care any longer; it just had to end, his family kept safe. It wasn't his war any more. His only concern was Ali and the children.

Tanner saw the figure of Osterman through the kitchen window.

That was it! Osterman was his point of departure, his break with Omega! He walked quickly back inside.

Leila sat at the table while Bernie stood by the stove boiling water for coffee.

"We're leaving," Bernie said. "Our bag's packed; I'll call for a taxi."

"Why?"

"Something's terribly wrong," said Leila, "and it's none of our business. We're not involved and we don't care to be."

"That's what I want to talk to you about. Both of you."

Bernie and Leila exchanged looks.

"Go ahead," said Bernie.

"Not here. Outside."

"Why outside?"

"I don't want Ali to hear."

"She's asleep."

"It's got to be outside."

The three of them walked past the pool to the rear of the lawn. Tanner turned and faced them.

"You don't have to lie any more. Either of you. I just want my part over with. I've stopped caring." He paused for a moment. "I know about Omega."

"About what?" asked Leila.

"Omega . . . Omega!" Tanner's voice—his whisper—was pained. "I don't *care!* So help me *God,* I *don't care!"*

"What are you talking about?" Bernie watched the news director, taking a step towards him. Tanner backed away. "What's the matter?"

"For God's sake, don't do this!"

"Don't do what?"

"I told you! It doesn't make any difference to me! Just please! *Please!* Leave Ali and the kids alone. Do whatever you want with *me! . . .* Just leave *them alone!"*

Leila reached out and put her hand on Tanner's arm. "You're hysterical, Johnny. I don't know what you're talking about."

Tanner looked down at Leila's hand and blinked back his tears. "How can you do this? Please! Don't lie any longer. I don't think I could stand that."

"Lie about what?"

"You never heard about any bank accounts in Switzerland? In Zurich?"

Leila withdrew her hand and the Ostermans stood motionless. Finally, Bernie spoke quietly. "Yes, I've heard of bank accounts in Zurich. We've got a couple."

Leila looked at her husband.

"Where did you get the money?"

"We make a great deal of money," answered Bernie cautiously. "You know that. If it would ease whatever's troubling you, why don't you call our accountant. You've met Ed Marcum. There's no one better . . . or cleaner . . . in California."

Tanner was confused. The simplicity of Osterman's reply puzzled him; it was so natural. "The Cardones, the Tremaynes. They've got Zurich accounts, too?"

"I guess they have. So do fifty percent of the people I know on the coast."

"Where did they get the money?"

"Why don't you ask them?" Osterman kept his voice quiet.

"You know!"

"You're being foolish," said Leila. "Both Dick and Joe are very successful men. Joe probably more than any of us."

"But why *Zurich? What's* in *Zurich?"*

"A degree of freedom," answered Bernie softly.

"That's it! That's what you were selling last night! 'What do you want most?,' you said. Those were your words!"

"There's a great deal of money to be made in Zurich, I won't deny that."

"With Omega! That's how you make it, *isn't it? Isn't it?"*

"I don't know what that means," said Bernie, now apprehensive himself.

"Dick and *Joe!* They're with *Omega!* So are *you!* The 'Chasm of Leather!' Information for Zurich! *Money for information!"*

Leila grabbed her husband's hand. "The phone calls, Bernie! The messages."

"Leila, please. . . . Listen, Johnny. I swear to you I don't know what you're talking about. Last night I offered to help you and I meant it. There

248

are investments being made; I was offering you money for investments. That's all."

"Not for *information?* Not for *Omega?*"

Leila clutched her husband's hand; Bernie responded by looking at her, silently commanding her to calm herself. He turned back to Tanner. "I can't imagine any information you might have that I could want. I don't know any Omega. I don't know what it is."

"Joe knows! Dick knows! They both came to Ali and me! They threatened us."

"Then I'm no part of them. *We're* no part."

"Oh, God, Bernie, something happened. . . ." Leila couldn't help herself. Bernie reached over and took her in his arms.

"Whatever it is, it hasn't anything to do with us. . . . Perhaps you'd better tell us what it's all about. Maybe we can help."

Tanner watched them, holding each other gently. He wanted to believe them. He wanted friends; he desperately needed allies. And Fassett had said it; not *all* were Omega. "You *really* don't know, do you? You *don't* know what Omega is. Or what 'Chasm of Leather' means."

"No," said Leila simply.

Tanner believed them. He had to believe them, for it meant he wasn't alone any more. And so he told them.

Everything.

When he had finished the two writers stood staring at him, saying nothing. It had begun to drizzle lightly but none of them felt the rain. Finally, Bernie spoke.

"And you thought I was talking about . . . we had something to do with *this?*" Bernie narrowed his eyes in disbelief. "My God! It's insane!"

"No it's not. It's real. I've seen it."

"You say Ali doesn't know?" asked Leila.

"I was told not to tell her, that's what they *told* me!"

"Who? Someone you can't even reach on the phone? A man Washington doesn't acknowledge? Someone who pumped you full of lies about us?"

"A man was *killed!* My family could have been killed last Wednesday! The Cardones and the Tremaynes were gassed last night!"

Osterman looked at his wife and then back at Tanner.

"*If* they really were gassed," he said softly.

"You've got to tell Alice." Leila was emphatic. "You can't keep it from her any longer."

"I know. I will."

"And then we've got to get out of here," said Osterman.

"Where to?"

"Washington. There are one or two Senators, a couple of Congressmen. They're friends of ours."

"Bernie's right. We've got friends in Washington."

The drizzle was beginning to turn into hard rain. "Let's go inside," said Leila, touching Tanner's shoulder gently.

"Wait! We can't talk in there. We can't say anything inside the house. It's wired."

Bernie and Leila Osterman reacted as though

they'd been slapped. "Everywhere?" asked Bernie.

"I'm not sure. . . . I'm not sure of anything anymore."

"Then we don't talk inside the house; or if we do we put on a radio loud and whisper."

Tanner looked at his friends. Thank God! Thank *God!* It was the beginning of his journey back to sanity.

24

In less than an hour the July storm was upon them. The radio reports projected gale force winds; medium-craft warnings were up from Hatteras to Rhode Island, and the Village of Saddle Valley was neither so isolated nor inviolate as to escape the inundation.

Ali awoke with the first thunder and John told her—whispered to her—through the sound of the loud radios, that they were to be prepared to leave with Bernie and Leila. He held her close to him and begged her not to ask questions, to trust him.

The children were brought into the living room; a television set moved in front of the fireplace. Ali packed two suitcases and placed them beside the garage entrance. Leila boiled eggs and wrapped celery and carrot sticks.

Bernie had said they might not stop driving for an hour or two.

Tanner watched the preparations and his mind went back a quarter of a century.

Evacuation!

The phone rang at two-thirty. It was a suppressed, hysterical Tremayne who—falsely, thought Tanner—recounted the events of the Lassiter depot and made it clear that he and Ginny were too shaken to come over for dinner. The Saturday evening dinner of an Osterman weekend.

"You've got to tell me what's going *on!*" Alice Tanner spoke to her husband in the pantry. There was a transistor radio at full volume and she tried to turn it down. He held her hand, preventing her, and pulled her to him.

"Trust me. Please *trust me,*" he whispered. "I'll explain in the car."

"In the car?" Ali's eyes widened in fright as she brought her hand to her mouth. "Oh, my God! What you're saying is . . . you *can't* talk."

"Trust me." Tanner walked into the kitchen and spoke, gestured really, to Bernie. "Let's load." They went for the suitcases.

When Tanner and Osterman returned from the garage, Leila was at the kitchen window looking out on the back yard. "It's becoming a regular gale out there."

The phone rang, and Tanner answered it.

Cardone was an angry man. He swore and swore again that he'd rip apart and rip apart once more the son of a bitch who'd gassed them. He was also confused, completely bewildered. His watch was worth eight hundred dollars and it wasn't taken. He'd had a couple of hundred in his wallet and it was left intact.

"The police said Dick had some papers stolen. Something about Zurich, Switzerland."

There was a sharp intake of breath from Cardone and then silence. When Joe spoke he could hardly be heard. "That's got nothing to do with *me!*" And then he rapidly told Tanner without much conviction that a call from Philadelphia had warned him that his father might be extremely ill. He and Betty would stay around home. Perhaps they'd see them all on Sunday. Tanner hung up the phone.

"Hey!" Leila was watching something out on the lawn. "Look at those umbrellas. They're practically blowing away."

Tanner looked out the window above the sink. The two large table umbrellas were bending under the force of the wind. The cloth of each was straining against the thin metal ribs. Soon they'd rip or invert themselves. Tanner knew it would appear strange if he didn't take care of them. It wouldn't be normal.

"I'll go get them down. Take two minutes."

"Want some help?"

"No sense both of us getting wet."

"Your raincoat's in the hall closet."

The wind was strong, the rain came down in torrents. He shielded his face with his hands and fought his way to the farthest table. He reached up under the flapping cloth and felt his fingers on the metal hasp. He started to push it in.

There was a shattering sound on the top of the wrought iron table. Pieces of metal flew up, searing his arm. Another report. Fragments of cement at his feet bounced off the base of the table. And then another shot, now on his other side.

Tanner flung himself under the metal table, crouching to the far side, away from the direction of the bullets.

Shots came in rapid succession, all around him, kicking up particles of metal and stone.

He started to crawl backwards onto the grass but the small eruptions of wet dirt paralyzed him. He grabbed for a chair and held it, clutched it in front of him as though it were the last threads of a disintegrating rope and he were high above a chasm. He froze in panic, awaiting his death.

"Let go! Goddamn it! Let go!"

Osterman was pulling at him, slapping him in the face and wrenching his arms from the chair. They scrambled back toward the house; bullets thumped into the wooden shingles.

"Stay away! Stay away from the door!" Bernie screamed. But he wasn't in time, or his wife would not heed the command. Leila opened the door and Bernie Osterman threw Tanner inside, jumping on top of him as he did so. Leila crouched below the window and slammed the door shut.

The firing stopped.

Ali rushed to her husband and turned him over, cradling his head, wincing at the blood on his bare arms.

"Are you hit?" yelled Bernie.

"No . . . no, I'm all right."

"You're not all right! Oh, God! Look at his arms!" Ali tried to wipe the blood away with her hand.

"Leila! Find some alcohol! Iodine! Ali, you got iodine?"

Tears were streaming down her cheeks, Alice could not answer the question. Leila grabbed her shoulders and spoke harshly.

"Stop it, Ali! *Stop* it! Where are some bandages, some antiseptic? Johnny needs help!"

"Some spray stuff . . . in the pantry. Cotton, too." She would not let go of her husband. Leila crept towards the pantry.

Bernie examined Tanner's arms. "This isn't bad. Just a bunch of scratches. I don't think anything's embedded . . ."

John looked up at Bernie, despising himself. "You saved my life. . . . I don't know what to say."

"Kiss me on my next birthday. . . . Good girl, Leila. Give me that stuff." Osterman took a medicine can and held the spray steady on Tanner's arms. "Ali, phone the police! Stay away from the window but get hold of that fat butcher you call a police captain!"

Alice reluctantly let her husband go and crawled past the kitchen sink. She reached up the side of the wall and removed the receiver.

"It's dead."

Leila gasped. Bernie leapt towards Ali, grabbing the phone from her hand.

"She's right."

John Tanner turned himself over and pressed his arms against the kitchen tile. He was all right. He could move.

"Let's find out where we stand," he said slowly.

"What do you mean?" asked Bernie.

"You girls stay down on the floor. . . . Bernie, the light switch is next to the telephone. Reach up and turn it on when I count to three."

"What are you going to do?"

"Just do as I say."

Tanner crept to the kitchen door, by the bar, and stood up out of sight of the window. The rain, the wind, the intermittent rumble of thunder were the only sounds.

"Ready? I'm going to start counting."

"What's he going to do?" Ali started up, but Osterman grabbed her and held her to the floor.

"You've been here before, Bernie," John said. "Infantry Manual. Heading: Night Patrols. Nothing to worry about. The odds are a thousand to one on my side."

"Not in any book *I* know."

"Shut up! . . . One, two, *three!*"

Osterman flipped the switch and the overhead kitchen light went on. Tanner leapt towards the pantry.

It came. The signal. The sign that the enemy was there.

The shot was heard, the glass shattered, and the bullet smashed into the wall, sending pieces of plaster flying. Osterman turned off the light.

On the floor, John Tanner closed his eyes and spoke quietly. "So, that's where we stand. The microphones were a lie. . . . Everything, a lie."

"No! Stay back! Get back!" screamed Leila before any of them knew what she meant. She lunged, followed by Alice, across the kitchen toward the doorway.

Tanner's children had not heard the shots outside; the sounds of the rain, the thunder, and the television set had covered them. But they'd heard the shot fired into the kitchen. Both women fell on them now, pulling them to the floor, shielding them with their bodies.

"Ali, get them into the dining room! Stay on the floor!" commanded Tanner. "Bernie, you don't have a gun, do you?"

"Sorry, never owned one."

"Me either. Isn't it funny? I've always disapproved of anyone buying a gun. So Goddamned primitive."

"What are we going to do?" Leila was trying to remain calm.

"We're going to get out of here," answered Tanner. "The shots are from the woods. Whoever is firing doesn't know whether we have weapons or not. He's not going to shoot from the front . . . at least I don't think so. Cars pass on Orchard pretty frequently. . . . We'll pile into the wagon and get the hell out."

"I'll open the door," said Osterman.

"You've been hero enough for one afternoon. It's my turn. . . . If we time it right, there's no problem. The door goes up fast."

They crept into the garage.

The children lay in the back section of the wagon between the suitcases, cramped but protected. Leila and Ali crouched on the floor behind the front seat. Osterman was at the wheel and Tanner stood by the garage door, prepared to pull it up.

"Go ahead. Start it!" He would wait until the engine was full throttle then open the door and jump into the wagon. There were no obstructions. The station wagon would clear the small Triumph and swing around easily for the spurt forward down the driveway.

"Go ahead, Bernie! For Christ's sake, start it!"

Instead, Osterman opened his door and got out. He looked at Tanner.

"It's dead."

Tanner turned the ignition key on the Triumph. The motor did not respond. Osterman opened the hood of the wagon and beckoned John over. The two men looked at the motor, Tanner holding a match.

Every wire had been cut.

"Does that door open from the outside?" asked Bernie.

"Yes. Unless it's locked."

"Was it?"

"No."

"Wouldn't we have heard it open?"

"Probably not with this rain."

"Then it's possible someone's in here."

The two men looked over at the small bathroom door. It was closed. The only hiding place in the garage. "Let's get them out of here," whispered Tanner.

Ali, Leila, and the two children went back into the house. Bernie and John looked around the walls of the garage for any objects which might serve as weapons. Tanner took a rusty axe; Osterman, a garden fork. Both men approached the closed door.

Tanner signaled Bernie to pull it open. Tanner rushed in, thrusting the blade of the axe in front of him.

It was empty. But on the wall, splotched in black spray paint, was the Greek letter Ω.

25

Tanner ordered them all into the basement. Ali and Leila took the children down the stairs, trying feebly to make a game of it. Tanner stopped Osterman at the staircase door.

"Let's put up a few obstacles, okay?"

"You think it's going to come to that?"

"I just don't want to take chances."

The two men crept below the sight-lines of the windows and pushed three heavy armchairs, one on top of another, the third on its side, against the front door. Then they crawled to each window, standing out of sight, to make sure the locks were secure.

Tanner, in the kitchen, took a flashlight and put it in his pocket. Together they moved the vinyl table against the outside door: Tanner shoved the aluminum chairs to Osterman, who packed them under the table, one chair rim braced under the doorknob.

"This is no good," Bernie said. "You're sealing us up. We should be figuring out how to get away!"

"Have *you* figured that out?"

In the dim light Osterman could see only the outline of Tanner's body. Yet he could sense the desperation in his voice.

"No. No, I haven't. But we've got to *try!*"

"I know. In the meantime we should take every precaution. . . . We don't know what's out there. How many or where they are."

"Let's finish it, then."

The two men crawled to the far end of the kitchen, beyond the pantry to the garage entrance. The outside garage door had been locked, but for additional security they propped the last kitchen chair under the knob and crept back into the hallway. They picked up their primitive weapons—the axe and the garden fork—and went down into the basement.

The sound of the heavy rain could be heard pounding on the small, rectangular windows, level with the ground outside the cellar. Intermittent flashes of lightning lit up the cinderblock walls.

Tanner spoke. "It's dry in here. We're safe. Whoever's out there is soaked to the skin, he can't stay there all night. . . . It's Saturday. You know how the police cars patrol the roads on weekends. They'll see there are no lights on and come investigate."

"Why should they?" asked Ali. "They'll simply think we went out to dinner. . . ."

"Not after last night. MacAuliff made it clear he'd keep an eye on the house. His patrol cars can't see through to the back lawn but they'll notice the front. They're bound to. . . . Look." Tanner took his wife's elbow and led her to the single front window just above ground level to the side of the flagstone steps. The rain made rivulets on the panes of glass; it was hard to see. Even the street lamp on Orchard Drive was not always visible. Tanner took the flashlight out of his pocket and motioned Osterman over. "I was telling Ali, MacAuliff said this morning that he'd have the house watched. He will, too. He doesn't want any more trouble. . . . We'll take turns at this window. That way no one's eyes will get tired or start playing tricks. As soon as one of us sees the patrol car, we'll signal up and down with the flashlight. They'll see it. They'll stop."

"That's good," said Bernie. "That's very good! I wish to hell you'd said that upstairs."

"I wasn't sure. Funny, but I couldn't remember if you could see the street from this window. I've cleaned this basement a hundred times, but I couldn't remember for sure." He smiled at them.

"I feel better," said Leila, trying her best to instill John's confidence into the others.

"Ali, you take the first shift. Fifteen minutes apiece. Bernie, you and I will keep moving between the other windows. Leila, sort of stay with Janet, will you?"

"What can I do, dad?" Raymond asked.

Tanner looked at his son, proud of him.

"Stay at the front window with your mother. You'll be permanent there. Keep watching for the police car."

Tanner and Osterman paced between the two windows at the rear of the house and the one at the side. In fifteen minutes, Leila relieved Ali at the front window. Ali found an old blanket which she made into a small mattress so Janet could lie down. The boy remained at the window with Leila, peering out, intermittently rubbing his hand on the glass as if the action might wipe away the water outside.

No one spoke; the pounding rain and blasts of wind seemed to increase. It was Bernie's turn at the front. As he took the flashlight from his wife he held her close for several seconds.

Tanner's turn came and went, and Ali once again took her place. None of them said it out loud but they were losing hope. If MacAuliff was patrolling the area, with concentration on the Tanner property, it seemed illogical that a police car hadn't passed in over an hour.

"There it is! There it is, Dad! See the red light?"

Tanner, Bernie and Leila rushed to the window beside Alice and the boy. Ali had turned on the flashlight and was waving it back and forth. The patrol car had slowed down. It was barely moving, yet it did not stop.

"Give me the light!"

Tanner held the beam steady until he could see, dimly but surely, the blurred reflection of the white car through the downpour. Then he moved the beam vertically, rapidly.

Whoever was driving had to be aware of the light. The path of the beam had to cross the driver's window, hit the driver's eyes.

But the patrol car did not stop. It reached the line of the driveway and slowly drove away.

Tanner shut off the flashlight, not wanting to turn around, not wanting to see the faces of the others.

Bernie spoke softly. "I don't like this."

"He had to see it! He *had* to!" Ali was holding her son, who was still peering out the window.

"Not necessarily," lied John Tanner. "It's a mess out there. His windows are probably just as clouded as ours. Maybe more so. Car windows fog up. He'll be around again. Next time we'll make sure. Next time, I'll run out."

"How," asked Bernie. "You'd never make it in time. We piled furniture in front of the door."

"I'll get through this window." Tanner mentally measured the space. It was far too small. How easily the lies came.

"I can crawl out of there, Dad!" The boy was right. It might be necessary to send him.

But he knew he wouldn't. He couldn't.

Whoever was in the patrol car had seen the beam of light and hadn't stopped.

"Let's get back to the windows. Leila, you take over here. Ali, check Janet. I think she's fallen asleep."

Tanner knew he had to keep them doing something, even if the action meant nothing. Each would have his private thoughts, his private panic.

There was a shattering crack of thunder. A flash of lightning lit up the basement.

"Johnny!" Osterman's face was against the left rear window. "Come here."

Tanner ran to Osterman's side and looked out. Through the whipping patterns of the downpour he saw a short, vertical beam of light rising from the ground. It was moving from far back on the lawn, beyond the pool, near the woods. The beam swayed slowly, jerkily. Then a flash of lightning revealed the figure holding the flashlight. Someone was coming toward the house.

"Someone's worried he's going to fall into the pool," whispered Bernie.

"What is it?" Ali's intense voice came from the makeshift mattress where she sat with her daughter.

"There's somebody out there," answered Tanner. "Everybody stay absolutely still. . . . It could be . . . all right. It might be the police."

"Or the person who shot at us! Oh, God!"

"Ssh! Be quiet."

Leila left the front window and went over to Alice.

"Get your face away from the glass, Bernie."

"He's getting nearer. He's going around the pool."

The two men moved back and stood at the side of the window. The man in the downpour wore a large poncho, his head sheltered by a rain hat. He extinguished the light as he approached the house.

Above them, the prisoners could hear the kitchen door rattling, then the sound of a body crashing against the wood. Soon the banging stopped and except for the storm there was silence. The figure left the area of the kitchen door, and Tanner could see from his side of the window the beam of light darting up and down. And then it disappeared around the far end of the house by the garage.

"Bernie!" Leila stood up beside Alice and the child. "Look! Over there!"

Through her side window came the intermittent shafts of another beam of light. Although it was quite far away, the beam was bright; it danced closer. Whoever was carrying that light was racing towards the house.

Suddenly it went out and again there was only the rain and the lightning. Tanner and Osterman went to the side window, one on each side, and cautiously looked out. They could see no one, no figure, nothing but rain, forced into diagonal sheets by the wind.

There was a loud crash from upstairs. And then another, this one sharper, wood slamming against wood. Tanner went toward the stairs. He had locked the cellar door, but it was thin; a good kick would break it from its hinges. He held the axe level, prepared to swing at anything descending those stairs.

Silence.

There were no more sounds from the house.

Suddenly, Alice Tanner screamed. A large hand was rubbing the pane of glass in the front window. The beam of a powerful flashlight pierced the darkness. Someone was squatting behind the light, the face hidden under a rain hood.

Tanner rushed to his wife and daughter, picking up the child from the blanket.

"Get back! Get back against the wall!"

The glass shattered and flew in all directions under the force of the outsider's boot. The kicking continued. Mud and glass and fragments of wood came flying into the basement. Rain swept through the broken window. The six prisoners huddled by the front wall as the beam of light flashed about the floor, the opposite wall and the stairs.

What followed paralyzed them.

The barrel of a rifle appeared at the edge of the window frame and a volley of ear-shattering shots struck the floor and rear wall. Silence. Cinderblock dust whirled about the basement; in the glare of the powerful flashlight it looked like swirling clouds of stone mist. The firing began again, wildly, indiscriminately. The infantryman in Tanner told him what was happening. A second magazine had been inserted into the loading clip of an automatic rifle.

And then another rifle butt smashed the glass of the left rear window directly opposite them. A wide beam of light scanned the row of human beings against the wall. Tanner saw his wife clutching their daughter, shielding the small body with her own, and his mind cracked with fury.

He raced to the window, swinging the axe toward the shattered glass and the crouching figure behind it. The form jumped back; shots pounded into the ceiling above Tanner's head. The shaft of light from the front window caught him now. It's over, Tanner thought. It was going to be over for him. Instead, Bernie was swinging the garden fork at the rifle barrel, deflecting shots away from Tanner. The news director crawled back to his wife and children.

"Get over here!" he yelled, pushing them to the far wall, the garage side of the basement. Janet could not stop screaming.

Bernie grabbed his wife's wrist and pulled her toward the basement corner. The beams of light crisscrossed each other. More shots were fired; dust filled the air; it became impossible to breathe.

The light from the rear window suddenly disappeared; the one from the front continued its awkward search. The second rifle was changing its position. And then from the far side window came another crash and the sound of breaking glass. The wide beam of light shone through again, now blinding them. Tanner shoved his wife and son toward the rear corner next to the stairs. Shots poured in; Tanner could feel the vibration as the bullets spiraled into the wall above and around him.

Crossfire!

He held the axe tightly, then he lunged forward, through the fire, fully understanding that any one bullet might end his life. But none could end it until he reached his target. Nothing could prevent that!

He reached the side window and swung the axe diagonally into it. An anguished scream followed; blood gushed through the opening. Tanner's face and arms were covered with blood.

The rifle in the front window tried to aim in Tanner's direction, but it was impossible. The bullets hit the floor.

Osterman rushed toward the remaining rifle, holding the garden fork at his shoulder. At the last instant he flung it through the outline of the broken glass as if it were a javelin. A cry of pain; the firing stopped.

Tanner supported himself against the wall under the window. In the flashes of lightning he could see the blood rolling down over the cinderblock.

He was alive, and that was remarkable.

He turned and went back toward his wife and children. Ali held the still screaming Janet. The boy had turned his face into the wall and was weeping uncontrollably.

"Leila! Jesus, God! *Leila!*" Bernie's hysterical roar portended the worst. *"Leila, where are you?"*

"I'm here," Leila said quietly. "I'm all right, darling."

Tanner found Leila against the front wall. She had not followed his command to move.

And then Tanner saw something which struck his exhausted mind. Leila wore a large greenish brooch—he hadn't noticed it before. He saw it clearly now, for it shone in the dark. It was iridescent, one of those mod creations sold in fashionable boutiques. It was impossible to miss in the darkness.

A dim flash of lightning lit up the wall around her. Tanner wasn't sure but he was close to being sure: there were no bullet markings near her.

Tanner held his wife and daughter with one arm and cradled his son's head with the other. Bernie ran to Leila and embraced her. The wail of a siren was heard through the sounds of the outside storm, carried by the blasts of wind through the smashed windows.

They remained motionless, spent beyond human endurance. Several minutes later they heard the voices and the knocking upstairs.

"Tanner! Tanner! Open the door!"

He released his wife and son and walked to the broken front window.

"We're here. We're here, you Goddamned filthy pricks."

26

Tanner had seen these two patrolmen numerous times in the Village, directing traffic and cruising in radio cars, but he didn't know their names. They had been recruited less than a year ago and were younger than Jenkins and McDermott.

Now he attacked. He pushed the first policeman violently against the hallway wall. The blood on his hands was smudged over the officer's raincoat. The second patrolman had dashed down the basement stairs for the others.

"For Christ's sake, let go!"

"You dirty *bastard!* You *fucking punk!* We could have been . . . *would* have been *killed* down there! All of us! My wife! My children! *Why did you do that?* You give me an answer and give it to me quick!"

"Goddamn it, let go! Do *what? What* answer, for God's sake?"

"You passed this house a half hour ago! You saw the Goddamn flashlight and you beat it! You raced out of here!"

"You're crazy! Me and Ronnie been in the north

272

end! We got a transmission to get over here not five minutes ago. People named Scanlan reported shots . . ."

"Who's in the other car? I want to know who's in the other *car!*"

"If you'll take your Goddamned hands off me I'll go out and bring in the route sheet. I forget who—but I know *where* they are. They're over on Apple Drive. There was a robbery."

"The Cardones live on Apple Drive!"

"It wasn't the Cardones' house. I know that one. It was Needham. An old couple."

Ali came into the hall from the stairs, holding Janet in her arms. The child was retching, gasping for air. Ali was crying softly, rocking her daughter back and forth in her arms.

Their son followed, his face filthy from the dust, smudged with his tears. The Ostermans were next. Bernie held on to Leila's waist, supporting her up the stairs. He held on to her as though he would never let her go.

The second patrolman came slowly through the doorway. His expression startled the other officer.

"Holy Mary Mother of God," he said softly. "It's a human slaughterhouse down there. . . . I swear to Christ I don't see how any of 'em are alive."

"Call MacAuliff. Get him over here."

"The line's dead," said Tanner, gently leading Ali to the couch in the living room.

"I'll go radio in." The patrolman named Ronnie went to the front door. "He won't believe this," he said quietly.

273

The remaining patrolman got an armchair for Leila. She collapsed into it and for the first time started to weep. Bernie leaned over behind his wife and caressed her hair. Raymond crouched beside his father, in front of his mother and sister. He was so terrified he could do nothing but stare into his father's face.

The policeman wandered toward the basement stairs. It was obvious he wanted to go down, not only out of curiosity, but because the scene in the living room was somehow so private.

The door opened and the second patrolman leaned in. "I told Mac. He picked up the radio call on his car frequency. Jesus, you should have heard him. He's on his way."

"How long will it be?" asked Tanner from the couch.

"Not long, sir. He lives about eight miles out and the roads are rotten. But the way he sounded he'll be here faster than anyone else could."

"I've stationed a dozen deputies around the grounds and two men in the house. One will stay downstairs, the other in the upper hallway. I don't know what else I can do." MacAuliff was in the basement with Tanner. The others were upstairs. Tanner wanted the police captain to himself.

"Listen to me! Someone, one of *your* men, passed this house and refused to stop! I know damned well he saw the flashlight! He saw it and drove away!"

"I don't believe that. I checked. Nobody in the

cars spotted anything around here. You saw the route sheet. This place is marked for extra concentration."

"I *saw* the patrol car *leave!* . . . Where's Jenkins? McDermott?"

"It's their day off. I'm thinking of calling them back on duty."

"It's funny they're off on weekends, isn't it?"

"I alternate my men on weekends. The weekends are very well covered. Just like the council ordered."

Tanner caught the tone of self-justification in MacAuliff's voice.

"You've got to do one other thing."

MacAuliff wasn't paying attention. He was inspecting the walls of the cinderblock cage. He stooped his immense frame down and picked up several lead slugs from the floor.

"I want every piece of evidence picked up here and sent down for analysis. I'll use the F.B.I. if Newark can't do it. . . . What did you say?"

"I said you've got to do one more thing. It's imperative, but you've got to do it with me alone. Nobody else."

"What's that?"

"You and I are going to find a phone, and you're going to get on it and make two calls."

"Who to?" MacAuliff asked the question because Tanner had taken several steps toward the cellar staircase to make sure no one was there.

"The Cardones and the Tremaynes. I want to know where they are. Where they *were*."

"What the hell . . ."

"Just do as I say!"

"You think . . ."

"I don't think *anything!* I just want to know where they are. . . . Let's say I'm still worried about them." Tanner started for the stairs, but MacAuliff stood motionless in the center of the room.

"Wait a minute! You want me to make the calls and then follow up with verification. Okay, I'll do it. . . . Now, it's my turn. You give me a pain. You aggravate my ulcer. What the hell's going on? There's too much crap here to suit me! If you and your friends are in some kind of trouble, come clean and tell me. I can't do a thing if I don't know who to go after. And I'll tell you this," MacAuliff lowered his voice and pointed his finger at the news director, his other hand on his ulcerated stomach, "I'm not going to have my record loused up because you play games. I'm not going to have mass homicide on my beat because you don't tell me what I should know so I can prevent it!"

Tanner stood where he was, one foot on the bottom step. He looked and wondered. He could tell in a minute, he thought.

"All right . . . Omega. . . . You've heard of Omega?" Tanner stared into MacAuliff's eyes, watching for the slightest betrayal.

"I forgot. You're not cleared for Omega, are you?"

"What the hell are you talking about?"

"Ask Jenkins. Maybe he'll tell you. . . . Come on, let's go."

276

Three telephone calls were made from MacAuliff's police car. The information received was clear, precise. The Tremaynes and the Cardones were neither at home nor in the vicinity.

The Cardones were in Rockland County, across the New York line. Dining out, the maid said; and if the police officer reached them would he be so kind as to ask them to call home. There was an urgent message from Philadelphia.

The Tremaynes, Virginia sick again, had returned to their doctor in Ridge Park.

The doctor confirmed the Tremaynes' visit to his office. He was quite sure they'd gone into New York City. As a matter of fact, he had prescribed dinner and a show. Mrs. Tremayne's relapse was primarily psychological. She had to get her mind on things other than the Lassiter depot.

It was all so specific, thought Tanner. So well established through second and third parties.

Yet neither couple was really accounted for.

For as Tanner reconstructed the events in the basement, he realized that one of the figures intent on killing them could have been a woman.

Fassett had said Omega was killers and fanatics. Men *and* women.

"There's your answer." MacAuliff's words intruded on Tanner's thoughts. "We'll check them out when they return. Easy enough to verify whatever they tell us . . . as you know."

"Yes. . . . Yes, of course. You'll call me after you talk to them."

"I won't promise that. I will if I think you should know."

The mechanic arrived to repair the automobiles. Tanner took him through the kitchen into the garage and watched the expression on his face as he inspected the severed wires.

"You were right, Mr. Tanner. Every lead. I'll splice in temporary connections and we'll make them permanent down at the shop. Somebody played you a rotten joke."

Back in the kitchen Tanner rejoined his wife and the Ostermans. The children were upstairs in Raymond's room where one of MacAuliff's policemen had volunteered to stay with them, play whatever games they liked, try to keep them calm while the adults talked.

Osterman was adamant. They *had* to get out of Saddle Valley, they had to get to Washington. Once the station wagon was repaired they'd leave, but instead of driving they'd go to Kennedy Airport and take a plane. They'd trust no taxis, no limousines. They'd give MacAuliff no explanations; they'd simply get in the car and go. MacAuliff had no legal right to hold them.

Tanner sat next to Ali, across from the Ostermans, and held her hand. Twice Bernie and Leila had tried to force him to explain everything to his wife and both times Tanner had said he would do so privately.

The Ostermans thought they understood.

Ali didn't and so he held her hand.

And each time Leila spoke Tanner remembered her shining brooch in the darkness of the basement —and the unmarked wall behind her.

The front door chimed and Tanner went to answer it. He came back smiling.

"Sounds from reality. The telephone repair crew." Tanner did not return to his seat. The blurred outlines of a plan were slowly coming in focus. He'd need Ali.

His wife turned and looked at him, reading his thoughts. "I'm going up to see the children."

She left and Tanner walked to the table. He reached down for his pack of cigarettes and put them in his shirt pocket.

"You're going to tell her now?" asked Leila.

"Yes."

"Tell her everything. Maybe she'll make some sense out of this . . . Omega." Bernie still looked unbelieving. "Christ knows, I can't."

"You saw the mark on the wall."

Bernie looked strangely at Tanner. "I saw a mark on the wall."

"Excuse me, Mr. Tanner." It was the downstairs policeman at the kitchen door. "The telephone men want to see you. They're in your study."

"Okay. Be right out." He turned back to Bernie Osterman. "To refresh your memory, the mark you saw was the Greek letter Omega."

He walked rapidly out the kitchen door and went to the study. Outside the windows, the storm clouds hovered, the rain, though letting up, was still strong. It was dark in the room; only the desk lamp was on.

"Mr. Tanner." The voice came from behind and he swung around. There was the man named Cole, dressed in the blue jacket of the telephone company, looking at him intently. Another man stood next to him. "Please don't raise your voice."

Tanner's shock was such that he lost control of himself. He lunged at the agent. "You son of a bitch . . ."

He was stopped by both men. They held his arms tightly behind him, pressed against the small of his back. Cole gripped his shoulders and spoke rapidly, with great intensity.

"Please! We know what you've been through! We can't change that, but we can tell you it's over! It's over, Mr. Tanner. Omega's cracked!"

"Don't you tell me anything! You bastards! You filthy bastards! You don't exist! They never heard of Fassett! Your phones are disconnected! Your . . ."

"We had to get out fast!" interrupted the agent. "We had to abandon both posts. It was mandatory. It will all be explained to you."

"I don't believe a thing you say!"

"Just listen! Make up your mind later, but *listen*. Fassett's not two miles from here putting the last pieces together. He and Washington are closing in. We'll have Omega by morning."

"What Omega? What Fassett? I called Washington! I talked to McLean, Virginia!"

"You spoke with a man named Dwight. In title, he's Andrews' superior, but not in fact. Dwight was never cleared for Omega. He checked with

Clandestine Services, and the call came to the Director. There was no alternative but to deny, Mr. Tanner. In these cases we always deny. We *have* to."

"Where are the guards outside? What happened to all your Goddamned taps? Your shock troops who wouldn't let us be touched?"

"It will all be explained to you. . . . I won't lie. Mistakes are made. One massive error, if you like. We can never make up for them, we know that. But we've never been faced with an Omega before. The main point is—the objective is right in front of us. We're on target now!"

"That's horseshit! The *main point* is my wife and children were almost killed!"

"Look. Look at this." Cole took a small metal disk from his pocket. His colleague let go of Tanner's arms. "Go on, take it. Look at it closely."

Tanner took the object in his hand, and turned it to catch the light. He saw that the tiny object was corroded, pock-marked.

"So?"

"That's one of the miniaturized pick-ups. The corrosion is acid. Acid dropped on it, to ruin it. The pick-ups have been messed up in every room. We're not getting any transmissions."

"How could anyone find them?"

"It's easy enough with the proper equipment. There's no evidence on any of these, no fingerprints. That's Omega, Mr. Tanner."

"Who is it?"

"Even I don't know that. Only Fassett does. He's

got everything under control. He's the best man in three continents. If you won't take my word ask the Secretary of State. The President, if you like. Nothing more will happen in this house."

John Tanner took several deep breaths and looked at the agent. "You realize you haven't explained anything."

"I told you. Later."

"That's not good enough!"

Cole returned Tanner's questioning look. "What choice have you got?"

"Call that policeman in here and start yelling."

"What good would that do you? Buy you a couple of hours of peace. How long would it last?"

Tanner would ask him one further question. Whatever the answer, it would make no difference. The plan in John Tanner's mind was crystallizing. But Cole would never know it.

"What's left for me to do?"

"Do nothing. Absolutely nothing."

"Whenever you people say that, the mortars start pounding the beach."

"No mortars now. That's over with."

"I see. It's over with. . . . All right. I . . . do . . . nothing. May I go back to my wife now?"

"Of course."

"Incidentally, is the telephone really fixed?"

"Yes, it is."

The news editor turned, his arms aching, and walked slowly into the hallway.

No one could be trusted any longer.

He would force Omega's hand himself.

27

Ali sat on the edge of the bed and listened to her husband's story. There were moments when she wondered if he were sane. She knew that men like her husband, men who functioned a great deal of the time under pressure, were subject to breakdowns. She could understand maniacs in the night, lawyers and stockbrokers in the panic of impending destruction, even John's compelling drive to reform the unreformable. Yet what he was telling her now was beyond her comprehension.

"Why did you agree?" she asked him.

"It sounds crazy, but I was trapped. I didn't have a choice. I had to go through with it."

"You volunteered!" said Ali.

"Not really. Once I agreed to let Fassett reveal the names, I signed an affidavit which made me indictable under the National Security Act. Once I knew who they were I was hung. Fassett knew I would be. It was impossible to continue normal relationships with them. And if I didn't, I might step over the line and be prosecuted."

"How awful," said Ali softly.

"Filthy is more to the point."

He told her about the succeeding episodes with Ginny and Leila outside by the pool. And how Dick Tremayne had followed him into the garage. Finally how Bernie had started to tell him something just before Janet's screams had wakened the household.

"He never told you what it was?"

"He said he was only offering me money for investments. I accused them both of being part of Omega. . . . Then he saved my life."

"No. Wait a minute." Ali sat forward. "When you went out for the umbrellas and we all watched you in the rain . . . and then the shots started and we all panicked. . . . I tried to go out and Leila and Bernie stopped me. So I screamed and tried to break away. Leila—not Bernie—held me against the wall. Suddenly she looked at Bernie and said, 'You can go, Bernie! It's all right, Bernie!' . . . I didn't understand, but she ordered him."

"A woman doesn't send her husband in front of a firing squad."

"That's what I wondered about. I wondered if I'd have the courage to send you out . . . for Bernie."

And so Tanner told his wife about the brooch; and the wall with no bullet marks.

"But they were *in* the basement, darling. They weren't *outside*. They weren't the ones who shot at us." Ali stopped. The memory of the horror was too much. She couldn't bring herself to speak further of it. Instead, she told him about Joe's hysterics in the living room and the fact that Betty Cardone had watched them through the window.

"So here we are," he said when she had finished. "And I'm not sure where that is."

"But the man downstairs said it would be over. He told you that."

"They've told me a lot of things. . . . But which one is it? Or is it all three?"

"Who?" she asked.

"Omega. It has to be in couples. They have to operate in couples. . . . But the Tremaynes and the Cardones were gassed in the car. They *were* left out on Lassiter. . . . Or were they?"

Tanner put his hands in his pockets and paced the floor. He went to the window and leaned against the sill, looking out on the front lawn.

"There are a lot of cops outside. They're bored to death. I bet they haven't seen the basement. I wonder—"

The glass shattered. Tanner spun around and blood spurted out of his shirt. Ali screamed, running to her husband as he fell to the floor.

More shots were fired but none came through the window. They were outside.

The patrolman in the hallway crashed through the door and raced to the fallen Tanner. No more than three seconds later the downstairs guard rushed into the room, his pistol drawn. Voices were heard yelling outside on the grounds. Leila entered, gasped, and ran to Ali and her fallen husband.

"Bernie! For God's sake, *Bernie!*"

But Osterman did not appear.

"Get him on the bed!" roared the patrolman from the upstairs hallway. "Please, ma'am, let go! Let me get him on the bed!"

Osterman could be heard yelling on the staircase. "What the hell happened?" He came into the room. "Oh, *Jesus!* Oh, Jesus *Christ!*"

Tanner regained consciousness and looked around. MacAuliff stood next to the doctor; Ali sat on the bed. Bernie and Leila were at the footrail, trying to smile at him reassuringly.

"You're going to be fine. Very superficial," said the doctor. "Painful, but not serious. Shoulder cartilage, that's what it is."

"I was shot?"

"You were shot." MacAuliff agreed.

"Who shot me?"

"We don't know that." MacAuliff tried to conceal his anger, but it surfaced. The captain was obviously convinced he was being ignored; that vital information was being withheld from him. "But I tell you this, I intend to question each one of you if it takes all night to find out what's happening here. You're all being damned fools and I won't permit it!"

"The wound is dressed," said the doctor, putting on his jacket. "You can get up and around as soon as you feel like it, only take it easy, Mr. Tanner. Not much more than a deep cut. Very little loss of blood." The doctor smiled and left rapidly. He had no reason to remain.

The moment the door was closed, MacAuliff made his abrupt statement. "Would you all wait downstairs, please? I want to be left alone with Mr. Tanner."

"Captain, he was just shot," said Bernie firmly. "You can't question him now; I won't let you."

"I'm a police officer on official business; I don't need your permission. You heard the doctor. He's not seriously hurt."

"He's been through enough!" Ali stared at Mac-Auliff.

"I'm sorry, Mrs. Tanner. This is necessary. Now will you all please . . ."

"No, we will *not!*" Osterman left his wife's side and approached the police chief. "He's not the one who should be questioned. *You* are. Your whole Goddamn police force should be put on the carpet. . . . I'd like to know why that patrol car didn't stop, Captain! I heard your explanation and I don't accept it!"

"You continue this, Mr. Osterman, I'll call in an officer and have you locked up!"

"I wouldn't try that. . . ."

"Don't tempt me! I've dealt with your kind before! I *worked* New York, sheenie!"

Osterman had grown very still. "What did you say?"

"Don't provoke me. You're provoking me!"

"Forget it!" said Tanner from the bed. "I don't mind, really. . . . Go ahead downstairs, all of you."

Alone with MacAuliff, Tanner sat up. His shoulder hurt, but he could move it freely.

MacAuliff walked to the end of the bed and held the footrail with both hands. He spoke calmly, "You talk now. You tell me what you know or I'll book you for witholding information in attempted murder."

"They were trying to kill *me*."

"That's still murder. M-u-r-d-e-r. It doesn't make any difference whether it's yours or that big Jew bastard's!"

"Why are you so hostile?" Tanner asked. "Tell me. You should be begging at my feet. I'm a taxpayer and you haven't protected my house."

MacAuliff made several attempts to speak but he was choking on his own anger. Finally he controlled himself.

"Okay. I know a lot of you don't like the way I run things. You bastards want to put me out and get some fucking hippie from a half-assed law school! Well, the only way you can do that is if I louse up. And I'm not *gonna* louse up! My record stays clean! This town stays clean! So you tell me what's going on and if I need help, I'll call it in! I can't do that without something to go on!"

Tanner rose from the bed, at first unsteadily, and then, to his surprise, firmly.

"I believe you. You're too frantic to lie. . . . And you're right. A lot of us *don't* like you. But that may be chemical, so let's let it go. . . . Still, I'm not answering questions. Instead, I'm giving you an order. You'll keep this house guarded night and day until I tell you to stop! Do you understand that?"

"I don't *take* orders!"

"You'll take them from me. If you don't, I'll plaster you across sixty million television screens as the typical example of the outdated, uneducated, unenlightened threat to real law enforcement! You're obsolete. Get that pension and run."

"You couldn't do that . . ."

"Couldn't I? Check around."

MacAuliff stood facing Tanner. The veins in his neck were so apparent the news director thought they would burst. "I hate you bastards!" he said coldly. "I hate your guts."

"As I do yours. . . . I've seen you in action. . . . But that doesn't matter now. Sit down."

Ten minutes later MacAuliff rushed out of the house into the diminishing July storm. He slammed the front door behind him and gave cursory orders to several police deputies on the lawn. The men acknowledged with feeble salutes, and MacAuliff climbed into his car.

Tanner took a shirt from his bureau drawer and awkwardly put it on. He went out of the bedroom and started down the stairs.

Ali was in the hallway talking to the police officer and saw him. She rushed up to meet him on the staircase landing.

"There are police crawling all over the place. I wish it were an army. . . . Oh, Lord! I'm trying to be calm. I really am! But I can't!" She embraced him, conscious of the bandage beneath his shirt. "What are we going to *do?* Who are we going to *turn* to?"

"Everything's going to be all right. . . . We just have to wait a little longer."

"What for?"

"MacAuliff is getting me information."

"What information?"

Tanner moved Ali against the wall. He spoke quietly, making sure the policeman wasn't watching them. "Whoever was outside those basement windows is hurt. One I know is badly wounded—in the leg. The other we can't be sure of, but Bernie thinks he hit him in the shoulder or the chest. MacAuliff's going out to see the Cardones and the Tremaynes. He'll phone me then. It may take quite a while, but he'll get back to me."

"Did you tell him what to look for?"

"No. Nothing. I simply asked him to follow up their stories about where they were. That's all. I don't want MacAuliff making decisions. That's for Fassett."

But it wasn't for Fassett, thought Tanner. It wasn't for anyone but him any longer. He'd tell Ali when he had to. At the last minute. So he smiled at her and put his arm around her waist and wished he could be free to love her again.

The telephone rang at ten-forty-seven.

"John? It's Dick. MacAuliff was over to see me." Tremayne was breathing hard into the telephone, but was keeping his voice reasonably calm. His control was stretched very thin, however.

". . . I have no idea what you're involved with—intended murder, for God's sake!—and I don't

290

want to know, but it's more than I can take! I'm sorry, John, but I'm getting the family out of here. I've got reservations on Pan Am at ten in the morning."

"Where are you going?"

Tremayne did not reply. Tanner spoke again. "I asked you where you were going."

"Sorry, John . . . this may sound rotten, but I don't want to tell you."

"I think I understand. . . . Do us a favor, though. Drop by on the way to the airport."

"I can't promise that. Good-bye."

Tanner held his finger down on the phone and then released it. He dialed the Saddle Valley police station.

"Police Headquarters. Sergeant Dale."

"Captain MacAuliff, please. John Tanner calling."

"He's not here, Mr. Tanner."

"Can you reach him? It's urgent."

"I can try on the car radio; do you want to hold?"

"No, just have him call me as soon as possible." Tanner gave his telephone number and hung up. MacAuliff was probably on his way to the Cardones. He should have arrived by now. He'd call soon. Tanner returned to the living room. He wanted to unnerve the Ostermans.

It was part of his plan.

"Who called?" asked Bernie.

"Dick. He heard what happened. . . . He's taking the family and leaving."

The Ostermans exchanged looks.

"Where?"

"He didn't say. They've got a flight in the morning."

"He didn't say where he was going?" Bernie stood up casually but couldn't hide his anxiety.

"I told you. He wouldn't tell me."

"That's not what you said." Osterman looked at Tanner. "You said 'didn't say.' That's different from not telling you."

"I suppose it is. . . . You still think we should head down to Washington?"

"What?" Osterman was looking at his wife. He hadn't heard Tanner's question.

"Do you still think we should go to Washington?"

"Yes." Bernie stared at Tanner. "Now more than ever. You need protection. Real protection. . . . They're trying to kill you, John."

"I wonder. I wonder if it's me they're trying to kill."

"What do you mean?" Leila stood up, facing Tanner.

The telephone rang.

Tanner returned quickly to the study and picked up the receiver. It was MacAuliff.

"Listen," said Tanner quietly. "I want you to describe exactly—*exactly*—where Tremayne was during your interrogation."

"In his study."

"*Where* in his study?"

"At his desk. Why?"

"Did he get up? Did he walk around? To shake your hand, for instance?"

"No. . . . No, I don't think so. No, he didn't."

"What about his wife? She let you in?"

"No. The maid. Tremayne's wife was upstairs. She was sick. We verified that; called the doctor, remember?"

"All right. Now tell me about the Cardones. Where did you find them?"

"Spoke first with his wife. One of the kids let me in. She was lying on the sofa, her husband was in the garage."

"Where did you talk with him?"

"I just told you. In the garage. I didn't get there too soon either. He's on his way to Philadelphia. His father's sick. They gave him last rites."

"Philadelphia? . . . Where exactly was he?"

"In the *garage*, I said! His bags were packed. He was in the car. He told me to be quick. He wanted to take off."

"He was *in* the car?"

"That's right."

"Didn't that seem strange to you?"

"Why should it? For Christ's sake, his father's dying! He wanted to get the hell to Philadelphia. I'll check it out."

Tanner hung up the phone.

Neither couple was seen by MacAuliff under normal conditions. None stood, none walked. Both had reasons not to be at his house on Sunday.

Tremayne behind a desk, frightened, immobile.

Cardone seated in an atuomobile, anxious only to drive away.

One or both *wounded*.

One or both, perhaps, Omega.

The time had come. Outside the rain had stopped; his traveling would be easier now, although the woods would still be wet.

In the kitchen, he changed into the clothes he'd carried down from the bedroom: black trousers, a black long-sleeved sweater, and sneakers. He put money in his pocket, making sure that his change included at least six dimes. Finally, he clipped a pencil-light to the top of his sweater.

Then he went to the hallway door and called Ali into the kitchen He dreaded this moment far more than anything which lay before him. Yet there was no other way. He knew he had to tell her.

"What are you doing? Why—"

Tanner held his finger to his lips and drew her close to him. They had walked to the far end of the kitchen by the garage door, the furthest point from the hallway. He whispered calmly to her.

"Remember I asked you to trust me?"

Ali nodded her head slowly.

"I'm going out for a while; just for a little while. I'm meeting a couple of men who can help us. MacAuliff made contact."

"Why can't they come here? I don't want you to go outside. You can't go outside!"

"There's no other practical way. It's been arranged," he lied, knowing she suspected the lie. "I'll phone you in a little while. You'll know everything's all right then. But until I do, I want you to tell the Ostermans I went for a walk. . . . I'm upset, anything you like. It's important they think *you* believe I went for a walk. That I'll be back any minute. Maybe I'm talking to some of the men outside."

"Who *are* you going to meet? You've got to tell me."

"Fassett's men."

She held his gaze. The lie was established between them now and she searched his eyes. "You have to do this?" she asked quietly.

"Yes." He embraced her roughly, anxious to leave, and walked rapidly to the kitchen door.

Outside he strolled about his property, establishing his presence with the police deputies in front and back of his house, to the point where he guessed he was no longer really watched. And then, when he felt no one was looking at him, he disappeared into the woods.

He made a wide circle towards the west, using the tiny beam of the pencil light to avoid obstacles. The wetness, the softness of the earth, made the going difficult, but eventually he saw the backyard lights of his neighbors the Scanlans, three hundred feet from his property line. He was soaked as he approached the Scanlans' back porch and rang the bell.

Fifteen minutes later—again longer than Tanner had anticipated—he climbed into Scanlan's Mercedes coupe and started the engine. Scanlan's Smith & Wesson magazine-clip pistol was in his belt, three extra clips of ammunition in his pocket.

Tanner swung left down Orchard Drive toward the center of the Village. It was past midnight; he was behind the schedule he had set.

He took momentary stock of himself and his actions. He had never considered himself an exceptionally brave man. Whatever courage he had ever displayed was always born of the moment. And he wasn't feeling courageous now. He was desperate.

It was strange. His fear—the profound, deeply felt terror he had lived with for days—now created its own balance, gave birth to its own anger. Anger at being manipulated. He could accept it no longer.

Saddle Valley was quiet, the main street softly lit by replicas of gas lamps, the storefronts in keeping with the town's image of quiet wealth. No neons, no floodlights, everything subdued.

Tanner drove past The Village Pub and the taxi stand, made a U-turn, and parked. The public telephone was directly across from the Mercedes. He wanted the car positioned far enough away so he could see the whole area. He walked across the street and made his first call.

"It's Tanner, Tremayne. Be quiet and listen to me. . . . Omega's finished. It's being disbanded. I'm calling it off. Zurich's calling it off. We've put you through the final test and you've failed. The stupidity displayed by everyone is beyond belief! I'm issuing the phase-out orders tonight. Be at the Lassiter depot at two-thirty. And don't try to call my home. I'm phoning from the Village. I'll take a taxi to the area. My house is being watched, thanks to *all* of you! Be at the depot at two-thirty and bring

Virginia. Omega's collapsed! If you want to get out alive, be there. . . . Two-thirty!"

Tanner pressed down the receiver. The Cardones next.

"Betty? It's Tanner. Listen closely. You get hold of Joe and tell him Omega is finished. I don't care how you do it, but get him back here. That's an order from Zurich. Tell him that! . . . Omega's collapsed. You've all been damn fools. Disabling my cars was stupid. I'm issuing phase-out orders tonight at the Lassiter depot at two-thirty. You and Joe be there! Zurich expects you. And *don't* try to phone me back. I'm calling from the Village. My house is watched. I'll take a taxi. Remember. The Lassiter depot—tell Joe."

Once more Tanner pressed the receiver down. His third call was to his own home.

"Ali? Everything's fine, darling. There's nothing to worry about. Now, don't talk. Put Bernie on the phone right away. . . . Ali, not *now!* Put Bernie on the *phone!* . . . Bernie, it's John. I'm sorry I took off but I had to. I know who Omega is but I need your help. I'm calling from the Village. I'll need a car later . . . not now; later. I don't want mine seen in the Village. I'll use a taxi. Meet me out at the Lassiter depot at two-thirty. Turn right out of the driveway and go east on Orchard—it curves north —for about a mile. You'll see a large pond, there's a white fence around it. On the other side is Lassiter Road. Go down Lassiter a couple of miles and you'll see the depot. . . . It's over, Bernie. I'll have Omega at the depot at two-thirty. For Christ's sake *don't, don't blow* it! Trust me! *Don't* call anybody or *do* anything! Just *be* there!"

Tanner hung up the telephone, opened the door and ran towards the Mercedes coupe.

28

He stood in the darkened doorway of a toy store. It occurred to him that Scanlan's Mercedes was a familiar car in the Village and the Tremaynes, the Cardones, and perhaps even the Ostermans knew Scanlan was his nearest neighbor. That might be to his advantage, he considered. If the assumption were made that he'd borrowed the automobile, it would be further assumed that he remained in the area. The hunt, then, would be thorough. There was nothing to do but wait now. Wait until a little after two o'clock before driving out to the Lassiter depot.

Wait in the center of the Village to see who came after him; who tried to stop him from making the rendezvous. Which couple? Or would it be all three? For Omega had to be frightened now. The unutterable had been said; the mystery brought out into the open.

Omega would have to try to stop him now. If anything Fassett had said was true, that was their only course of action. To intercept him before he reached the depot.

He counted on it. They wouldn't stop him—he'd make sure of that, but he wanted to know in advance who the enemy was.

He looked up and down the street. There were only four people visible. A couple walking a Dalmatian, a man emerging from the Pub, and the driver asleep in the front seat of his taxi.

From the east end of town Tanner saw the headlights of a car approaching slowly. Soon he saw it was his own station wagon. He pressed back into the recessed, unlit doorway.

The driver was Leila Osterman. Alone.

Tanner's pulse quickened. What had he done? It had never occurred to him that any of the couples would separate in a crisis! Yet Leila was alone! And there was nothing to prevent Osterman from holding his family as hostages! Osterman was one of those being protected, not one of the hunted. He could move about freely, leave the premises if he wished. Force Ali and the children to *go* with him if he thought it necessary!

Leila parked the station wagon in front of the Pub, got out, and walked rapidly over to the taxi driver, shaking him awake. They talked quietly for a moment; Tanner couldn't hear the voices. Eventually Leila turned back to the Pub and went in. Tanner remained in the doorway, fingering the dimes in his pocket, waiting for her to come out. The waiting was agony. He had to get to the phone. He had to get through to the police! He had to make sure his family was safe!

Finally she appeared, got in the wagon, and

drove off. Five or six blocks west she turned right; the car disappeared.

Tanner raced across the street to the telephone booth. He dropped in a dime and dialed.

"Hello?"

Thank God! It was Ali!

"It's me."

"Where are you . . ."

"Never mind that now. Everything's fine. . . . Are you all right?" He listened carefully for any false note.

"Of course, I am. We're worried sick about you. What are you doing?"

She sounded natural. It was all right.

"I don't have time. I want . . ."

She interrupted him. "Leila went out looking for you. You've made an awful mistake. . . . We've talked. You and I were wrong, darling. Very *wrong*. Bernie got so worried he thought . . ."

He cut her off. He didn't have the seconds to waste; not on the Ostermans, not now. "I've got to get off the phone. Stay with the guards. Do as I say. Don't let them out of your sight!"

He hung up before she could speak. He had to reach the police. Every moment counted now.

"Headquarters. Jenkins speaking."

So the one man on the Saddle Valley police force cleared for Omega was back. MacAuliff had recalled him.

"Headquarters," repeated the patrolman testily.

"This is John Tanner . . ."

"Jesus Christ, where have you been? We've been looking all over for you!"

"You won't find me. Not until I want you to. . . . Now, listen to me! The two policemen in the house—I want them to stay with my wife. She's never to be left alone! The children either! Never! None of them can be alone with Osterman!"

"Of course! We know that! Now, where are you? Don't be a damned fool!"

"I'll phone you later. Don't bother to trace this call. I'll be gone."

He slammed down the receiver and opened the door, looking for a better vantage point than the storefront. He couldn't run unobserved from the doorway. He started back across the street. The taxi driver was asleep again.

Suddenly, without warning, Tanner heard the roar of an engine. The blurred outline of a car without headlights sped toward him. It came out of nowhere at enormous speed; he was its target. He raced toward the opposite sidewalk only feet ahead of the rushing car. He threw himself toward the curb, twisting his body away from the automobile.

At the same instant he felt a great blow on his left leg. There was a piercing sound of tires braking on asphalt. Tanner fell, rolling with his plunge, and saw the black car narrowly miss the Mercedes, then speed away down Valley Road.

The pain in his leg was excruciating; his shoulder was throbbing. He hoped to Christ he could walk! He had to be able to *walk!*

The cab driver was running toward him.

"Jesus! What happened?"

"Help me up, will you, please?"

"Sure! Sure! You okay? . . . That guy must've had a load on! Jesus! You could've been killed. You want me to get a doctor?"

"No. No, I don't think so."

"I got a telephone right over there! I'll call the cops! They'll have a doctor here in no time!"

"No! No, don't! I'm all right. . . . Just help me walk around a bit." It was painful for him, but Tanner found he could move. That was the important fact. The pain didn't matter now. Nothing mattered but Omega. And Omega was out in the open!

"I better call the police anyway," said the driver, holding on to Tanner's arm. "That clown should get yanked off the road."

"No. . . . I mean, I didn't get the license. I didn't even see what kind of car. It wouldn't do any good."

"I guess not. Serve the bastard right, though, if he plows himself into a tree."

"Yeah. That's right." Tanner was walking by himself now. He'd be all right.

The telephone at the taxi stand rang across the street.

"There goes my phone. . . . You okay?"

"Sure. Thanks."

"Saturday night. Probably the only call I'll get on the whole shift. Only keep one cab on duty Saturday night. That's one too many." The driver moved away. "Good luck, buddy. You sure you don't want a doctor?"

"No, really. Thanks."

He watched the driver take down an address, then heard his voice as he repeated it.

"Tremayne. Sixteen Peachtree. Be there in five minutes, ma'am." He hung up and saw Tanner watching him. "How d'you like that? She wants to go to a motel at Kennedy. Who do you suppose she's shacking up with out there?"

Tanner was bewildered. The Tremaynes had two cars of their own. . . . Had Tremayne intended to ignore the command to meet at the Lassiter depot? Or, by making sure the single Saturday night taxi was away, was Tremayne hoping to isolate him in the Village?

Either was possible.

Tanner hobbled toward an alley running alongside of the Pub, used primarily for deliveries. From there, since it led to a municipal parking lot, he could escape undetected if it were necessary. He stood in the alley and massaged his leg. He'd have a huge welt in an hour or so. He looked at his watch. It was twelve-forty-nine. Another hour before he would drive to the depot. Perhaps the black car would return. Perhaps others would come.

He wanted a cigarette, but did not want to strike a match near the street. He could cup the glow of a cigarette, not the flame of a match. He walked ten yards into the alley and lit up. He heard something. Footsteps?

He inched his way back toward the Valley Road entrance. The Village was deserted. The only sounds were muted, coming from the Pub. Then

304

the Pub's door opened and three people came out. Jim and Nancy Loomis with a man he didn't recognize. He laughed sadly to himself.

Here he was, John Tanner, the respected Director of News for Standard Mutual, hiding in a darkened alley—filthy, soaked, a bullet crease in his shoulder and a swelling bruise on his leg from a driver intent on murder—silently watching Jim and Nancy come out of the Pub. Jim Loomis. He had been touched by Omega and he'd never know it.

From the west end of Valley Road—the direction of Route Five—came an automobile traveling quietly at no more than ten miles an hour. The driver seemed to be looking for someone or something on Valley Road.

It was Joe.

He hadn't gone to Philadelphia. There was no dying father in Philadelphia. The Cardones had lied.

It was no surprise to Tanner.

He pressed his back against the alley wall and made himself as inconspicuous as he could, but he was a large man. For no other reason than that it gave him security, Tanner withdrew the pistol from his belt. He'd kill Cardone if he had to.

When the car was within forty feet of him, two short blasts from a second automobile, coming from the other direction, made Cardone stop.

The second car approached rapidly.

It was Tremayne. As he passed the alley, Tanner could see the look of panic on his face.

The lawyer pulled up beside Cardone and the two men spoke quickly, softly. Tanner couldn't make out the words, but he could tell they were spoken rapidly and with great agitation. Tremayne made a U-turn, and the automobiles raced off in the same direction.

Tanner relaxed and stretched his pained body. All were accounted for now. All he knew about and one more he didn't. Omega plus one, he considered. Who was in the black automobile? Who had tried to run him down?

There was no point in putting it off any longer. He'd seen what he had to see. He'd drive to within a few hundred yards of the Lassiter depot and wait for Omega to declare themselves.

He walked out of the alley and started for the car. And then he stopped.

There was something wrong with the car. In the subdued light of the gas lamps he could see that the automobile's rear end had settled down to the surface of the street. The chrome bumper was inches above the pavement.

He ran to the car and unclipped his pencil light. Both back tires were flat, the metal rims supporting the weight of the automobile. He crouched down and saw two knives protruding from the deflated rubber.

How? When? He was within twenty yards every second! The street was deserted! No one! No one could have crept behind the Mercedes without being seen!

Except, perhaps, those few moments in the alley.

306

Those moments when he lit a cigarette and crouched by the wall watching Tremayne and Cardone. Those seconds when he'd thought he'd heard footsteps.

The tires had been slashed not five minutes ago!

Oh Christ! thought Tanner. The manipulation hadn't stopped at all! Omega was at his heels. Knowing. Knowing every move he made. Every second!

What had Ali started to say on the phone? Bernie had . . . what? He started toward the booth, taking the last dime out of his pocket. He pulled the pistol out of his belt and looked around as he crossed the street. Whoever punctured the tires might be waiting, watching.

"Ali?"

"Darling, for God's sake come home!"

"In a little while, hon. Honest, no problems. No problems at all. . . . I just want to ask you a question. It's important."

"It's just as important that you get *home!*"

"You said before that Bernie had decided something. What was it?"

"Oh . . . when you called the first time. Leila went out after you; Bernie didn't want to leave us alone. But he was worried that you might not listen to her and since the police were here, he decided to go find you himself."

"Did he take the Triumph?"

"No. He borrowed a car from one of the police."

"Oh, Christ!" Tanner didn't mean to explode into

the phone but he couldn't help it. The black automobile out of nowhere! The *plus-one* was really part of the three! "Is he back?"

"No. Leila is, though. She thinks he may have gotten lost."

"I'll call you." Tanner hung up. Of course Bernie was "lost." There hadn't been time for him to get back. Not since Tanner had been in the alley, not since the tires were slashed.

And now he realized that somehow he had to reach the Lassiter depot. Reach it and position himself before any part of Omega could stop him, or know where he was.

Lassiter Road was diagonally northwest, about three miles from the center of the Village. The depot perhaps another mile or two beyond. He'd walk. It was all he could do.

He started as quickly as he could, his limp diminishing with movement, then ducked into a doorway. No one followed him.

He kept up a zigzag pattern northwest until he reached the outskirts of town—where there were no sidewalks, only large expanses of lawn. Lassiter wasn't far away now. Twice he lay on the ground while automobiles raced past him, drivers oblivious to anything but the road in front of them.

Finally, through a back stretch of woods behind a well-trimmed lawn, neither unlike his own, he reached Lassiter Road.

On the rough tarred surface he turned left and started the final part of his journey. It wasn't any farther than a mile or a mile and a half by his calculations. He could reach the deserted depot in fifteen minutes if his leg held out. If it didn't, he'd simply slow down, but he'd get there. His watch read one-forty-one. There was time.

Omega wouldn't arrive early. It couldn't afford to. It—or they—didn't know what was waiting for them.

Tanner limped along the road and found he felt better—more secure—holding Scanlan's pistol in his hand. He saw a flicker of light behind him. Headlights, three or four hundred yards away. He crossed into the woods bordering on the road and lay flat on the muddy ground.

The car passed him traveling slowly. It was the same black car that had run him down on Valley Road. He couldn't see the driver; the absence of street lights made any identification impossible.

When it was out of sight, Tanner went back to the road. He had considered walking in the woods but it wasn't feasible. He could make better time on the cleared surface. He went on, hobbling now, wondering whether the black automobile belonged to a policeman currently stationed at 22 Orchard Drive. Whether the driver was a writer named Osterman.

He had gone nearly half a mile when the lights appeared again, only now in front of him. He dove into the brush, hoping to God he hadn't been seen, unlatching the safety of his pistol as he lay there.

The automobile approached at incredible speed. Whoever was driving was racing back to find someone.

Was it to find him?

Or Leila Osterman?

Or was it to reach Cardone, who had *no* dying father in Philadelphia. Or Tremayne, who *wasn't* on his way to the motel at Kennedy Airport.

Tanner got up and kept going, his leg about to collapse under him, the pistol gripped tightly in his hand.

He rounded a bend in the road and there it was. A single sagging street lamp lit the crumbling station house. The old stucco depot was boarded up, giant weed drooping ominously from the cracks in the rotted wood. Small ugly leaves grew out of the foundation.

There was no wind, no rain, no sound but the rhythmic drip of water from thousands of branches and leaves—the last exhausted effects of the storm.

He stood on the outskirts of the decayed, overgrown parking area trying to decide where to position himself. It was nearly two o'clock and a secluded place had to be found. The station house itself! Perhaps he could get inside. He started across the gravel and weeds.

A blinding light flashed in his eyes; his reflexes lurched him forward. He rolled over on his wounded shoulder, yet felt no pain. A powerful searchlight had pierced the dimness of the depot grounds, and gunshots echoed throughout the deserted area. Bullets thumped into the earth around him and whistled over his head. He kept rolling, over and over, knowing that one of the bullets had hit his left arm.

310

He reached the edge of the sunken gravel and raised his pistol toward the blinding light. He fired rapidly in the direction of the enemy. The searchlight exploded; a scream followed. Tanner kept pulling the trigger until the clip was empty. He tried to reach into his pocket with his left hand for a second clip and found he couldn't move his arm.

There was silence again. He put down the pistol and awkwardly extracted another clip with his right hand. He twisted the pistol on its back and with his teeth holding the hot barrel, pushed the fresh clip into the chamber, burning his lips as he did so.

He waited for his enemy to move. To make any sound at all. Nothing stirred.

Slowly he rose, his left arm now completely immobile. He held the pistol in front of him, ready to pull the trigger at the slightest movement in the grass.

None came.

Tanner backed his way towards the door of the depot, holding his weapon up, probing the ground carefully with his feet so that no unexpected obstacle would cause him to fall. He reached the boarded-up door, knowing he couldn't possibly break it down if it was nailed shut. Most of his body was inoperative. He had little strength left.

Still, he pushed his back against the door and the heavy wood gave slightly, creaking loudly as it did so. Tanner turned his head just enough to see that the opening was no more than three or four inches. The ancient hinges were caked with rust. He slammed his right shoulder against the edge of the door and it gave way, plunging Tanner into the darkness, onto the rotted floor of the station.

He lay where he was for several seconds. The station house door was three-quarters open, the upper section snapped away from its hinges. The street lamp fifty yards away provided a dull wash of illumination. Broken and missing boards from the roof were a second, inadequate source of light.

Suddenly Tanner heard a creaking behind him. The unmistakable sound of a footstep on the rotted floor. He tried to turn around, tried to rise. He was too late. Something crashed into the base of his skull. He felt himself grow dizzy, but he saw the foot. A foot encased in bandages.

As he collapsed on the rotted floor, blackness sweeping over him, he looked upward into a face.

Tanner knew he had found Omega.

It was Laurence Fassett.

29

He couldn't know how long he'd been unconscious. Five minutes? An hour? There was no way to tell. He couldn't see his watch, he couldn't move his left arm. His face was against the rough splintered floor of the crumbling station house. He could feel the blood slowly trickling from his wounded arm; his head ached.

Fassett!

The manipulator.

Omega.

As he lay there, isolated fragments of past conversations raced through his mind.

". . . we should get together . . . our wives should get together . . ."

But Laurence Fassett's wife had been killed in East Berlin. Murdered in East Berlin. That fact had been his most moving entreaty.

And there was something else. Something to do with a Woodward broadcast. . . . The broadcast about the C.I.A. a year ago.

". . . I was in the States then. I saw that one."

But he wasn't "in the States" then. In Washington Fassett had said he'd been on the Albanian border a year ago. ". . . forty-five days of haggling." In the field. It was why he'd contacted John Tanner, the solid, clean news director of Standard Mutual, a resident of the target, Chasm of Leather.

There were other contradictions—none as obvious, but they were there. They wouldn't do him any good now. His life was about to end in the ruins of the Lassiter depot.

He moved his head and saw Fassett standing above him.

"We've got a great deal to thank you for. If you are as good a shot as I think you are you've created the perfect martyr out there. A dead hero. If he's only wounded, he'll soon be dead at any rate. . . . Oh, he's the other part of us, but even he'd recognize the perfect contribution of his sacrifice. . . . You see, I didn't lie to you. We are fanatics. We have to be."

"What now?"

"We wait for the others. One or two are bound to show up. Then it'll be over. Their lives and yours, I'm afraid. And Washington will have its Omega. Then, perhaps, a field agent named Fassett will be given another commendation. If they're not careful, they'll make me Director of Operations one day."

"You're a traitor." Tanner found something in the dark shadows by his right hand. It was a loose piece of flooring about two feet long, an inch or so wide. He awkwardly, painfully, sat up, pulling the plank to his side.

"Not by my lights. A defector, perhaps. Not a traitor. Let's not go into that. You wouldn't understand or appreciate the viewpoint. Let's just say in my opinion you're the traitor. *All* of you. Look around you . . ."

Tanner lashed out with the piece of wood and crashed it with all his might across the bandaged foot in front of him. Blood erupted instantly, spreading through the gauze. Tanner flung himself upward into Fassett's groin, trying desperately to reach the hand with the gun. Fassett screamed in anguish. Tanner found the agent's wrist with his right hand, his left arm immobile, serving only as a limping tentacle. He drove Fassett back against the wall and ground his heel into Fassett's wounded foot, stamping it over and over again.

Tanner wrenched the gun free and it fell to the floor, sliding towards the open door and the dim shaft of light. Fassett's screams shattered the stillness of the station house as he slumped against the wall.

John lunged for the pistol, picked it up and held it tightly in his hand. He got up, every part of his body in pain, the blood flowing now out of his arm.

Fassett was barely conscious, gasping in agony. Tanner wanted this man alive, wanted Omega alive. But he thought of the basement, of Ali and the children, and so he took careful aim and fired twice, once into the mass of blood and flesh which was Fassett's wound, once into the knee cap of the leg.

He lurched back toward the doorway, supporting himself in the frame. Painfully, he looked at his watch: two-thirty-seven. Seven minutes after Omega's appointed time.

No one else would come now. Half of Omega lay in agony in the station house; the rest in the tall, wet grass beyond the parking lot.

He wondered who it was.

Tremayne?

Cardone?

Osterman?

Tanner tore off part of his sleeve and tried to wrap it around the wound in his arm. If only he could stop the bleeding, even a bit. If he could do that perhaps he could make it across the old parking area to where the searchlight was.

But he couldn't, and, off balance, fell backwards to the floor. He was no better off than Fassett. Both their lives would ebb away right there. Inside the ancient depot.

A wailing began; Tanner wasn't sure if it was a trick of his brain or if it was real. Real! It was growing louder.

Sirens, then the roar of engines. Then the screeching of brakes against loose gravel and wet dirt.

Tanner rose to his elbow. He tried with all his strength to get up—only to his knees, that would be good enough. That would be sufficient to crawl. Crawl to the doorway.

The beams of searchlights filtered through the loose boards and cracked stucco, one light remaining on the entrance. Then a voice, amplified by a bull horn.

"This is the police! We are accompanied by federal authorities! If you have weapons, throw them out and follow with your hands up! . . . If you are holding Tanner hostage, release him! You are surrounded. There's no way for you to escape!"

Tanner tried to speak as he crawled toward the door. The voice sounded once again.

"We repeat. Throw out your weapons . . ."

Tanner could hear another voice yelling, this one not on a horn.

"Over here! Throw a light over here! By this automobile! Over here in the grass!"

Someone had found the rest of Omega.

"Tanner! John Tanner! Are you inside!?"

Tanner reached the entrance and pulled himself up by the edge of the door into the spill of light.

"There he is! Jesus, *look* at him!"

Tanner fell forward. Jenkins raced to his side.

"There you are, Mr. Tanner. We've tied you up as best we can. It'll hold till the ambulance gets here. See if you can walk." Jenkins braced Tanner around the waist and pulled him to his feet. Two other policemen were carrying out Fassett.

"That's him. . . . That's Omega."

"We know. You're a very impressive fellow. You did what no one else was able to do in five years of trying. You got Omega for us."

"There's someone else. Over there. . . . Fassett said he was the other part of them."

"We found him. He's dead. He's still there. You want to go over and see who it is? Tell your grandchildren some day."

317

Tanner looked at Jenkins and replied haltingly. "Yes. Yes, I would. I guess I'd better know."

The two men walked over into the grass. Tanner was both fascinated and repelled by the moment that approached, the moment when he would see for himself the second face of Omega. He sensed that Jenkins understood. The revelation had to be of his own observation, not second hand. He had to bear witness to the most terrible part of Omega.

The betrayal of love.

Dick. Joe. Bernie.

Several men were examining the black automobile with the ruined searchlight. The body lay face down by the sedan's door. In the dark, Tanner could see it was a large man.

Jenkins turned on his flashlight and kicked the body over. The beam of light shone into the face.

Tanner froze.

The riddled body in the grass was Captain Albert MacAuliff.

A police officer approached and spoke to Jenkins from the edge of the parking area.

"They want to come over."

"Why not? It goes with their territories. The beach is secured." Jenkins spoke with more than a trace of contempt.

"Come on!" yelled McDermott to some men in the shadows on the other side of the parking lot.

Tanner could see the three tall figures walking across the gravel. Walking slowly, reluctantly.

Bernie Osterman. Joe Cardone. Dick Tremayne.

He limped with Jenkins' help out of the grass, away from Omega. The four friends faced each other; none knew what to say.

"Let's go," said Tanner to Jenkins.

"Pardon us, gentlemen."

PART FOUR

SUNDAY AFTERNOON

Sunday afternoon in the Village of Saddle Valley, New Jersey. The two patrol cars roamed up and down the streets as usual, but they remained at cruising speeds, lazily turning into the shady roads. The drivers smiled at the children and waved at the residents doing their Sunday chores. Golf bags and tennis rackets could be seen in small foreign convertibles and in gleaming station wagons. The sun was bright; the trees and the lawns glistened, refreshed by the July storm.

Saddle Valley was awake, preparing for a perfect Sunday afternoon. Telephones were dialed, plans made, a number of apologies offered for last evening's behavior. They were laughed off—what the hell, last evening was Saturday night. In Saddle Valley, New Jersey, Saturday nights were quickly forgiven.

A late model dark blue sedan with whitewall tires drove into the Tanner driveway. Inside the house John Tanner got up from the couch and walked painfully to the window. His upper chest and his entire left arm was encased in bandages.

So, too, was his left leg, from thigh to ankle.

Tanner looked out the window at the two men walking up the path. One he recognized as Patrolman Jenkins—but only on second glance. Jenkins was not in his police uniform. Now he looked like a Saddle Valley commuter—a banker or an advertising executive. Tanner didn't know the second man. He'd never seen him before.

"They're here," he called toward the kitchen. Ali came out and stood in the hallway. She was dressed casually in slacks and a shirt, but the look in her eyes wasn't casual at all.

"I suppose we've got to get it over with. The sitter's out with Janet. Ray's at the Club. . . . I suppose Bernie and Leila are at the airport by now."

"If they made it in time. There were statements, papers to sign. Dick's acting as everyone's attorney."

The chimes rang and Ali went to the door. "Sit down, darling. Just a little at a time, the doctor said."

"Okay."

Jenkins and his unfamiliar partner came in. Alice brought coffee and the four of them sat across from each other, the Tanners on the couch, Jenkins and the man he introduced as Grover in the armchairs.

"You're the one I talked to in New York, aren't you?" John asked.

"Yes, I am. I'm with the Agency. Incidentally, so is Jenkins. He's been assigned here for the past year and a half."

324

"You were a very convincing policeman, Mr. Jenkins," said Ali.

"It wasn't difficult. It's a pleasant place, nice people."

"I thought it was the Chasm of Leather." Tanner's hostility was apparent. It was time for explanations. He had demanded them.

"That, too, of course," added Jenkins softly.

"Then we'd better talk about it."

"Very well," said Grover. "I'll summarize in a few words. 'Divide and kill.' That was Fassett's premise. Omega's premise."

"Then there really was a Fassett. That was his name, I mean."

"There certainly was. For ten years Laurence Fassett was one of the finest operatives in the Agency. Excellent record, dedicated. And then things happened to him."

"He sold out."

"It's never that simple," said Jenkins. "Let's say his commitments changed. They altered drastically. He became the enemy."

"And you didn't know it?"

Grover hesitated before replying. He seemed to be searching for the least painful words. His head nodded, imperceptibly. "We knew. . . . We found out gradually, over a period of years. Defectors of Fassett's caliber are never revealed overnight. It's a slow process; a series of assignments with conflicting objectives. Sooner or later a pattern emerges. When it does, you make the most of it. . . . Which is exactly what we did."

"That seems to me awfully dangerous, complicated."

"A degree of danger, perhaps; not complicated, really. Fassett was maneuvered, just as he maneuvered you and your friends. He was brought into the Omega operation because his credentials warranted it. He was brilliant and this was an explosive situation. . . . Certain laws of espionage are fundamental. We correctly assumed that the enemy would give Fassett the responsibility of keeping Omega *intact*, not *allowing* its destruction. He was at once the defending general and the attacking force. The strategy was well thought out, take my word for it. Do you begin to see?"

"Yes." Tanner was barely audible.

" 'Divide and Kill.' Omega existed. Chasm of Leather *was* Saddle Valley. The checks on residents *did* uncover the Swiss accounts of the Cardones and the Tremaynes. When Osterman appeared, he, too, was found to have an account in Zurich. The circumstances were perfect for Fassett. He had found three couples allied with each other in an illegal—or at least highly questionable—financial venture in Switzerland."

"Zurich. That's why the name Zurich made them all nervous. Cardone was petrified."

"He had every reason to be. He and Tremayne. One the partner in a highly speculative brokerage house with a lot of Mafia financing; and the other an attorney with a firm engaged in unethical mergers—Tremayne, the specialist. They could have been ruined. Osterman had the least to lose, but, nevertheless, as part of the public media, an indictment might have had disastrous effects. As you know better than we do, networks are sensitive."

"Yes," said Tanner again without feeling.

"If, during the weekend, Fassett could so intensify mistrust between the three couples that they began hurling accusations at each other—the next step would be violence. Once *that possibility* was established, the real Omega intended to murder at least two of the couples, and Fassett could then present us with a substitute Omega. Who could refuse him? The subjects would be dead. It . . . was brilliant."

Tanner rose painfully from the couch and limped to the fireplace. He gripped the mantel angrily.

"I'm glad you can sit there and make professional judgments." He turned on the government men. "You had no right, *no right!* My *wife,* my *children* were damn near *killed!* Where were your men outside on the grounds? What happened to all that protective equipment from the biggest corporation in the world? Who listened on those electronic . . . *things* which were supposedly installed all over the house? *Where was everybody? We were left in that cellar to die!*"

Grover and Jenkins let the moment subside. They accepted Tanner's hostility calmly, with understanding. They'd been through such moments before. Grover spoke quietly, in counterpoint to Tanner's anger.

"In operations such as these, we anticipate that errors—I'll be honest, generally one massive error

—occur. It's unavoidable when you consider the logistics."

"What error?"

Jenkins spoke. "I'd like to answer that. . . . The error was mine. I was the senior officer at 'Leather' and the only one who knew about Fassett's defection. The only one. Saturday afternoon McDermott told me that Cole had unearthed extraordinary information, and had to see me right away. I didn't check it out with Washington, I didn't confirm it. I just accepted it and drove into the city as fast I could. . . . I thought that Cole, or someone here at 'Leather,' had discovered who Fassett really was. If that had been the case a whole new set of instructions would have to come from Washington. . . ."

"We were prepared," interrupted Grover. "Alternate plans were ready to be implemented."

"I got into New York, went up to the hotel suite . . . and Cole wasn't there. I know it sounds incredible, but he was out to dinner. He was simply *out to dinner*. He left the name of the restaurant, so I went there. This all took time. Taxis, traffic. I couldn't use the phone; all conversations were recorded. Fassett might have been tipped. Finally I got to Cole. He didn't know what I was talking about. He'd sent no message."

Jenkins stopped, the telling of the story angered and embarrassed him.

"That was the error?" asked Ali.

"Yes. It gave Fassett the time he needed. *I* gave him the time."

"Wasn't Fassett risking too much? Trapping himself? Cole denied the message."

"He calculated the risk. Timed it. Since Cole was constantly in touch with 'Leather,' a single message, especially second hand, could be garbled. The fact that I fell for the ruse also told him something. Put simply, I was to be killed."

"That doesn't explain the guards outside. Your going to New York doesn't explain their not being there."

"We said Fassett was brilliant," continued Grover. "When we tell you why they weren't there, why there wasn't a single patrol within miles, you'll understand just how brilliant he was. . . . He systematically withdrew all the men from your property on the grounds that *you were Omega*. The man they were guarding with their lives was, in reality, the enemy."

"What?"

"Think about it. Once you were dead, who could disprove it?"

"Why would they believe it?"

"The electronic pick-ups. They'd stopped functioning throughout your house. One by one they stopped transmitting. You were the only one here who knew they existed. Therefore, *you* were eliminating them."

"But I wasn't! I didn't know where they were! I still don't!"

"It wouldn't make any difference if you did." It was Jenkins who spoke. "Those transmitters had operating capacities of anywhere from thirty-six to forty-eight hours only. No more. I showed you one last night. It was treated with acid. They all were. The acid gradually ate through the miniature plates and shorted out the transmissions. . . . But all the men in the field knew was that they weren't functioning. Fasset *then* announced that he'd made the error. *You* were Omega and he hadn't realized it. I'm told he did it very effectively. There's something awesome about a man like Fassett admitting a major mistake. He withdrew the patrols and then he and MacAuliff moved in for the kill. They were able to do it because I wasn't here to stop them. He'd removed me from the scene."

"Did you know about MacAuliff?"

"No," answered Jenkins. "He wasn't even a suspect. His cover was pure genius. A bigoted small town cop, veteran of the New York police, and a right-winger to boot. Frankly, the first hint we had of his involvement was when you said the police car didn't stop when you signaled from the basement. Neither patrol car was in the vicinity at the time; MacAuliff made sure of that. However, he carries a red signal light in his trunk. Simple clamp device that can be mounted on top. He was circling your house, trying to draw you out. . . . When he finally got here, two things struck us. The first was that he'd been reached by car radio. Not at home. The second was a general description supplied by those on duty. That MacAuliff kept holding his stomach, claimed to be having a severe ulcer attack. MacAuliff had no history of ulcers. It was possible that he'd been wounded. It turned out to be correct. His 'ulcer' was a gash in his stomach. Courtesy of Mr. Osterman."

Tanner reached for a cigarette. Ali lit it for him.

"Who killed the man in the woods?"

"MacAuliff. And don't hold yourself responsible. He would have killed him whether you got up and turned on the light or not. He also gassed your family last Wednesday. He used the police riot supply."

"What about our dog? In my daughter's bedroom."

"Fassett," said Grover. "You had ice cubes delivered at one-forty-five; they were left on the front porch. Fassett saw the chance to create further panic and so he simply took them in. You were all at the pool. Once he got inside, he could maneuver; he's a pro. He was just a man delivering ice cubes. Even if you saw him, he could have told you it was extra precaution on his part. You certainly wouldn't have argued. And Fassett obviously was the man on the road who gassed the Cardones and the Tremaynes."

"Everything was calculated to keep us *all* in a constant state of panic. With no let up. Force my husband to think it was each of them." Ali stared at Tanner and spoke quietly. "What have we done? What did we say to them?"

"At one time or another I was convinced each person had given himself . . . or herself . . . away. I was positive."

"You were looking for that desperately. The relationships in this house, during the weekend, were

331

intensely personal. Fassett knew that." Grover looked over at Jenkins. "Of course, you must realize that they were all frightened. They had good reason to be. Regardless of their own personal, professional guilts, they shared a major one."

"Zurich?"

"Precisely. It accounted for their final actions. Cardone wasn't going to a dying father in Philadelphia last night. He'd called his partner Bennett to come out. He didn't want to talk on the phone and he thought his house might be watched. Yet he wasn't about to go far away from his family. They met at a diner on Route Five. . . . Cardone told Bennett about the Zurich manipulation and offered his resignation for a settlement. His idea was to turn state's evidence for the Justice Department in return for immunity."

"Tremayne said he was leaving this morning . . ."

"Lufthansa. Straight through to Zurich. He's a good attorney, very agile in these sorts of negotiations. He was getting out with what he could salvage."

"Then they both—separately—were leaving Bernie with the mess."

"Mr. and Mrs. Osterman had their own plans. A syndicate in Paris was prepared to assume their investment. All it would have taken was a cablegram to the French attorneys."

Tanner rose from the couch and limped toward the windows overlooking his backyard. He wasn't sure he wanted to hear any more. The sickness was everywhere. It left no one, it seemed, untouched. Fassett had said it.

It's a spiral, Mr. Tanner. No one lives in a deep freeze anymore.

He turned slowly back to the government men. "There are still questions."

"We'll never be able to give you all the answers," said Jenkins. "No matter what we tell you now, the questions will be around for a long time. You'll find inconsistencies, seeming contradictions, and they'll turn into doubts. The questions will become real again. . . . That's the difficult part. Everything was too subjective for you. Too personal. You operated for five days in a state of exhaustion, with little or no sleep. Fassett counted on that, too."

"I don't mean that. I mean physical things. . . . Leila wore a brooch that could be seen in the dark. There were no bullet marks in the wall around her. . . . Her husband wasn't here when I was in the Village last night. Someone slashed the tires then and tried to run me down. . . . The rendezvous at the Lassiter depot was *my* idea. How could Fasset have known if one of them hadn't told him? . . . How can you be so sure? You didn't know about MacAuliff. How do you know they aren't . . ." John Tanner stopped as he realized what he was about to say. He looked at Jenkins, who was staring at him.

Jenkins had spoken the truth. The questions were real again, the deceptions too personal.

Grover leaned forward in his chair. "In time everything will be answered. Those questions aren't difficult. Fassett and MacAuliff worked as a team. Fassett had the telephone taps moved to his new location once he left the motel. He easily could have radioed MacAuliff in the Village to kill you and then gone out to the depot when MacAuliff told him he'd failed. Obtaining other automobiles is no problem, slashing tires no feat. . . . Mrs. Osterman's brooch? An accident of dress. The unmarked wall? Its location, as I understand it, makes direct fire almost impossible."

" 'Almost,' 'could have' . . . oh, God." Tanner walked back to the sofa and awkwardly sat down. He took Ali's hand. "Wait a minute." He spoke haltingly. "Something happened in the kitchen yesterday afternoon . . ."

"We know," interrupted Jenkins gently, "Your wife told us."

Ali looked at John and nodded. Her eyes were sad.

"Your friends, the Ostermans, are remarkable people," continued Jenkins. "Mrs. Osterman saw that her husband wanted to, *had* to go out and help you. He couldn't stand by and watch you killed. . . . They're very close to each other. She was giving him permission to risk his life for you."

John Tanner closed his eyes.

"Don't dwell on it," said Jenkins.

Tanner looked at Jenkins and understood.

Grover got out of his chair. It was a signal for Jenkins, who did the same.

"We'll go now. We don't want to tire you out. There'll be plenty of time later. We owe you that. . . . Oh, by the way. This belongs to you." Grover reached into his pocket and withdrew an envelope.

"What is it?"

"The affidavit you signed for Fassett. Your agreement with Omega. You'll have to take my word that the recording is buried in the archives. Lost for a millenium that way. For the sake of both countries."

"I understand. . . . One last thing." Tanner paused, afraid of his question.

"What is it?"

"Which of them called you? Which of them told you about the Lassiter depot?"

"They did it together. They all met back here and decided to phone the police."

"Just like that?"

"That's the irony, Mr. Tanner," said Jenkins. "If they had done what they should have done earlier, none of this would have happened. But it was only last night that they got together and told each other the truth."

Saddle Valley was filled with whispers. In the dimly lit Village Pub men gathered in small groups and talked quietly. At the Club, couples sat around the pool and spoke softly of the terrible things which had touched their gracious haven. Strange rumors circulated—the Cardones had taken a long vacation, no one knew where; there was trouble in his firm, some said. Richard Tremayne was drinking more than usual, and his usual was too much. There were other stories about the Tremaynes, too. The maid was no longer there, the house a far cry from what it had been. Virginia's garden was going to seed.

But soon the stories stopped. Saddle Valley was nothing if not resilient. People forgot to ask about the Cardones and the Tremaynes after a while. They never fitted in, really. Their friends were hardly the kind a person wanted at the Club. There simply wasn't the time for much concern. There was so much to do. Saddle Valley, in summer, was glorious. Why shouldn't it be?

Isolated, secure, inviolate.

And John Tanner knew there'd never be another Osterman weekend.

Divide and kill.

Omega had won, after all.